Georges Louis Lecler

Buffon's Natural History
Volume 4

Georges Louis Leclerc de Buffon

Buffon's Natural History
Volume 4

1st Edition | ISBN: 978-3-75234-067-9

Place of Publication: Frankfurt am Main, Germany

Year of Publication: 2020

Outlook Verlag GmbH, Germany.

Reproduction of the original.

Buffon's Natural History.

VOL. IV.

INFANCY CONTINUED.

Infants, when newly born, sleep much, though with frequent interruptions. As they are also in frequent want of nourishment, they ought in the day to receive the breast every time they awake. The greatest part of the first month they pass in sleep, and do not seem to awake, but from a sense of pain or hunger; their sleep, therefore, generally terminates with a fit of crying. As they are compelled to remain in the same position in the cradle, confined by shackles, their situation soon becomes painful. Their excrements, whose acrimony is offensive to their tender and very delicate skin, often render them wet and chilly; and in this distress, by their cries alone can they call for relief. With the utmost assiduity ought this relief to be given them; or rather such inconveniences ought to be prevented by frequently changing part of their cloathing both night and day. The Savages deem this an object so essential, that though their changes of skins cannot possibly be so frequent as ours of linen, yet they supply this deficiency by the use of other substances; of which there is no necessity to be sparing. In North-America, a quantity of dust obtained from wood that has been gnawed by worms is placed at the bottom of the cradle, and which they renew as often as appears requisite. On this powder the infant is laid, and covered with skins; and though a bed of feathers, it is pretended, cannot be more soft and easy, yet it is not used to indulge the delicacy of the child, but to keep it clean; which in effect it does, by drawing off the moisture of every kind. In Virginia, they place the child naked upon a plank covered with cotton, and provided with a hole as a passage for the excrement. Here the cold is often unfavourable to such a practice; but it is almost general in the East of Europe, and especially in Turkey. This custom has this further advantage, it precludes all care, and is the most certain method of preventing the ill effects which too frequently result from the usual negligence of nurses. It is maternal affection alone which is capable of supporting that continual vigilance, that minute attention, which a new-born infant requires. How then can such vigilance, such care, be expected from a mercenary groveling nurse?

Some nurses desert their children for several hours without feeling the smallest anxiety; and others are so cruel as to be unaffected with their cries; then do the helpless innocents seem to be in a kind of despair; then do they exert every effort of which they are capable; and, till their strength actually forsakes them, implore assistance by their cries. If these violent agitations do not create some distemper, they discompose, however, the temperament and constitution of the child, and even influence perhaps its disposition.

There is another abuse which lazy nurses are frequently guilty of: instead of employing effectual methods for pleasing the infant, they rock it furiously in the cradle; this procures a momentary cessation of its cries, by confusing its brain, and if long continued stuns the child into a sleep. But this sort of sleep is merely a palliative, and so far is the agitation by which it was obtained from removing the cause of complaint, that it may disorder the head and stomach, and be the foundation of future disorders of very fatal consequence.

Before children are put into the cradle, we ought to be certain they want nothing, and they should never be rocked with such violence as to confound or stun them. If their sleep is not sound, a slow and equal motion of the cradle is sufficient to render it so; nor ought they to be rocked often, for if accustomed to this motion they will not sleep without it. Though children in good health should sleep long and spontaneously, yet the temperament of the body may be injured by too much. In this case they should be roused by gentle motion; their ears ought to be amused with some soft and agreeable sounds, and their eyes with some brilliant and striking objects. It is at this age they receive their first impressions from the sense, and these are, perhaps, of more future importance than many may imagine.

The eyes of infants are always directed to the strongest light in the room, and if from the child's situation only one eye can be directed to it, the other, for want of exercise, will remain more weak. To prevent this inconvenience the foot of the cradle ought to be so placed that the light, whether it comes from a window or a candle, may front it. In this position both eyes receive it alike, and thus by exercise acquire equal strength. If one eye becomes stronger than the other, the child will squint; for it is incontestably proved, that the inequality of strength in the eyes is the cause of squinting.

For the first and second months, and even for the third and fourth, the infant, especially when its constitution is weak and delicate, ought to receive no nourishment but milk from the breast. Whatever be its strength, it may receive material injury if any other food is given it during the first month. In Holland, in Italy, in Turkey, and in general over all the Levant, children have nothing but the breast for a whole year. The savages of Canada suckle them till they are four or five, and sometimes six or seven years of age. With us most nurses have not a sufficiency of milk to satisfy the demands of their children; and in order to be frugal of what they have, they feed them, even from the first, with a composition of boiled flour and milk. This nourishment allays their hunger; but as their stomachs and bowels are yet too weak to digest a gross and viscous substance, they suffer by it, and not unoften die by indigestions.

The milk of animals may supply the deficiency of that of the mother in cases of necessity; but then it is highly necessary the child should receive it, by sucking the animal's teat, in order that it may be of an equal and proper warmth, and that by the action of the muscles in sucking it may mix with the saliva, which facilitates digestion. In the country I have known several peasants who had no other nurses but ewes; and these peasants were as vigorous as any that had been suckled by their mothers.

After two or three months, when the child has acquired strength, they begin to give it food a little more solid, consisting of a kind of bread made of flour and milk, which disposes the stomach to receive the common bread, and such other nutriment as it will afterwards be accustomed to.

As an introduction to the use of solid food, the consistency of liquid food is gradually increased, and therefore, after having habituated the child to flour and milk boiled, they next give it bread diluted in some convenient fluid. During the first year infants are incapable of mastication, their teeth still continuing enveloped in the gums, which are so soft that their feeble resistance can produce no effect on any solid matter. Some nurses, especially among the common people, chew the food first, and then give it to the child, a practice from which, before we reflect upon it, we ought to banish every idea of disgust, which can make no impression upon infants. So far from feeling anything of that kind, they as readily receive food from the mouth of the nurse as from her breasts; nay it seems to proceed, from a natural propensity, by its being introduced in a number of countries widely different from each other. We find it in Italy, in Turkey, in the greatest part of Asia, in America, in Canada, &c. I conceive it to be highly useful, from being the only method by which the stomach of children can be furnished with the saliva that is required for the digestion of solid food. If the nurse chews a bit of bread, her saliva dilutes it, and renders it more nutritious than if it had been moistened in any other liquid, yet this practice is only necessary till they are supplied with teeth to chew their food, and dilute it with their own saliva.

The incisores, or fore teeth, are eight in number, four in the front of each jaw-bone. These generally appear first, though seldom till seven, eight, or ten months. Some few infants have been born with teeth so sharp as to cut their nurse's nipple. The original substance of the teeth is lodged in sockets, and covered by the gums, to the bottom of which it extends its roots, and pressing forward by little and little, at length forces its way through them. Though this operation is natural, it is not, however, consonant to the general laws of Nature, which constantly operate upon the human body, without exciting any painful sensation. Here Nature makes a violent and an excruciating effort, which is sometimes attended with fatal consequences. In breeding their teeth children lose their sprightliness, and become peevish and restless. The gums are at first red and swelled, and afterwards, when the pressure is ready to intercept the course of the blood in the veins, they appear white. They are constantly applying their fingers to the affected part as if endeavouring to assuage its irritation: they obtain further relief by putting into their mouth a bit of ivory, coral, or any other hard and polished substance they are supplied with, which they rub on that part of the gums that is most affected. This action relaxes the parts, and affords a momentary cessation of the pain; it also helps to attenuate the membrane of the gum, which, from the double pressure it then sustains, must break the more easily; yet this laceration, or rupture of the gums, is frequently attended with no small degree of pain and danger. When the gums are more firm than usual, by the solidity of the fibres of which they are composed, their resistance to the action of the tooth is more obstinate, and occasions an inflammation, with all its deadly symptoms. In order to preclude this, an incision may be successfully made on the gum, by means of which minute operation the inflammation ceases, and the teeth obtain a free passage.

The canine, or dog teeth, which are next to the incisores, are in number four, and commonly appear in the ninth or tenth month. About the end of the first, or in the course of the second year, sixteen other teeth appear, which are called molares, or grinders, four of which are situated on each side of the dog teeth. The periods for the cutting of the teeth vary in different children, and though it is pretended that those of the upper jaw usually appear first, yet it often happens that they are preceded by those of the under.

The incisores, the canine, and the first four of the molares, are generally shed in the fifth, sixth, or seventh year, but they are commonly replaced by others in the seventh year, though sometimes not till the age of puberty. The shedding of these sixteen teeth is occasioned by the expansion in the gums for the new set which are at the bottom of the sockets, and by their growth press out the first. There not being any beneath the other grinders they remain, unless forced out by accident, and when lost they are hardly ever recovered.

There are four other teeth still, which are situated at the extremity of each jaw, but which every person does not have. These seldom appear till the age of puberty, and sometimes later; they are called dentes sapientiæ, or wisdom-teeth, and either appear one after another, or two at a time. The only reason of there being a variety in the number of teeth, which is from 28 to 32, is the irregularity of the wisdom-teeth. Women, it has been observed, have generally fewer teeth than men.

Some authors pretend that the teeth would continue to grow through life, if it were not for their continual attrition, occasioned by the food on which man subsists, and increase in size (as is the case in several animals) in proportion as he advances in age. But this opinion is contradicted by experience; for persons who live wholly on liquid nutriment have not teeth longer than those who live on solid food, and if any thing is capable of wearing the teeth, it is rather their mutual friction one against another than mastication. Besides, they possibly deceive themselves by confounding teeth with tusks, as to the growth of the former in certain animals. The tusks of the wild boar and elephant, for example, continue to grow during life, but it is highly improbable that the teeth of either, when once arrived at their natural size, should afterwards increase. Tusks have a greater affinity, by far, with horns than with teeth; but this is not the proper place to enter into their specific differences, nor shall any thing further be added, than that the first set of teeth in children is of a substance less solid than the subsequent one, and more loosely fixed in the jaws.

It is often asserted, that the first hair of children is always brown, but that it presently falls off, and is succeeded by hair of a different colour. Whether the remark is just or not I cannot determine, but the hair of most children is fair, and, in many instances, almost white. In some it is red, and in others black, yet in those who are to have fair or brown complexions, the hair in the earliest stage of infancy, is fair in a greater or less degree. Those who give a promise of future fairness have generally blue eyes, those likely to be red have a yellowish shade in their eyes, and those who will be brown have a darker yellow; but colours are very imperfectly distinguished in the eyes of new-born infants, because they have almost all the semblance of blue.

When a child is suffered to cry too violently, and too long, it may in consequence be afflicted with a rupture, in which case an early application of bandages is necessary; with this assistance the complaint is removed with ease, without it the disease may last for life.

The limits of my plan admit not a detail of every disease incidental to children. I shall only remark, that worms, and all verminous diseases, very evidently owe their origin to the nature of their food. Milk is a kind of chyle, an unadulterated nutriment; it consists of organic and generative substances, and, therefore, if not digested by the stomach, and made use of in the expansion and growth of the body, it assumes, by its essential activity, other forms, and produces animated beings, particularly worms, in such quantities, that the infant is often in danger of falling a victim to them. A part of the bad effects that accrue from worms, might probably be prevented, by allowing children to drink a little wine, because all fermented liquors counteract the generation of worms, and besides contain but few organic nutritive particles: it is chiefly by its action upon the solids that wine gives strength, and it may be rather said to fortify the body than to strengthen it. Besides, the generality of children are fond of wine, at least easily accustomed to drink it.

However delicate the frame may be in infancy, it is yet less sensible of cold than during any other period of life. As the pulse of infants is more quick than that of adults, it may, from this circumstance alone, be concluded, that the internal heat is proportionally greater. On the same principle it is hardly to be doubted, that of this heat small animals have a greater share than the large; it has invariably been found, that, in the same degree the animal is small, the motion of the heart and arteries is proportionally vigorous and quick; and this is ever the case in the same as well as in different species. The pulse of an infant, or of a man of small stature, is more frequent than that of a grown person, or a man of a large size. The pulse of an ox is slower, and a dog quicker than that of a man; and so precipitate are the motions in the heart of an animal still smaller, as a sparrow, for instance, they can hardly be counted.

Till the age of three years the life of an infant is highly precarious. In the course of the ensuing two or three years, however, it becomes more certain; and at the age of six or seven a child has a greater probability of living than at any other age. By consulting Simpson's tables of the degrees of mortality, at different ages, as applicable to London, it appears, that, of a certain number of children, born at one time, above a fourth of them died in the first year, above a third in two years, and, at least, one half in the first three years. If this calculation is just a wager might be proposed, that an infant, when born, would not live three years. A man who dies at the age of twenty-five is to be lamented for the short duration of his life; and yet, according to these tables, one half of mankind die before the age of three years, consequently, every individual who has passed his third year, far from repining at his fate, ought to consider himself as treated with superior favour by his Creator. But this mortality in children is by no means so great in every place as in London. M. Dupré de St. Maur has proved, by a number of experiments made in France, that one half of the children born at the same time are not extinct in less than seven or eight years. By these experiments it is also shewn, that at the age of five, six, or seven years, the life of a child is more certain than at any other age, and that an equal bet may be laid for 42 years more, whereas in proportion as a child lives beyond five, six, or seven years, the probable number of years it will live decreases. At twelve years, for instance, the equal chance is only for 39 years; at 20, for $33^1/_2$; at 30, for 20; and thus forward, till the age of 85, when there is an equal chance of living three years longer.[A]

[A] In the course of this volume we shall present our readers with a table, at large, of the different probabilities of human life.

There is one thing very remarkable in the growth of the human body. The fœtus in the womb continues to increase more and more in equal periods, till the birth. The infant, on the contrary, increases less and less, that is in the same period of time, till the age of puberty, to which it seems to bound, as it were, at once. The fœtus, for example, is an inch long in the first month, two inches and a quarter in the second; three inches and a half in the third; five inches and upwards in the fourth; six inches and a half, or even seven inches, in the fifth; eight inches and a half, or nine inches, in the sixth; eleven inches, in the seventh; fourteen inches, in the eighth; and eighteen inches, in the ninth. Although this measurement may vary in different children, yet if the child be 18 inches at its birth, it will hot increase more than six or seven inches in the first year after: that is, at the end of the first year, it will be 24 or 25 inches; of the second, 28 or 29 inches; of the third, only 30, or, at most 32 inches; and from this age till that of puberty, it will not advance more than one inch and a half, or two inches, in the course of each year. From these remarks it is evident that the fœtus increases more in a month, towards the close of its residence in the matrix than the infant does in a year, till it arrives at the age of puberty; when Nature seems to make one grand effort to unfold the animal machine, and render her work complete.

So essential is it, that the constitution of the nurse should be sound, and her juices untainted that we have many instances of diseases being imparted from the nurse to the infant, and from the infant to the nurse. Whole villages have been infected with the venereal virus, by nurses suckling the children of other women.

Were mothers to suckle their own offspring it is probable the latter would be more strong and vigorous. The milk of a stranger must be less proper for them than that of the mother, for as the fœtus is nourished in the matrix by a fluid, which bears a strong resemblance to the milk that is formed in the breasts, the infant, therefore, is already, as it were, habituated to the milk of its mother. The milk of any other woman, on the contrary, is a nourishment new to the child, and sometimes so different from the other that it is difficult to make the child take it: and if forced will sicken and languish, from not being able to digest the milk of the nurse; a circumstance which, if the consequences are not seasonably prevented by the substitution of another nurse, soon proves fatal.

I cannot help observing, that the custom of crowding a multitude of children into one place, as in the hospitals of large cities, is highly repugnant to what ought to be the grand object proposed, their preservation. The greatest part of such children fall victims to a kind of scurvy, or to other diseases, from which they might have been exempted, had they been brought up in different houses, or rather in the country. The same expence would be sufficient for their support, and an infinity of lives, in which it is well known consist the real riches of a state, would be saved.

At twelve or fifteen months infants begin to lisp. *A* is the vowel which they articulate with most ease, as it requires nothing more than the opening of the lips, and forcing out the breath. *E* requires that the tongue should be raised as the lips are opened; and is therefore pronounced with a degree of more trouble. *I* is attended with greater difficulty, as in the articulation of the vowel the tongue is elevated still more, and made to approach the teeth of the upper jaw. In the pronunciation of *O*, the tongue must be lowered, and the lips contracted; and in that of *U*, the latter must be also contracted, and in some degree extended. The first consonants which children pronounce are those which require the least motion in the organs. Of these the most easy of articulation are *B M* and *P*. For that of *B* and *P* it is simply requisite that the lips should be closed and then opened with quickness, and for that of *M*, that they should be first opened and then closed with celerity. The articulation of the other consonants supposes motions more complicated. The pronunciation of *C D G L N Q R S* and *T* depend each on a particular action of the tongue, which it would be very difficult to explain; and for the pronunciation of *F*, a more continued sound is necessary, than for that of any other consonant. *A* being the most easily articulated of the vowels, as are *B P* and *M*, of the consonants, we need not wonder that the first words which children pronounce, in every country, should be composed of, that vowel, and of those consonants; and that, for example, in every language, *Baba, Mama, Papa,* should be the primitive articulations. They are the most familiar sounds to man, and the most natural to him, because the most easily pronounced, and the letters of which they are composed must exist wherever there is any typical mode for the denotation of sounds.

It is to be observed, however, that as the sounds of several consonants are nearly similar; those, for instance, of *E* and *P*, of *C* and *S*, of *K* and *Q*, in certain cases; of *D* and *T*, of *F* and *V*, of *G* and *J*, of *G* and *K*, of *L* and *R*, so there may be many languages in which such consonants are not to be found. But in every language, there must be a *B* or a *P*, a *C* or an *S*, a *K* or a *Q*, a *D* or a *T*, an *F* or a *V* consonant, a *G* or a *J* consonant; an *L* or an *R*, and in the most contracted of all alphabets, there cannot be less than six or seven consonants, for of that number there are simple sounds, which have all a very sensible difference from each other. Those children who do not readily articulate *R*, substitute *L* for it; and in the place of *T* they articulate *D*. Indeed *L* and *D* require more difficult movements in the organs than either *R* or *T*; and it is from this difference, and from the choice of consonants more or less easy of articulation, that the softness or the harshness of a language proceeds. But on this subject it would be superfluous to enlarge.

Some children pronounce distinctly, and repeat whatever is said to them, at two years, though the generality do not speak for the first two years and a half, and often not so early. It has been observed, that those who are most backward, never speak with the same facility as those who begin to articulate more early, and that those who are in that respect the most forward, may learn to read before the expiration of the third year. Some I have myself known, who had begun to read at two years, and who read to admiration at four. After all, it is difficult to determine whether there is any advantage to be derived from such premature education. With so little success indeed, is it generally attended, that we see and hear of numbers, who, though they had been prodigies at the age of four, eight, twelve, and sixteen years, are found, however, at those of twenty-five, or thirty, to be downright block-heads, or men of very inferior abilities. *I* am convinced, therefore, that education is the best, which does not compel Nature, and which is proportioned to the strength and capacity of the child.

CHAPTER III.

OF PUBERTY.

Puberty immediately succeeds childhood and attends us to the end of our days. Till this period arrives the sole object of Nature seems to have been the growth and preservation of her work. She supplies the infant with nothing but what is necessary for its bodily increase. Wrapped up, as it were, within itself, its existence, in some respects, resembles that of a vegetable, and which it has not the power to communicate. Presently, however, the principles of life multiply; and it not only possesses what is necessary for its own being but sufficient to give existence to others. This superabundance of life, this source of strength and vigour, impatient of its internal restraint, vents itself abroad, and the age of puberty is announced by a number of external and internal marks; it is the spring of life and the season of pleasure. Of that age may we be enabled to write the history with such circumspection as to excite in the imagination none but philosophical ideas! Puberty, however, and the circumstances that accompany it, as circumcision, castration, virginity, and impotency, are of too essential consequence in the History of Man to allow a suppression of facts to which they relate. In giving a detail of them we shall endeavour to maintain that modest reserve which constitutes the true decorum of style, that philosophical apathy which may destroy loose ideas, and give it in words confined to their literal import and original signification.

Circumcision is a custom very ancient, and which still subsists in the greatest part of Asia. Among the Hebrews this operation was performed within eight days after the birth. In Turkey they never perform it before the age of seven or eight years, and often not even till that of eleven or twelve. In

Persia, the practice is general at the age of five or six. The wound thus occasioned is healed with caustic or astringent powders, or with burned paper, which, according to Chardin, is the most effectual remedy; he adds, that circumcision is attended with infinite pain when performed on grown persons; that they cannot stir abroad after it for three weeks or a month, and that sometimes it proves fatal to them.

In the Maldivia islands they circumcise their children at the age of seven; and previous to this operation they bathe them in the sea for six or seven hours, in order to render their skin more soft. The Israelites made use of a sharpened flint, a custom which the Jews still continue in most of their synagogues. The Mahometans, however, use a common knife, or a razor.

Were it not for their precaution in cutting it in childhood, the Turks, it is alledged, and the inhabitants of many other countries in which circumcision is practised, would naturally have their prepuces too long. Boulaye tells us, that in the deserts of Mesopotamia and Arabia, on the banks of the Tigris and the Euphrates, he saw a number of Arabian boys, whose prepuces were so long, that, without the aid of circumcision, he imagined they would be unfit for procreation.

The skin of the eye-lids is also longer in the Oriental than in other nations. The skin is a substance similar to that of the prepuce; but what relation, in point of growth, can subsist between two so distant parts?

Girls in several parts of Arabia, towards the Gulph of Persia and the Red Sea, are equally subjected to this operation as boys. But in these countries, as there is no previous overgrowth of the *nymphæ*, they are not circumcised till they have passed the age of puberty. In other climates this exuberance is indeed far more early; and it is so general among the inhabitants of certain countries, as those near the river Benin, that they circumcise girls as well as boys within eight, or at most fifteen days after their birth. The circumcision of females is of great antiquity in Africa; and even Herodotus mentions it as being a custom of the Ethiopians.

Circumcision may have been founded on necessity, yet infibulation and castration could never have taken place but from jealousy, or from some gloomy and superstitious frenzy, some wretched antipathy to the human race, or from some envious tyrant who enacted laws to make privation a virtue, and mutilation a merit.

Infibulation is performed upon boys by drawing the prepuce forward, making an incision, and putting a coarse thread through it, till the cicatrice is healed; and then, in the room of that, is substituted a kind of ring, which remains as long as the person pleases who gave orders for the operation, and sometimes for life. The Oriental monks, who have made a vow of chastity, wear rings of a large size, in order that they may be compelled to observe this vow inviolate. We shall hereafter speak on the infibulation of girls; on this head nothing can be supposed too fantastic or absurd, which men, borne away by passion, or immersed in superstition, have scrupled to put in practice.

Though in infancy there is sometimes but one testicle in the scrotum, and sometimes not any, yet we must not suppose in either case that this is a real defect. It often happens, that the testicles are retained in the abdomen, from whence they at length extricate themselves, and descend to the natural place. This generally happens at the age of eight or ten years, though sometimes not till that of puberty. They are scarcely ever concealed after this age, when Nature makes violent efforts to bring them forward: the same effect is sometimes produced by some violent motion, as a leap, a fall, &c. Even when the testicles do not manifest themselves, the procreative powers are not the less perfect; and it has been observed, that persons in that situation are often the most vigorous.

There are men who have but one testicle, but this defect is of little consequence, and in that case is much larger than the usual size. Others have three, and such are said to possess a vast superiority of bodily force and vigour. From a view of the animal, creation, we perceive how much these parts contribute to strength and courage; how great, for example, is the difference between a bull and an ox, a wether and a ram, a capon and a cock.

The custom of castrating the human species is of great antiquity. Among the Egyptians it was the established punishment of adultery. Among the Romans eunuchs were very numerous; and to this day in Asia, and a part of Africa, men thus mutilated are employed to attend and act as guards to the chastity of the women. In Italy, the sole object of this infamous and cruel operation is to perfect the voice. The Hottentots cut out one testicle, by the privation of which they imagine they will become more nimble racers. In other countries, the poor people adopt the practice in order to prevent their children from being able to generate, and by that means save them from that distress and anguish which they themselves experience when they cannot procure food for their support.

The different kinds of castration are numerous; those intended for vocal perfection only suffer the extraction of the two testicles; but those who are instigated by the gloomy distrust of jealousy think their females far from being safe if guarded by such eunuchs, nor will they countenance any but what have had the external parts of generation utterly exterminated.

Amputation is not the only method used for this purpose. Formerly some people prevented the growth of the testicles, and rendered them useless by bathing their children in warm water, or in decoctions of plants, and then pressing and rubbing the testicles till the organization was destroyed. Others compressed them with an instrument, and it is pretended, that from this mode of castration the life is not exposed to the smallest danger.

The amputation of the testicles is not very hazardous; it may be performed at any age, yet that of infancy is esteemed the most favourable. The amputation of the whole external parts of generation, however, is more often mortal than otherwise, especially if performed after the age of fifteen; and even at the most favourable age, which is from, seven to ten, it is still attended with danger. The difficulty of preserving them renders the eunuchs of this species by far the most valuable. Tavernier says, that in Turkey and Persia they cost five of six times more than any others. Chardin observes, that the entire amputation is always accompanied with the most agonizing pain; that it is performed with tolerable safety on children, but with great danger after the age of fifteen; that more than a fourth fall victims to it; and that it takes at least six weeks to heal the wound. Pietro della Valle, on the other hand, asserts that those who undergo this operation in Persia, as a punishment for rapes, or other crimes of that nature, recover from it with ease, even when they are advanced in years, and that they apply to the wound nothing but a few ashes. Whether those who suffered the same punishment formerly in Egypt, as related by Diodorus Siculus, found the consequences of it equally mild, we know not; but, according to Thevenot, numbers of the children of negroes perish, whom the Turks force to undergo this operation, although performed at the early age of between eight to ten.

Besides negro eunuchs, there are others in Turkey, Persia, &c. who chiefly come from the kingdom of Golconda, the Peninsula on this side the Ganges, the kingdoms of Assan, Pegu, and Malabar, where their complexion is grey, and from the Gulph of Bengal, where it is of an olive colour. There are also white eunuchs from Georgia and Circassia, tho' not in great numbers. Tavernier says, that during his residence in Golconda, in 1657, there were not less than 22,000 eunuchs made. The black ones come from Africa, and chiefly from Ethiopia. Those are the most prized whose appearance is the most ugly and horrible; a flat nose, a countenance ghastly, thick large lips and protuberant, and black straggling teeth are the esteemed qualities. These people have commonly very fine teeth; but such would be a very great defect in a black eunuch, who must be a hideous monster.

Eunuchs who have been deprived of only their testicles, still feel an irritation in the parts that are left, and have the external mark of desire even more frequently than other men. Those parts, however, remain, as to size, nearly in the same state as before the operation; and if this is performed at the

13

age of seven years, an eunuch of twenty is, in this respect, as a child of seven. If it is not, on the contrary, performed till the time of puberty, or a little after, the size is nearly the same as that in other men.

Between the parts of generation and the throat there are particular connections, altho' we know not the cause. Eunuchs have no beard, their voice, though shrill and powerful, is never of a deep tone; and not unoften does the throat become the seat of the secret distemper. The correspondence which certain parts of the body have with others, widely remote and of a different nature, ought to be more generally observed; but we pay too little attention to effects, when we do not surmise their causes. Thus it is, that though in effect the action of the animal machine in a great measure depends upon them, these different affinities remain unexamined with that care they deserve. In women, there is a great correspondence between the matrix, the breasts and the head: and how many beneficial facts of this kind might, be found if a few able physicians would direct their studies to such discoveries! These muscles, veins, arteries,, and nerves, which they describe with so much accuracy, and with so much fidelity, are not the springs which give life to our organization. There resides in organized bodies certain internal powers, which are by no means guided by the laws of gross mechanism; instead of attempting to know the nature of those powers by their effects, the very ideas of them have been treated as ideal, and endeavours have been made to discard and banish them from philosophical researches. These very powers, nevertheless, have maintained their importance in gravitation, in the phenomena of electricity, &c. But, however evident and universal they may be, as their action is wholly internal, and they are solely objects of reason, it is with a kind of unwillingness that they are admitted; inclination still leads us to judge from external appearances; we form a notion, that in those appearances every thing consists, and that we are not allowed to penetrate farther; and thus we effectually turn our hacks upon that which might lead to refined information.

The ancients, whose genius was less limited, and whose philosophy was more extended, were not embarrassed at meeting with things they were at a loss to explain. More intimately acquainted with Nature; with them, a sympathy, a particular correspondence, was only a phenomenon; but with us, if we cannot reduce it to our pretended laws of motion, it is a paradox. They knew that most of the effects of Nature were produced by means beyond human foresight, they knew it was impossible to reduce them to any particular principles of action, and modes of operation; and therefore with them it was sufficient to have remarked a certain number of relative effects, in order to constitute a cause.

Whether, with the ancients, we call sympathy this peculiar correspondence of the different parts of the body, or, with the moderns, we consider it as an unknown relation in the action of the nerves, it exists through the whole animal economy; and, were the perfection of the theory of physic our object, too much attention could not be paid to its effects. But this is not a place to enlarge on a subject of so much importance. I shall only observe, that this correspondence between the voice and the organs of generation is discovered not only in eunuchs but in other men, and even in women. In men, the voice changes at the age of puberty; and in women, a strong voice is suspected to indicate a superior propensity to love.

The first sign of puberty is a kind of stiffness in the groin, which becomes more sensible in walking, or in bending the body forward. This stiffness is frequently accompanied with pungent pains in the joints, and also with a new sensation in the parts which characterize the sexes. The voice is, for some time, harsh and unequal, and afterwards it becomes more full, strong, and articulate. This change is very perceptible in boys, but less so in girls, because the sound of their voices is naturally more acute.

These signs of puberty are common to both the sexes, but there are others peculiar to each; as in females, the menstrual discharge and the expansion of the breasts; and in males, the beard, and power of generating. These signs, it is true, are not alike certain. The beard, for example, does not always appear precisely at the age of puberty; and there even exist whole nations where the men have hardly any beard. There is no nation, however, in which the puberty of the female sex is not indicated by the enlargement of the breasts.

Universally through the human species women arrive at puberty sooner than men. But that age is different in different countries, and seems to depend on the temperature of the climate and the quality of the food. Among people who live at their ease, and feed plentifully, children arrive at this state two or three years sooner than those in the country, and among the poorer classes of people, whose food is less nourishing and more scanty. In the southern parts of Europe, and in cities, the majority of girls attain puberty at about twelve years, and boys at fourteen; but in the regions of the north, and in country places, the former are hardly so at fourteen, or the latter at sixteen.

Should it be asked why females in every climate are capable of engendering more early than men? It might be satisfactorily replied, that men are much larger and stronger, their bones more hard, their muscles more firm and compact, and therefore a longer time is required for their growth. And as it is not till after the growth is completed that the superfluity of the organic particles is dispersed into the parts of generation, females must of course arrive at maturity sooner than the males.

In the hot climates of Asia, Africa, and America, girls are generally mature at ten years of age, and often at nine; and though the menstrual discharge is less copious in warm countries it is yet more early. The intervals between are nearly the same in every country, and in this respect there seems to be a greater difference between individuals than between nations. In the same climate and nation some women are subject to the menstrua at the end of every fifteenth day, while others are free from them for six weeks; but a month, however, two or three days over or under, is the usual period.

The quantity of the discharge seems to depend on the quantity of nourishment, and of insensible perspiration. Women who eat much, and exercise little, have the most copious discharge? in warm countries it is always least, because the perspiration is great. As to its duration, it is generally from three to four or five days, though sometimes to six, seven, and even eight days.

The *material* causes of it are supposed to be a superfluity of blood and nutritive particles. The symptoms which precede are certain indications of repletion; as heat, tension, swelling, and the pains which women feel, not only in the parts themselves, and the adjoining ones, but also in the breasts, which swell and discover a surplus of blood by the *areolæ*, or the circle about the nipple, becoming of a deeper colour. The eyes are oppressed, and underneath their orbits the skin assumes a blue or violet tint; the cheeks are flushed; the head is heavy and full of pain; and the whole body in general is in a state of oppression from the surcharge of blood.

At the age of puberty the body usually attains its full growth in length. Just before, young people sometimes increase several inches, but the quickness of growth is most sudden and perceptible in the genitals of both sexes. This growth in males is an expansion merely, but in females it is often attended with a contraction, to which different appellations have been given in explaining the signs of virginity.

Mankind, jealous of every kind of pre-eminence, have always put a superior value on what they could first possess, and that to the exclusion of others. This species of folly has given a positive entity to the virginity of women. Virginity, which is nothing but a *moral*, being a virtue that solely consists in the purity of the heart, men have, as with one consent, converted into a *physical* object, and in which they also fancy themselves much interested. From these absurd opinions, usages, ceremonies, superstitions, and even awards and punishments, have been established: abuses the most illicit, and customs the most shocking and disgraceful, have been authorized. To ignorant matrons, and to prejudiced physicians, have young women been obliged to submit the most secret parts of Nature for examination, without their reflecting that such acts of indecency is a downright attack upon chastity, and that every immodest, every indelicate situation, which caused an internal blush, was little less than prostitution.

The prejudices that have been formed on this head I despair of removing. Things which mankind take a pleasure in believing, however nugatory and unreasonable they may be, they will always believe; yet, as it is the province of history to relate not only the accession of events, and the circumstances of facts, but also the origin of predominant opinions and errors, I think it my indispensable duty, in the History of Man, to examine this favourite idol to which he sacrifices; to consider what the reasons are by which he is prompted to pay that adoration, and to enquire whether virginity, as he understands it, is a real or merely a fabulous divinity.

Fallopius, Vesalus, Bartholin, Heister, Ruysch and many other anatomists, pretend, that the membrane of the hymen is a substance which actually exists, and which ought to be numbered among the parts of generation peculiar to women. They maintain further, that this membrane is fleshy, very thin in children, but more thick in grown girls; that it is situated under the orifice of the urethra, and that it partly closes the passage of the vagina; that there is a hole pierced through it, sometimes round, sometimes long, so small that a pea can hardly be passed through in infancy, or a bean at puberty. The hymen, according to Winflow, is a membranous kind of wrinkle, more or less circular, and sometimes semi-lunar, with an aperture, in some very small, and in others more large. Dulaurent, Graaf, Pineus, Mauricea, and other anatomists, of at least equal reputation and authority with those first quoted, insist, on the other hand, that the membrane of the hymen is nothing but a chimera, a part by no means natural to girls, and express their astonishment that it should have ever been mentioned as a thing which has an actual and real existence. In confirmation of this doctrine they adduce a multitude of observations made on girls of different ages, whom they had dissected, in none of whom this membrane was to be found. They confess that they have seen, though very rarely, a membrane that united certain fleshy protuberances, which they call *carunculæ myrtiformes*; but this membrane they insist is by no means consonant to the natural state of the parts. Anatomists are not more united as to the quality and number of these *carunculæ*. Are they merely wrinkles of the vagina? Are they distinct and separate parts? Do they belong to the membrane of the hymen? Is their number certain? Is there only one, or are there many, in the state of virginity? Each of these questions has been asked, and to each a different answer has been given.

This contrariety of opinion, as to a fact which depends upon a simple inspection, is a proof of the eagerness of mankind to discover in Nature things which alone exist in their own imaginations. Several anatomists frankly declare they never found either the hymen or *carunculæ*, even before the age of puberty, while others, in maintaining that this membrane, and these *carunculæ* do exist, confess, that they are substances which vary in form, size, and consistency, in different subjects; that sometimes in the place of the hymen there is only a single *caruncula*; that at other times there are two or more united by a membrane, and that the shape of the aperture is of different forms. From all these observations what conclusions are to be drawn, but that the causes of the pretended contraction in the passage of the vagina are not certain, and that when they do exist their effect is transient and susceptible of different modifications? Anatomy leaves no entire certainty as to the existence of this membrane of the hymen and these *carunculæ*, of course it authorizes us to reject such tokens of virginity, not only as uncertain but as imaginary. The effusion of blood, though a more common sign, is not less equivocal. In every age this has been deemed a certain proof of virginity; and yet all such proof is nothing, where the entrance of the vagina is naturally relaxed or dilated. Neither is it confined to virgins, as many women who pretend not to that denomination, frequently experience an effusion off blood. From some it flows copiously, and repeatedly; from others in a very small quantity, and only once; and from some it never flows at all. This diversity depends on the age, the health, the conformation of the parts, and a number of other circumstances. A few of these we shall enumerate, and at the same time endeavour to investigate the causes of those physical tokens which have been laid down as certain proofs of virginity.

At the age of puberty, the parts of both sexes undergo a considerable change. Those of man advance so quickly, that in two or three years they attain their full growth, those of women also increase at this period, especially the *nymphæ*, which though before almost imperceptible, become now large and evident. The menstrual discharge happens at the same time; and all the parts being still in a state of growth, swell by an increase of blood, and mutually compress each other. The orifice of the vagina contracts, though the vagina itself has considerably increased. The form of this contraction must be very different in different subjects, for from the information of anatomists, it appears, there are sometimes four, at others only three or two *carunculæ*, and that sometimes there is found a circular, or semi-lunar series of folds and wrinkles. But one thing anatomists have never told us; namely, that whatever form this contraction may assume, it never appears before the age of puberty.

In the young girls whom I have had occasion to see dissected, nothing of that kind was to be found; and having collected several facts on this subject, I can with confidence maintain, that when a girl has conversed with a man before puberty, there is no effusion of blood, provided the disproportion of the parts had not been too great, or the efforts had not been too violent. At full puberty, on the other hand, that effusion often happens, even from trifling causes; especially if she is of a full habit, and regular. This sign of virginity is rarely observed in such as are meagre or subject to the *fluor albus*; and, what evidently proves it to be fallacious, is the frequency of its repetition. In some women four, and even five times, has this pretended virginity been renewed in the space of two or three years; and often been successfully practised by some on their deluded husbands upon being suspected of incontinency, and that purely by abstinence. This renovation, however, only happens from the fourteenth to about the eighteenth year. When the growth of the body is finished the parts remain in the state they then are; and when they assume a different appearance, it is only by such expedients and artifices as, to mention here, would be alike unnecessary and improper.

As nothing, therefore, can be more chimerical than the prejudices of men, with respect to virginity, so nothing can be more uncertain than the pretended signs of it. A young woman may have commerce with a man, before the years of puberty, and yet discover no signs of virginity; yet afterwards, the period of puberty being arrived, this same woman shall exhibit all these pretended signs, while a real virgin may not have the smallest effusion whatever. Men, therefore, ought to make themselves very easy as to this point, and not give a loose, as they often do, to unjust and idle suspicions.

Were we desirous to obtain an evident and undoubted sign of virginity, we should search for it among those barbarous nations who, incapable of instilling, by education, the sentiments of virtue and honour into their children, secure the chastity of their daughters by expedient which nothing could have suggested but the rudeness of their manners. The people of Ethiopia, and other parts of Africa, of Pegu, Arabia Petræa and other nations of Asia, draw together by a kind of needle-work, the part which Nature has separated, leaving only a space sufficient for the necessary evacuations. As the child grows, the parts gradually adhere; insomuch that, when the time of marriage arrives, they must unavoidably be disunited by incision. For this infibulation of girls, as it is a substance not subject to corruption, they use the fibres of the asbestos. Some tribes only use a kind of ring; to this practice, wives as well as girls are subjected, with this single difference, that the ring alloted to the latter cannot be removed, and in that alloted to the former there is a lock of which the husband alone possesses the key. But why quote barbarous nations, when we have similar examples so much nearer home? What is the delicacy on which some of our neighbours pique themselves, with respect to the chastity of their wives, but a jealousy, equally barbarous and criminal?

How various are the dispositions, manners, and opinions of different nations? After what has been here related of the high estimation in which virginity is held by the bulk of mankind, and of the precautions and ignomious methods they employ, in order to secure it, could it be imagined there were other nations who despise it, and who consider the trouble of removing it as a servile office?

Prompted by superstition, the inhabitants of certain countries resign the first fruits of virginity to their priests, and sometimes to their very idols. This privilege is enjoyed by the priests of Cochin and Calicut; and in Goa, virgins are prostituted, either voluntarily or forcibly, by their nearest relations to an idol of iron. Of these vile excesses, gross superstition and a blind sense of the duties of religion, have been the sources, while motives more earthly have induced people of other countries eagerly to devote their daughters to their chiefs. In this manner, without any dishonour, do they prostitute their daughters in the kingdom of Congo. Nearly the same is the custom in Turkey, in Persia, and in several other countries, both of Asia and Africa, where the most eminent nobles deem themselves, in the highest degree, honoured by receiving from their sovereign, women with whom he is himself already disgusted.

In the kingdom of Arracan, and in the Philippine islands, a man would think himself much disgraced were he to espouse a female who had not been defloured; and it is only by dint of money that a person can be prevailed with to precede the husband. In the province of Thibet, a mother will search for a stranger, and earnestly beg of him to put her daughter in a situation for obtaining a husband. The Laplanders also prefer such women as have already had a commerce with strangers, from an idea that they must be possessed of more merit than others, otherwise they could not have pleased men whom they consider as better judges of beauty than themselves. In Madagascar, and in several other countries, women the most dissolute and debauched are those who are married the soonest. Many more instances might be produced of this peculiar fancy, which could never have subsisted but from a gross and utter depravation of manners.

Marriage is the natural state of man after puberty. A man ought to have but one wife, and a woman but one husband; This is the law of Nature, the number of females being nearly equal with that of males, and ignorance and tyranny must have been the leading features where men have established laws in opposition to it. Reason, humanity, and justice, complain aloud of those odious seraglios, in which the liberty and the affections of many women are sacrificed to the brutal passion of one individual. Are these tyrants of mankind the more happy by this pre-eminence?—No; surrounded with eunuchs, and with women, useless to themselves and to other men, the misery they have created is a constant source of torment and perplexity.

Marriage, therefore, as it is established among us, and among every other people who are guided by the light of reason and revelation, is a state which is suited to man, and in which he ought to employ the additional faculties he has acquired by puberty: by obstinately persisting in celibacy they will become troublesome, and even fatal. From a too long continence in either sex diseases may arise, or at least create irritations so violent, that reason and religion would not be sufficient to counteract the impetuosity of the passions which they excite, and thus man may be reduced to a level with the brutes, which, under the impression of such sensations, become furious and ungovernable.

The most violent effect of this irritation in women is the *furor uterinus*, a kind of mania, which disorders their reason and bereaves them of all sense of shame. With words the most lascivious, and with actions the most indecent, is this melancholy distemper accompanied and its origin revealed. I have seen a girl at the age of twelve years, of a brown but lively and florid complexion, small in size, yet strong and plump, commit the most indecent actions at the very sight of a man, from which nothing could divert her, neither the presence of her mother, expostulation, nor punishment. Her reason, however, forsook her not, and the paroxysms, which were so violent as to excite horror, ceased the minute she was left with her own sex. Aristotle says, it is at this age the irritation is greatest, and girls ought then to be most attentively watched. The remark may be applicable to the climate in which he lived, but in countries more cold, the female constitution does not become warm so early.

When the *furor uterinus* increases to a certain degree marriage is no remedy for it and instances there are of its being fatal. Happily the force of Nature is rarely of itself the cause of such dreadful passions, even when the temperament inclines to them; and before they arrive at this extremity many causes must concur, of which the principal is, an imagination inflamed by licentious conversation and obscene representations. The contrary temperament is infinitely more common among women, the generality of whom are, with respect to this passion, exceedingly cool or indifferent. Of men too, there are many in whose chastity there is little merit; and some I have known, who, at the age of twenty-five and thirty, enjoyed a good state of health without having ever experienced this passion so urgent as to render a gratification necessary.

From continence there is less to be feared than from excess, as is strikingly evinced in a number of men, some of whom, by the effects of the latter, lose their memory; some are deprived of sight; some become bald, and many have dwindled into a consumption and died.

21

Of the irreparable injury done to their health by venereal indulgences, young persons can never be sufficiently warned. How many cease to be men, or who at least cease to enjoy the faculty of manhood, before the age of thirty? And how many at fifteen, or eighteen, have received the infection of a disease, which is not only in itself disgraceful, but often incurable.

It has already been observed, that at the age of puberty, the growth usually ceases. It often happens, however, that in the course of a tedious illness, the body increases more in length, than would have been the case in a state of perfect health. This is probably occasioned by the external organs of generation remaining without action during that period. The organic nutriment, having no irritation to determine it to those parts, does not reach them; and the want of this irritation is owing to an imbecility and lassitude of the parts, which prevent the secretion of the seminal fluid. As the organic particles, therefore, remain in the mass of blood, the extremities of the bones are necessarily enlarged, nearly in the same manner as those of eunuchs. Thus young people, on their recovery from along course of sickness, are frequently taller, but worst shaped, than formerly. Some, for instance, become crooked-backed, others crook-legged; and this, because the still ductile extremities of the bones have been necessarily extended by the superfluity of the organic particles, whose only office, in a state of health, would have been the formation of the seminal fluid.

To produce children is the object of marriage, though this object is sometimes frustrated. Among the different causes of sterility there are some alike common to men and women; but as in men they are more apparent, to men they are more commonly attributed. In both sexes, sterility is occasioned either by an inherent defect in the conformation of the organs, or by accidental injuries to the organs themselves. Among men, the most essential imperfections in the conformation are those which affect the testicles, or those parts called the *erectores penis*. The false direction of the urethra, which is sometimes not only oblique, but badly perforated, is another obstacle to generation; as is the adherence of the prepuce to the bridle, which may, however, be corrected. In women, the conformation of the matrix may likewise be imperfect; and the perpetual closure or expansion of the orifice of the matrix, are defects which are alike repugnant to generation. But the most frequent cause of sterility, both in men and women, is the corruption of the seminal liquid in the *testes*; for if the secretion, by which the semen be formed, is vitiated, the fluid must be incapable of impregnation; in which case, though the organs may have every appearance of being properly qualified for it, there will be no procreation; but these causes have no external appearance.

In cases of sterility, different means have been employed to discover whether the defect was to be imputed to the man or the woman. Of these, inspection is the chief; and indeed, if the sterility be occasioned by an external fault in the conformation, this is sufficient. But if the defect is in the internal organs, it is almost impossible to discover or remove it. There are men, to all appearance well formed, who want the genuine sign of a proper conformation; and others who have it in so slight a degree as to make the mark of virility extremely equivocal. This is the most animal part of the human frame, and is constantly under the influence of instinct, and not governed by that of the mind. Many young persons of the purest ideas have been subjected to the liveliest sensations, though ignorant of pleasure, or the cause, and others remain cold and languid notwithstanding the efforts of imagination.

When sterility does not arise from any defect in external conformation, it more frequently proceeds from the women than the men; for, besides the injurious effects of the fluor albus, I conceive there is another material cause. In the course of my experiments, as related in the preceding volume, I observed there were small protuberances in the female testicles which I called glandular bodies; they originate under the membrane of the testicle, in a short time begin to swell, and then opening, a fluid issues therefrom; from this time they begin to decay, and having disappeared, they are immediately succeeded by others, from which the testicles are constantly undergoing a kind of alteration; and I am inclined to think, that if any circumstance takes place to interrupt the necessary exercise of the vessels, the seminal liquor will become corrupt, and sterility also will follow.

Sometimes conception precedes puberty. Numbers of women have become mothers before the smallest appearance of the menstrua: and some to whom this evacuation was never known have brought forth children. Instances of this occur in our own climate, without travelling for them to Brazil; where whole nations, we are told, are perpetuated without any woman being subject to the menstrual discharge; an evident proof, that it is not the substance of this discharge, but the seminal liquid of male and female which are essentially necessary to generation. It is also known that the cessation of the menses, which generally happens about the age of forty or fifty, does not always disqualify women from conceiving, and that some women have really become pregnant at the age of sixty or seventy. These examples, however frequent, may be considered as exceptions to the general rule; but they are sufficient to convince us that the menstrual blood is by no means the constituent principle of generation.

In the ordinary course of Nature women do not conceive before the menses appear, nor after they have ceased. The age at which men first acquire the powers of procreation is less distinctly marked. His body must obtain a certain degree of growth, before the seminal fluid can be produced; and before it can be formed and perfected, that growth must become still greater. This usually happens between the age of twelve and eighteen; but the period at which the procreative faculty of man ceases, Nature seems to have left undetermined. At sixty or seventy, when age begins to enfeeble the body, the seminal fluid is less copious, and often unprolific; yet there are many instances of men still continuing to procreate at the age of eighty or ninety.

There also are examples of boys who have propagated at eight, nine, and ten years; and of girls who have conceived at seven, eight, and nine. But such facts are exceedingly rare, and ought to be classed as singular phenomena. The external sign of virility appears in infancy, but that is not sufficient; in order to accomplish the act of generation, there must be a previous production of semen; and this is never effected till the growth of the body is nearly finished. At first the quantity is very small, and for the most part unfruitful.

Some authors have mentioned two signs of conception. The one is, a kind of tremor which they say begins at the time of conception, and continues for several days after; the other is taken from the orifice of the matrix, which they assure us is entirely closed after conception. These signs are, however, in my opinion, very equivocal, if not altogether imaginary.

This tremor is mentioned by Hippocrates, and, according to him, it is so violent as to make the teeth chatter. Galen, on the authority of some women, imputes this symptom to a contraction of the matrix; others explain it by a vague sensation of cold over the whole body, and almost all establish the fact, like Galen, from the testimony of different women.

Opinions, however, vary as to the changes which happen in the matrix after conception, some maintaining, that the edges of the orifice are drawn together so closely that there is not the smallest vacancy left between them; and others, that these edges are not exactly close till after the two first months of pregnancy. They nevertheless agree, that immediately after conception the orifice is closed by a glutinous humour; that the matrix, which, but for the pregnancy, might receive through its orifice a substance of the size of a pea, has no longer any perceptible aperture, and that the difference is so evident that a skilful midwife may distinguish it. If these assertions were true, even in the first days of pregnancy, its certainty or uncertainty might be ascertained.

The advocates on the other side urge, that if after conception the orifice of the matrix were closed, there could be no superfœtation. To this it may be replied, that the seminal liquor may penetrate through the membranes of the matrix; that even the matrix itself may open to admit the superfœtation; and that at any rate superfœtations happen so rarely, that they make a very trifling exception to the general rule. Other authors have maintained, that this change never appears but in women who have conceived before, and borne children. In first conceptions, indeed, the difference must be less sensible; but be it as conspicuous as it may, ought we thence to conclude that it is a certain and positive sign? No; it is unaccompanied with sufficient evidence.

Neither from the study of anatomy, nor from experiments, can we, as to this point, acquire more than general conclusions, which on a particular examination are often found to be highly erroneous. It is the same also with respect to the tremor or convulsive cold, which some women have said they felt at the time of conception. As most women do not experience this sensation; as others assure us, on the contrary, that they have felt a burning heat; and, as others still confess, that they are utter strangers to all such feelings; the natural conclusion is, that such signs are highly dubious, and that when they do happen, it is less perhaps in consequence of conception, than of other consequences.

On this subject I shall add but one fact, from "Parson's Lectures on Muscular Motion," which proves that the orifice of the matrix does not close immediately after conception; or that at least the seminal fluid may even then find a passage into it. A woman of Charles-Town, in South-Carolina, was delivered, in 1714, of two children, one immediately after the other. To the utter astonishment of all present, one child was black and the other white. From this evident testimony of her infidelity to her husband, the woman acknowledged that a negro had one day entered her chamber, where her husband had just left her in bed, and by threats of immediate death compelled her to gratify his desires. This fact proves that the conception of two or more children does not always happen at one time, and gives great weight to my opinion, that the semen penetrates through the texture of the matrix.

Many other equivocal symptoms of pregnancy are said to distinguish it in the first months; as a slight pain in the region of the matrix and loins; a numbness over the whole body; a continual drowsiness; a melancholy and capricious disposition; the tooth-ach, head-ach, and vertigo; yellow eyes, with the pupils contracted, and lids oppressed; paleness of countenance, with spots upon it; a depraved appetite, with loathing, vomiting, and spitting; hysteric symptoms; the fluor albus; stoppage of the menstrual discharge, or instead of it hæmorrhage; the secretion of milk in the breasts, &c. Many other symptoms might be adduced, which are supposed to be the signs of pregnancy, but which are frequently nothing more than the effects of particular maladies.

Of these we shall leave the discussion to physicians. Were we to consider each of them in particular, we should deviate too far from our subject; nor could we do it with advantage, without entering into a lengthened series of profound investigation. It is with this as with a number of other subjects that relate to physiology and animal economy, the authors, very few excepted, who have written on these subjects, have treated them in a manner so vague, and explained them by affinities so remote, and hypotheses so false, that it is not surprising their remarks should have been attended with as little information as utility.

CHAPTER IV.
A DESCRIPTION OF MAN.

The body attains its full height at the age of puberty, or at least a few years after. Some young people cease growing at fourteen or fifteen; while others continue their growth till two or three and twenty. During this period most men are of slender make; their thighs and legs small, and the muscular parts are as yet unfilled; but by degrees the fleshy fibres augment, the muscles swell, the limbs assume their figure, and become more proportioned, and before the age of thirty the body, in men, has acquired its most perfect symmetry.

In women, the body sooner attains this symmetry; their muscles and other parts being less strong, compact, and solid than those of men; and being also less in size, they require less time in coming to maturity. Hence it is that a woman is as completely formed at twenty, as a man at thirty.

The body of a well-shaped man ought to be square, the muscles expressed with boldness, and the lines in the face distinctly marked. In woman superior elegance prevails; her form is more soft, and her features more delicate. Strength and majesty belong to the former, grace and softness are the peculiar embellishments of the latter.

In both, their external forms declare their sovereignty over every living creature. Man supports his body erect; his attitude is that of command; and his face, which is turned towards the heavens, displays a superior dignity. The image of his soul is painted in his countenance; the excellence of his nature penetrates through the material form in which it is enclosed, and gives to his features a lively animation. His majestic port, his firm and resolute step, announce the superiority of his rank. He touches the earth only with his extremity, and beholds it as if at a disdainful distance. His arms are not given to him for pillars of support; nor does he render his hands callous by their treading on the ground, and losing that delicacy of feeling for which they were originally designed. His arms and hands are formed for very different purposes; they are formed to second every intention of his will; to defend himself, and to enable him to seize and enjoy the gifts of Nature.

When the mind is at rest, all the features of the visage are in a state of profound tranquillity. Their proportion, their union, their harmony, seem to mark the sweet serenity, and to give a true information of what passes within. When the soul, however, is agitated, the human visage becomes a living picture, where the passions are expressed with as much delicacy as energy; where every motion is expressed by some corresponding feature; where every impression anticipates the will, and betrays those hidden agitations, that he would often wish to conceal.

It is particularly in the eyes that the passions are painted, and most readily discovered. The eye seems to belong to the soul more than any other organ; it seems to participate of all its emotions; the softest and most tender as well as the most violent and tumultous. These if not only receives, but transmits by sympathy into the soul of the observer all that secret fire with which its mind is agitated; and thus does passion often become general. In short the eye is the lively index of the mind, and forcibly speaks the language of intelligence.

Those who are short-sighted labour under a particular disadvantage in this respect, being in a manner deprived of the intelligent expression of the eye; and which frequently gives an air of stupidity to the finest face. It is strong and violent passions alone that we ever see marked on such countenances, and which often produce very unfavourable prepossessions. However intelligent we may afterwards find such persons, it is with difficulty we renounce our former prejudices. We are so habituated to judge by external appearances that we too often decide on men's talents by their physiognomy; and having perhaps at first, caught up our judgments prematurely, they mechanically influence us all our lives after; nay the colour, or cut of the clothes will sometimes influence conclusions as to their abilities; and that not always without reason: therefore since strangers may decide upon understanding by so trifling an article as dress, we ought not to be totally inattentive to it, trifling as it may appear.

The vivacity, or the languid motion of the eyes, gives the strongest marks to the countenance; and their colour contributes still more to enforce the expression. The different colours of the eyes are dark-hazle, light-hazle, green, blue, grey, and whitish grey. These different colours arise from the different colours of the little muscles, that serve to contract the pupil, and they very often change colour with disorder, and with age.

Those most frequent are, the hazle and the blue, and very often both these colours are found in the same eye. Those eyes which are called black are only dark-hazle, which may be easily seen upon close inspection, and only appear black from the contrast with the white of the eye; in all those which have a blue shade that colour becomes the most predominant. Those eyes are reckoned the most beautiful where the shade is the deepest; and either in the black or the blue, the fire, which gives to the eye its finest expression, is most distinguishable. For this reason, the black eyes, as they are called, have the greatest force and vivacity; but the blue are the most delicate, and have the most powerful effect in beauty, as they reflect a greater variety of rays from the tints of which they are composed.

This variety in the colour of the eyes, is peculiar to man, and one or two of the brute-creation; in other animals, the colour in any one individual is the same in all the rest. The eyes of the ox are brown; those of sheep of a watery colour; those of goats are grey, &c. and it may also be remarked, that the eyes of most white animals are red; as the rabbit, ferret, &c. "According to Aristotle, in the human species grey eyes are the strongest; blues eyes are weak; full eyes are near sighted, and brown ones require a good light."

Though the eye, when put in motion, seems to be drawn towards either side, yet it only moves round its centre; by which its coloured part moves nearer, or farther from the angle of the eye-lids, and is thus elevated or depressed. The distance between the eye is less in man than in any other animal; in some it is so great that it is almost impossible that they should ever view the same object with both eyes at once.

Next to the eyes, that which gives most character to the face are the eye-brows, which being, in some measure, totally different from the other features, their effect is most readily distinguished. The eye-lashes have an effect in giving expression to the eye, particularly when long and close, they soften its glances, and improve its sweetness. Man and apes are the only animals that have eye-lashes both upon the upper and lower lids, all other animals want them on the lid below, and even man has less on the under than on the upper.

The eye-lids serve to guard the ball of the eye, and to furnish it with a proper moisture. The upper lid rises and falls; the lower has scarce any motion; and though their being moved depends on the will, yet the will is unable to keep them open when sleep, or fatigue, oppresses the mind. In birds and amphibious quadrupeds the lower lid alone has motion; and fishes and insects have no eye-lids whatsoever.

The forehead makes a large part of the face, and chiefly contributes to its beauty. It ought to be justly proportioned, neither too round nor too flat, neither too narrow nor too low, and it should be regularly surrounded with the hair. The hair tends greatly to improve the face, and baldness takes away from beauty. Borrowed locks, however, do not justly supply the place of real ones, as the true character cannot be so well traced in the countenance when the one is substituted for the other. The highest part of the head, and that immediately above the temples, first becomes bald; the hair under the temples, and at the back of the head, is seldom known to fail.

It has been observed by some authors that baldness was peculiar to man, and that it never happens to women in the most advanced periods of life. The hair is, in general, thickest where the constitution is strongest, and more glossy and beautiful where the health is most permanent. The ancients supposed the hair to be produced like the nails, the part next the root pushing out that immediately contiguous. But the moderns have found that every hair may be truly said to live and to receive nutriment like other parts of the body. The roots do not turn grey sooner than the extremities, but the whole hair changes colour nearly at the same time, and we have many instances of persons who have grown grey in one night's time. When turned white it gradually loses its strength and falls off. Aristotle asserts, that no man ever became bald previous to his intercourse with women.

The nose is the most prominent feature in the face, but as it has scarce any motion, even in the strongest passions, it rather adds to the beauty, than to the expression of the countenance. The form of this feature, and its advanced position, are peculiar to the human visage alone. Other animals, for the most part, have nostrils with a partition between them, but none of them have an elevated nose. Apes themselves have scarce any thing else of this feature but the nostrils, the rest of the feature lying flat upon the visage, and scarce higher than the cheek-bones. This organ serves man and most animals not only to breathe but to enjoy odoriferous scents. Birds have merely two holes for these purposes.

The mouth and lips, next to the eyes, are found to have the greatest expression. The passions have great power over this part of the face, and the mouth marks its different degrees by its different forms. The organ of speech still more animates this part, and gives it more life than any other feature in the face. The ruby colour of the lips, and the white enamel of the teeth, have such a superiority over every other feature that they seem to form the principal object of our regard. In fact, the whole attention is fixed upon the lips of the speaker; however rapid his discourse, and however various the subject, the mouth takes correspondent situations, and deaf men have been often found to *see* the force of those reasonings, which they could not *hear*, by attending to the motions of the lips.

Notwithstanding the opinion of Aristotle, with regard to the crocodile, I am convinced, that in that, as well as in man, and other animals, the under jaw alone has the power of motion. In the human embrio, and in monkeys, the under jaw is very much advanced before the upper. In instances of the most violent passion this jaw has often an involuntary quivering motion; and often also pain and pleasure, as well, as languor produces another, which is that of yawning.

When the mind is affected with ardent desire, or reflects with regret upon some good unattained or lost, it feels an internal emotion, which acting upon the diaphragm, elevates the lungs, and produces a sigh; when the mind perceives no prospect of relief the sighs are repeated, sorrow succeeds, and tears often follow; the air rushes into the lungs, and gives rise to an inspiration stronger than sighs, termed sobbing, in which the voice becomes more evident; from this it proceeds to groans, which are a species of sobs continued to some length, and are longer or shorter according to the degree of anxiety the mind is labouring under. The plaintive shriek is a groan expressed with a sharp tone of voice; which when violently excited, generally continues the same tone throughout, but when moderate, usually falls at the end.

Laughter is a sound of the voice, interrupted and pursued for some continuance. The muscles of the belly, and the diaphragm, are employed in its weaker exertions; but those of the ribs are violently agitated in the stronger; the head and breast are sometimes thrown forward, in order to raise them with the greater ease. The chest remains undisturbed, the cheeks swell, the mouth naturally opens, and the belly becoming depressed, the air issues out with a noise, and which in violent fits continues for some time, and is often repeated; but in more tranquil emotions, although the cheeks swell, the lips remain close, and in some persons dimples are formed near the corners of the mouth. This smile is often an indication of kindness and good-will; it is also often used as a mark of contempt and ridicule.

The cheeks are features without any particular motion, and rather seem as an ornament to the face than for the purpose of expression, as may also be said of the chin and temples. The former indeed may be considered in some measure a picture of the mind, from the involuntary paleness and redness with which they are at limes overspread. Blushing proceeds from different passions; being produced from shame, anger, pride, Or joy, while paleness is ever an attendant on fright, fear, and sorrow. These alterations in the colour are entirely involuntary; all the other expressions of the passions are, in some small degree, under control; but blushing and paleness betray our secret thoughts, and we might as well attempt to stop the circulation of our blood, by which they are caused, as to prevent their appearance.

The whole head, as well as the features of the face, takes peculiar attitudes from different passions; it bends forward to express humility, shame, or sorrow; it is turned to one side, in languor, or in pity; it is thrown with the chin forward, in arrogance and pride; erect in self-conceit and obstinacy; it is thrown backwards in surprize or astonishment; and combines its motions to the one side and the other, to express contempt, ridicule, anger, and resentment.

The parts of the head which give least expression to the face are the ears. These which are immoveable, and make so small an appearance in man, are very distinguishing features in quadrupeds: they serve in them as the principal marks of the passions, and discover their joys or their terrors with tolerable precision. The smallest ears in men are said to be most beautiful; but the largest are found the best for hearing. Some savage nations bore their ears, and so draw down the tips to rest upon their shoulders.

The different customs of men appear still more extravagant in their manner of wearing their beards. Some, and among others the Turks, cut the hair off their heads, and let their beards grow. The Europeans, on the contrary, shave their beards and wear their hair. The American savages pluck the hairs off their beards, but are proud of those on the head; the Negroes shave their heads in figures at one time, in stars at another, and still more commonly in alternate stripes. The Talapoins of Siam shave the heads and the eye-brows of such children as are committed to their care. Every nation seems to have entertained different prejudices, at different times, in favour of one part or another of the beard. Some have preferred the hair upon the upper lip to that on the chin; some like the hair hanging down; some chuse it curled; and others like it straight.

Though fashions have arisen in different countries from fancy and caprice, yet when they have become general they deserve examination. Mankind have always considered it as a matter of moment, and they will ever continue desirous of drawing the attention of each other, by such ornaments as mark the riches, the power, or the courage of the wearer. The value of shining stones is entirely founded upon their scarceness or their brilliancy. It is the same with respect to shining metals, of which the weight is so little regarded when spread over our cloaths. These ornaments are designed to draw the attention of others, and to excite the idea of wealth and grandeur; and few there are who, undazzled by the glitter of an outside, can coolly distinguish between the metal and the man.

All things rare and brilliant will, therefore, continue to be fashionable, while men derive greater advantage from riches than virtue, and while the means of appearing considerable are more easily acquired than the title to merit. The first impression we make on strangers arises from our dress; and this varies in conformity to the character we are ambitious to obtain. The modest man, or he who would wish to be thought so, endeavours to shew the simplicity of his mind by the plainness of his dress; the vain man, on the contrary, takes a pleasure in displaying his superiority in finery and external appearance.

Another object of dress is, to encrease the size of our figure, and to take up more room in the world than Nature seems to have allotted us. We desire to enlarge our dimensions by swelling out our cloaths and raising our heels; but how bulky soever our dress may be, our vanities still exceed them. The largeness of the doctor's wig arises from the same pride as the smallness of the beau's queue. Both want to have the size of their understanding measured by the external dimensions of their heads.

There are some fashions that seem to have a more reasonable origin, which is to hide or to lessen the defects of Nature. To take men altogether, there are many more ordinary faces and deformed bodies, than beautiful countenances and handsome figures. The former, as being the most numerous, give laws to fashion, and their laws are generally such as are made in their favour. Women begin to colour their checks with red when the natural roses are faded, and the younger are obliged to follow the example, though not compelled by the same necessity. In all parts of the world this custom prevails more or less, and powdering and frizzing the hair, though not so general, seems to have arisen from a similar desire of displaying the features to most advantage.

But, leaving the draperies of the human picture, let us return to the figure unadorned by art.

The head of man, whether considered externally or internally, is differently formed from that of all other animals. The head of the monkey has some similitude, but in that there are differences, which we shall take notice of in another place. The bodies of almost all quadrupeds are covered with hair, but the head of man alone has this ornament before puberty, and that more abundantly than any other animal.

There is a great variety in the teeth of all animals, some have them above and below, others have them in the under jaw only: in some they stand separate from each other, while in others they are close and united. The palate of some fishes is nothing but a bony substance studded with points, which perform the office of teeth. All these substances, that is, the teeth of men, quadrupeds, and fishes, the saws, &c. of insects, like the nails, horns, and hoofs, derive their origin from the nerves. We before remarked that the nerves harden by being exposed to the air; and as the mouth gives free access to it, the nerves that terminate therein, being thus exposed, acquire a solidity. In this manner the teeth and nails are formed in man, and the beaks, hoofs, horns, and talons of other animals are produced.

The neck supports the head, and unites it to the body. This part is more considerable in the generality of quadrupeds, than in man. Fishes and other animals that have not lungs similar to ours, have no neck. Birds in general have the neck longer than any other kind of animal; those of them which have short claws have also short necks, and so on the contrary.

The human breast is larger in proportion than that of other animals; and none but man, and those animals which make use of their fore feet as hands, such as monkeys, squirrels, &c. have collar-bones. The breasts, in women are larger than in men; they however seem formed in the same, manner; and sometimes milk is found in the breasts of the latter. Of this there have been many instances about the age of puberty, and I have seen a young man press a considerable quantity out of one of his breasts. Among animals there, is a great variety in this part of the body. Some, as the ape and the elephant, have but two teats, which are placed on each side of the breast, Bears have four. Sheep have but two, placed between the hinder legs. Other animals, such as the bitch and sow, have them all along the belly. Birds and other oviparous animals have no teats; but viviparous fishes, as the whale and the dolphin, have both teats and milk. The form also of the teats varies in different animals, and in the same animal at different ages. Those women whose breasts are shaped like a pear, are said to make the best nurses. In the belly of the human race the naval makes a conspicuous figure, but which is scarcely perceptible in other animals.

The arms of men but very little resemble the fore legs of quadrupeds, and much less the wings of birds. The ape is the only animal that is possessed of hands and arms; and they are fashioned more rudely, and with less exact proportion, than in men. The shoulders are also much larger in man than in any other animal, and of a form widely distinct.

The form of the back differs not much from that of many quadrupeds, only that the reins are more muscular and strong. The buttock, however, in man is different from that of all animals whatsoever. What goes by that name in other creatures is only the upper part of the thigh, and by no means similar: man being the only animal that can support himself perfectly erect, the peculiar hardness of this part enables him to sustain that position.

The human feet are also different from those of all animals, even apes not excepted. The foot of the ape is rather a kind of aukward hand; its toes, or rather fingers, are long, and that in the middle longest of all; the foot also wants the heel. In man the sole of the foot is broader and more adapted to maintain the equilibrium of the body in walking, dancing, or running.

The nails are smaller in man than those of any animal. If they were much longer than the extremities of the fingers, they would obstruct the management of the hand. Such savages as suffer them to grow long, make use of them in flaying and tearing animals, but though their nails are considerably larger than ours, they are yet by no means to be compared to the hoofs or the claws of other animals.

There is little known exactly with regard to the proportion of the human figure, for the same parts do not bear similar proportions in any two individuals; nor even in the same, for seldom is it that the right leg or arm is of equal dimensions with the left. It is not by taking an exact *resemblance* that we can determine on the best proportion of the human figure; we must seek for it in taste and sentiment, which have exceeded the laws of mechanism in the imitation of Nature; and in which imitation we recognize her perfections more conspicuously than in her own productions; and by the same rule the beauty of the best statues is much better conceived by observation than by measurement. The ancients executed statues in so high a degree of perfection, that they have ever been considered as exact representations of the most perfect human figures. These statues, which were at first copied after the human form, are now considered as the most perfect models of it; and for this plain reason, that they were not formed after any one individual, but from a diligent observation of the perfect symmetry that was to be collected, as it were, from the whole species. In doing this, these artists also considered each part of the human frame should be of certain dimensions to become the standard of perfection; for instance, that the body should be ten times the length of the face; and that the face should also be divisible into three equal parts, the first form the hair on the forehead to the nose, the second the nose, and the third from the nose to the end of the chin. In measuring the body they use the term nose as the third of the face, one of which they reckon in height, from the top of the forehead to the crown of the head, therefore from the top of the head to the bottom of the chin is a face and one third, and from the chin to the upper part of the breasts two thirds more, which of course makes two tenths of the whole body; to the bottom of the paps another, to the navel a fourth, and from thence to the division of the lower extremities a fifth, or half the body; two more faces are assigned to the thighs, half a one to the knee, two from the knee to the top of the foot, and the other half from thence to the sole, which completes the ten. This division does not hold good in men of a more than ordinary size, in whom about half a face is allowed between the paps and the commencement of the thighs, which in them is not the middle of the body. The arms being stretched out, measure from the ends of the middle fingers ten faces, or exactly the length of the body. The hand is the length of the face, the thumb that of the nose, as is also the longest toe, and the bottom of the foot, is one sixth part of the length of the body. The space between the eyes is the breadth of the eye. the breadth of the thickest part of the thigh is double that of the thickest part of the leg, and treble the smallest. Were any individual measured by these rules, those we consider as the most perfect would be found highly deficient.

These correspondences are, however, extremely arbitrary. In infants the upper parts of the body are larger than the lower; the legs and thighs do not constitute any thing like half the length of the body; as the child increases in age the inferior parts increase more than in proportion, so that the body is not equally divided till it has acquired its full growth. In women the anterior part of the chest is more prominent than in men; but as in the former the chest is more thick, so in the latter it is more broad. In women too the hips are considerably more bulky, and so different is the conformation of those two parts, that it is sufficient to distinguish the skeleton of a woman from that of a man.

The total height of the human figure varies considerably. Men are said to be tall who are from five feet eight or nine inches to six feet. The middle stature is from five feet two to five feet seven inches; and such as fall under these measures are said to be of small stature. Women in general are two or three inches shorter than men. As for giants and dwarfs, of them we shall have occasion to speak in another place.

Though the body of a man is more externally delicate than that of any animal, it is exceedingly muscular, and for its size perhaps more strong. Were we to compare the strength of a lion with that of a man, we ought to consider that the former is armed with teeth and talons, which give a false idea of its power. The arms which man has received from Nature are not offensive; and happy were it if Art had never furnished him with weapons more terrible than those which arm the paws of the lion.

But there is another, and perhaps a more just manner of comparing the strength of man with that of animals, namely by the weights which either can carry. We are assured that the porters of Constantinople carry burthens 900 pounds weight; and M. Desaguliers tells us of a man in an upright posture, who, by distributing a certain number of weights, in such a manner that every part of his body bore its share, was able to support a weight of 2000 pounds. By the same expedient a horse, which is at least six or seven times our bulk, ought to be enabled to carry a load, of 12 or 14,000 pounds; an enormous weight in comparison of what that animal can support, even when the weight is distributed with every possible advantage.

The strength of a man may be still further estimated by agility and the continuance of his labour. Men accustomed to running outstrip horses, or at least continue their speed for a greater length of time. A man will walk down a horse if they continue together, and perform a long journey much sooner, and with less fatigue. The royal messengers of Ispahan, who are runners by profession, go 36 leagues in 14 or 15 hours. Travellers assure us, that the Hottentots out-run lions in the chace, and that the savages, who live by hunting, pursue the elk and other animals with such speed as to take them. Many other surprising things are told of the nimbleness of savages, and of the long journeys they accomplish on foot, over the most craggy mountains, and the most unfavourable roads, where there is no path to direct, and every obstacle to oppose. A thousand leagues are these people said to travel in less than six weeks, or two months. Birds excepted, whose muscles are indeed stronger in proportion than those of any other animal, no other creature could support such a continuance of fatigue. The civilized man is ignorant of his own strength; nor is he sensible how much he loses of it by effeminacy, and how he might add to it by the habit of vigorous exercise.

Sometimes we find men of extraordinary strength; but this gift of Nature, which would be valuable to them in a primitive state, is of very trifling service with the polished part of mankind, among whom mental perfections are held in higher estimation than bodily, and manual exertions are confined to persons of the lowest classes.

Men are much stronger than women; and this superiority they have too often employed, by tyrannically enslaving a sex, which was formed to partake with them the pleasures as well as the pains of life. Savage nations subject their women to a continued series of labour. On them is imposed every office of drudgery, while the husband indolently reclines in his hammock. From this inactive situation he is seldom roused but by the calls of hunger, when he is obliged to seek food by fishing or hunting. A savage has no idea of taking pleasure in exercise; and nothing surprises him more than to see an European walk backwards and forward, merely for his amusement or recreation. All men have a tendency to laziness; but the savages of hot countries are not only lazy to an extreme, but tyrannical to their women, beyond any other classes of men. In civilized countries men dictate laws to women, which are the more severe, as their manners are rough and untaught, and it is only among nations highly polished that women are raised to that equality of condition which is naturally their due, and so necessary to the true enjoyment of society. These refinements flow from themselves; and to strength they oppose arms more sure to conquer, when by modesty they teach us to pay homage to the empire of beauty; a natural advantage, superior to strength. But much skill is requisite to manage and increase its influence, as is evident from the different ideas which different nations entertain of beauty. These indeed are so widely opposite, so palpably contradictory, that there is every reason to suppose the sex have gained more by rendering themselves amiable, than even by this gift of Nature, about which men are so much divided. As from the difficulty of obtaining it, the value of a thing still increases, so beauty has always had its admirers, and its votaries, respect necessarily encreased as soon as the possessors of it maintained a becoming dignity, and turned a deaf ear to every address of which virtue was not the positive basis; this naturally introduced a delicacy of sentiment, and polished manners followed of course.

So widely did the ancients disagree with us in respect of beauty, that, with them, a small forehead, and eye-brows joined, were accounted ornaments in the female countenance; and even to this day, in Persia, the union of the eye-brows is held in high estimation. In several parts of the Indies, it is necessary that the teeth should be black, and the hair white, to form a beauty; and, in the Marian islands, it is a principal occupation of the women, to blacken the teeth with herbs, and to whiten the hair by certain lotions. In China and Japan, the essential ingredients of beauty are, a large visage, small eyes, and almost concealed, a nose flat and bulky, little feet, and a belly enormously big. Some of the Indians of America and Asia, in order to enlarge the countenance, compress the heads of their children between two planks, others flatten them from the crown only, and others exert every effort to render them round. Every nation, and every individual, has a peculiar prejudice, or taste, with respect to beauty, which probably originates from some pleasing impression received in infancy, and therefore depends more, perhaps, on habit and chance than on the disposition of our organs.

When we come to treat of the different senses, we shall perhaps be able to determine what stress is to be laid on the ideas of beauty which we receive from the eyes. In the mean time let us examine the human countenance as it appears when agitated by the passions. In grief, joy, love, shame, and compassion, the eyes swell, and overflow with tears. The effusion of these is always accompanied with a tension of the muscles of the face, which opens the month. The natural moisture in the nose becomes increased by the tears flowing through the lachrymal ducts; they do not, however, flow uniformly, but burst out by intervals.

In sorrow the corners of the mouth are lowered, the under lip raised, the eye-lids nearly closed, the pupil elevated, and almost covered with the eye-lid; the other muscles of the face are relaxed, so that the space between the mouth and the eyes is larger than ordinary, and of consequence the .countenance appears lengthened. [See *fig.* 13.]

In fear, terror, or horror, the forehead is wrinkled, the eye-brow raised, the eye-lids are extended as much as possible, and discover a part of the white over the pupil, which is lowered, and somewhat concealed by the lower eye-lid: the mouth, at the same time, is widely opened, and the lips separating, both the upper and under teeth are seen. [See *fig.* 14.]

In contempt and derision the upper lip is raised on one side, and on the other there is a little motion, resembling a supercilious smile; the nose is shrivelled on the same side that the lip is raised, and the corner, of the mouth is extended; the eye on the same side is almost shut, while the other is open as usual, but the pupils of both are lowered as when looking from a height. [See *fig.* 15.]

In jealousy, envy, and malice, the eye-brows fall down, and are wrinkled; the eye-lid is raised and the pupil lowered; the upper lip is raised on each side, while the corners of the mouth are rather lowered; and the middle of the under lip is raised, in order to join the middle of the upper lip. [See *fig. 16.*]

In laughter the two corners of the mouth are drawn back and somewhat raised; the upper part of the cheeks is raised; and the eyes are more or less closed; the upper lip is raised, while the under one is lowered; and in immoderate laughter the mouth is opened, and the skin of the nose is shrivelled. [See *fig. 17.*]

The arms, the hands, and the body in general, likewise assist the countenance by different gestures, in the expression of the emotions of the soul. In joy, for example, the eyes, the head, the arms, and the whole body, are agitated by quick and varied movements. In languor and melancholy the eyes are sunk, the head is reclined, and the whole body is motionless. In admiration, surprize, and astonishment, all motion is suspended, and we remain in one and the same attitude. These expressions of the passions are independent on the will; but there is another sort of expression, which seems to be produced by a reflection of the mind, by a command of the will, and by which the eyes, the head, the arms, and the whole body, are put in action. They appear to be so many efforts of the mind to defend the body, or at least so many secondary signs sufficient to express particular passions. In love, desire, and hope, we raise the head and eyes towards heaven, as if to implore the good we wish for; we bend the head forward, as if to hasten, by this approach, the possession of the desired object; and we extend the arms, and open the hands, in order to embrace and seize it. On the contrary, in fear, hatred, and horror, we advance the arms with precipitation, as if to repel the object of our aversion; and in order to shun it we turn aside the eyes and head, and shrink back. These movements are so quick that they appear involuntary: but it is by habit we are deceived, for they are motions which depend on reflection, and which mark the perfection of the springs of the human body, by the readiness with which each member obeys the dictates of the will.

As the passions are agitations of the mind, and as most of them have an affinity to the impressions of the senses, they may be expressed by the movements of the body, and especially by those of the visage. Of what passes within we may form a judgment from the external motions of the body, and can know the actual situation of the soul by inspecting the changes of the countenance. But as the soul has no form which can have any relation to that of matter we cannot judge of it by the figure of the body, or by the features of the countenance. An ill-formed body may contain an amiable mind; nor is the good or bad disposition of a person to be determined by the features of the face, these features having no analogy with the nature of the soul on which any reasonable conjectures may be founded.

To this kind of prejudice, nevertheless, the ancients were strongly attached; and in all ages there have been men who have attempted to form into a science of divination their pretended skill in physiognomy; but it is evident that this divination can only extend to the situation of the mind when expressed by the motion of the eyes, visage, and other parts of the body, and that the form of the nose, the mouth, and other features, are no more connected with the natural disposition of the person, than is the largeness or the thickness of the limbs to that of thought. Shall a man have more genius because he has a better-shaped nose? Shall he have less wisdom because his eyes are little, and his mouth is large? It must be acknowledged, therefore, that the divination of physiognomists is without foundation, and that nothing can be more chimerical than their pretended observations.

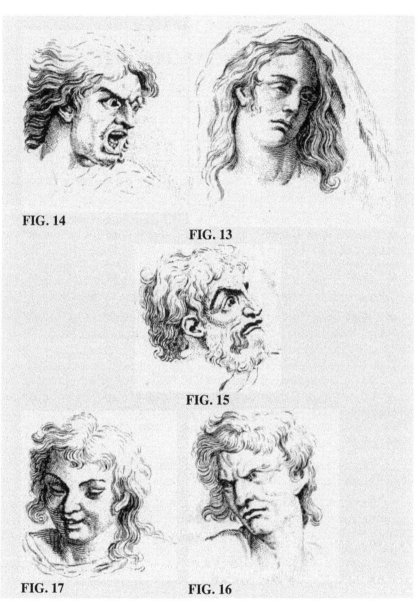

FIG. 14

FIG. 13

FIG. 15

FIG. 17

FIG. 16

Click on image to view larger version.

CHAPTER V.
OF OLD AGE AND DEATH.

Every object in Nature has its improvement and its decay. No sooner does the human form arrive at its limited perfection, than it begins to decline. The alteration is at first insensible, and even several years elapse before it becomes perceptible. Yet we ought to feel the weight of our years better than other people can estimate the number of them; and, as those are rarely deceived who judge of our age from external appearances, we would be still less so, as to the internal effect, if we did but observe ourselves more, and flatter ourselves less with false and idle hopes.

When the body has attained its full length, by the final expansion of all its parts, it begins to receive an additional bulk, which rather incommodes than assists it, and may be considered as the first step towards decay. This is formed from a superfluous substance termed fat, and generally appears about the age of thirty-five, or forty, and by which, in proportion to its encrease, the body becomes less nimble, active, and unconstrained in its motions.

The bones also, and the other solid parts of the body, encrease in solidity. The membranes become cartilaginous, or gristly, the cartilages become bony, the fibres become more hard, the skin dries up, wrinkles are gradually formed in it, the hair grows grey, the teeth fall out, the visage becomes haggard, and the body stoops. The first approach of these alterations is perceived before the age of forty; by slow degrees they advance till that of sixty, and by rapid ones till that of seventy: after which period, decrepitude soon follows, and continues to augment to the age of ninety, or a hundred, when the life of man is generally terminated.

Having already traced the causes of the formation, growth, and expansion of the human frame, we shall now proceed to consider those of its decay.

At first the bones of the fœtus are only small threads, of a ductile matter, and of little more substance than the flesh; by degrees they acquire solidity, and may be considered as a kind of small tubes, lined both within and without by a thin membrane which supplies the osseous matter. A pretty exact idea might be formed of the growth of bones, by comparing them with the manner in which the wood and solid parts of vegetables are produced. These bones, or, as we have said, tubes, are covered at both ends by a soft substance, and in proportion as they receive nutritious juices, the extremities extend from the middle point which always preserves its original station. The ossification begins at the middle and gradually follows the extension until the whole is converted into bone. Having acquired their full growth, and the nutritious juices no longer being necessary for their augmentation, they serve the purpose of increasing their solidity; in time the bones become so solid as not to admit the circulation of these juices which are highly essential to their nourishment; and this being stopped, they undergo a change like that perceived in old trees; and this change is the first cause that renders the decay of the human body inevitable.

The cartilages, which may be considered as soft and imperfect bones, grow also more rigid as we increase in years; and as they are generally placed near the joints, the motion of these must of consequence become more difficult. Thus, in old age, every action of the body is performed with labour; and the cartilages, which in youth were elastic, and in manhood pliant, will now sooner break than bend, and may be considered as the second cause of our dissolution.

The membranes become likewise as we grow old more dense and more dry. Those, for example, which surround the bones cease to be ductile, and are incapable of extension so early as the age of 18 or 20. It is also the same with the muscular fibres, and though to the external touch the body seems, as we advance in years, to grow more soft, yet in reality it is increasing in hardness. On such occasions it is the skin, and not the flesh, that communicates this perception. The fat which increases when the body is arrived at maturity, being interspersed between the skin and muscles, gives an appearance of softness which the flesh is far from possessing in reality; an undeniable proof of which is to be found in comparing the flesh of young and old animals; the former is tender and delicate; the latter hard, dry, and unfit for eating.

While the body increases, the skin will stretch to any degree of tension; but when the former diminishes, the latter never contracts; and hence the source of wrinkles, which cannot be prevented. Those of the face proceed from this cause, though as to shape they depend in a greater measure on its form, features, and habitual movements. By examining the countenance of a man at the age of 25 or 30, we may discover in it the origin of all the wrinkles it will have in old age; particularly when the features are in a state of agitation by laughing, weepings or any strong grimace. All the little furrows formed by these agitations will one day become wrinkles, which no art shall be able to remove.

In proportion then as we advance in years, the bones, the cartilages, the membranes, the flesh, the skin, and all the fibres of the body grow more solid, hard, and dry. Every part shrinks, and every motion becomes more slow; the circulation of the fluids is performed with less freedom, the perspiration diminishes, the secretions alter, the digestion becomes slow and laborious, the nutritive juices become less plentiful, and no longer serving to convey their accustomed nourishment, are wholly useless, as if they did not exist. Thus the body dies by little and little, all its functions diminish by degrees, and death only at last seizes upon that little which is left.

As the bones, the cartilages, the muscles, and all the other parts of the body, are naturally softer in women than in men, they do not acquire so soon that hardness which hastens death. Women, therefore, ought to live longer than men. This is actually the case; for by consulting the tables which have been formed respecting the duration of human life, we shall find that, after a certain age, women have a greater chance for long life than men of the same number of years. From this it may also be inferred, that such men as are weak in appearance, and whose constitution rather resembles that of women, have a probability of living longer than those who seem to be more strong and robust; as likewise, that in either sex such persons as have been slow in their advances to maturity, will be slow in their advances to the infirmities of old age, because in both cases, the bones, the cartilages, and all the fibres, require a longer time to arrive at that degree of solidity, which must be the foundation of their destruction. This natural cause of death is common to all animals, and even to vegetables. An oak only perishes because its more ancient parts, which are in the centre, become so hard and so compact, that they can no longer receive any nourishment; and the moisture they contain, being deprived of circulation, becomes corrupted, and gradually alters the fibres of the wood, which become red, and at length crumble into dust.

The duration of life may be determined, in some measure, by the time that was employed in the attainment of maturity. A tree, or an animal, which takes but a short time to finish its growth, perishes much sooner than those which are longer in coming to maturity. Neither animals nor plants begin to spread in bulk till they have acquired their summit of height. Man grows in stature till the age of 17 or 18; but his body is not completely unfolded in all its parts till that of 30; while a dog is at its full length in one year, and at its full thickness in another. The man whose growth is so tedious, lives for 90 or an 100 years; whereas the dog seldom survives its 10 or 12th year. To the generality of other animals this observation is equally applicable. Fishes, whose growth continues for a number of years, live for centuries; and this from no other known certain cause, but the particular constitution of their bones, which do not admit of the same solidity as the bones of terrestrial animals.

Whether there are any exceptions to this kind of rule, which Nature seems to have adopted in proportioning the duration of life to that of the bodily growth, we shall enquire when we come to the particular history of animals, as also whether crows and stags live for such a number of years as is commonly pretended. In the mean while, as a general truth, let it be remarked, that large animals live longer than small ones, and this because they require a longer time to come to maturity.

The causes of our decay then are inevitable; nor can we avoid the fatal arrow of death, or even avert it, without changing the laws of Nature. The ideas which a few visionaries have formed of perpetuating life by some particular panacea, as that of the transfusion of the blood of one living creature into the body of another, must have died with themselves, did not self-love constantly cherish our credulity, even to the persuasion of some things which are in themselves impossible, and to the doubt of others, of which every day there are demonstrative proofs.

When the constitution of the body is sound, it is perhaps possible, by moderation in the passions, by temperance and sobriety, to lengthen life for a few years. But even of this there seems to be an uncertainty, for if it is necessary that the body should employ its whole strength, that it should consume all its powers by labour and exercise, whence could any benefit accrue from regimen and abstinence? Men no doubt there are who have surpassed the usual period of human existence, and not to mention Par, who lived to the age of 144, and Jenkins to that of 165, as recorded in the Philosophical Transactions, we have many instances of the prolongation of life to 110, and even to 120 years; yet this longevity was occasioned by no peculiar art or management; on the contrary, it appears that the generality of them were peasants, huntsmen, or labourers, men who had employed their whole bodily strength, and even abused it, if to abuse it is possible, otherwise than by continual idleness and debauchery.

Besides, if we reflect that the European, the Negro, the Chinese, and the American, the civilized man and the savage, the rich and the poor, the inhabitant of the city, and the inhabitant of the country, however different in other respects, are yet entirely similar as to the period allotted for their existence; if we reflect that the difference of race, of climate, of nourishment of accommodation, makes no difference in the term of life; that men who feed on raw flesh, or on dried fish, on sago, or on rice, on cassava, or on roots, live as long as those who feed on bread and prepared meats, we must be still more strongly convinced that the duration of life depends not either on habits, customs, or on the qualities of particular food, and that nothing can change the laws of that mechanism, by which the number of our years are regulated, but excesses of luxury or intemperance.

If in the duration of life there is any difference, it ought seemingly to be ascribed to the quality of the air. In elevated countries there are commonly found more old people than in low. The mountains in Scotland and Wales, of

Auvergne and Switzerland, have furnished more instances of extreme longevity than the plains of Holland, Flanders, Germany, or Poland. In general, however, the period of human existence may be said to be the same in every country. If not cut off by accidental diseases man is found to live to the years of 90 or an 100. Beyond that date our ancestors did not live, nor has it, in any degree varied since the time of David.

Should it be asked, why, in the early ages, men lived to 900, 930, and even 960 years? it may, with great probability of reason, be answered, that the productions of the earth might then be of a different nature; as, at the creation, the surface of the globe must have been far less solid and compact than it afterwards became, so it is possible that the productions of Nature, and even the human body itself, being more ductile and more susceptible of extension, their growth was not so soon accomplished as at present. Every kind of nourishment being in itself more soft and more ductile, the bones, the muscles, &c. necessarily retained their primitive softness and ductility longer. As the body, therefore, did not attain its complete expansion, nor its generative powers, for 120 or 130 years, the duration of life would be proportioned to that time, required for the growth, as it is to this day. In the supposition, for example, that the age of puberty was originally at the years of 130, as it is now at the age of 14, it will appear, that the period of human existence has always been proportionally the same as it is at present, since by multiplying those two numbers by seven, for instance, we shall find that the age of the present race will be 98 years, as those in the first age 910. It is probable, then, that the duration of human life decreased in proportion as the solidity of the surface of the earth increased, and that the ages from the creation, to the time of David, having been sufficient to communicate to terrestrial substances all the consistency which they are capable of acquiring by the pression of gravity, the surface of the earth has ever since remained in the same condition, and the limits of the growth of its different productions have been fixed, as well as those of the duration of life.

Independent of accidental maladies which happen at every age, but become more dangerous and more frequent at the latter periods of life, all men are subject to natural infirmities, that originate solely from a decay of the different parts of the body. The muscular powers lose their firmness, the head shakes, the hands tremble, the legs totter, and the sensibility of the nerves decreasing, every sense becomes blunted. But the most striking infirmity is, that men very aged, are unequal to the office of generation. Of this inability two causes may be assigned, a defect of tension in the external organs, and a decay of the seminal fluid.[B] The latter defect, however, may be supplied by a young woman; and thus it is that we sometimes see men at an advanced period of life become fathers, but then they have a much less share in their children than young ones; and thence it happens, that young persons, when married to old men, decrepid and deformed, often bring forth monsters, and children more defective still than their fathers.

[B] Our author here enters into a repetition of the nature of the organic animalcules, and to account for the defect of tension in the external organs, but which we have passed over, not doubting our readers would feel the propriety of his concluding remark, that this was an improper place for such discussions.

The scurvy, dropsy, and such diseases as proceed from a vitiated state of the blood and other fluids, are the most fatal to mankind; but these fluids depend upon the solids, which are the real organic parts. As we become advanced in life the vessels contract, the muscles lose their strength, and the secretory organs are obstructed; from which causes the blood, and other fluids, become viscid, and occasion those diseases which are generally supposed to arise from vitiated humours. The natural decay of the solids are, therefore, the original causes of those disorders; nevertheless, if the fluids become stagnated, or are obstructed in their circulation, by a contraction of the vessels, they produce alarming symptoms, and soon corrupt and corrode the weakest parts of the solids. Thus do the causes of dissolution continually multiply until they put a period to our existence.

All these causes of decay act continually upon our material existence, and contribute to its dissolution. Nature, however, approaches to this much-dreaded period by slow and imperceptible degrees. Day after day is life consuming, and every hour is some one or other of our faculties, or vital principles, perishing before the rest. Death, therefore, is only the last shade in the picture; and it is probable that man suffers a greater change in passing from youth to age, than from age into the grave. In the instant of the formation of the fœtus life is as yet nothing, or next to nothing. It extends and acquires consistence and force as the body increases, and as soon as the latter begins to decrease the former decreases also, till its final extinction. As our life begins by degrees, so by degrees it is terminated.

Why, then, be afraid of death, if our lives have been such as not to make us apprehend the consequences of futurity? Why be afraid of that moment which is preceded by an infinity of others of the same kind? Death is as natural as life, and both happen to us in the same manner, without our having the smallest sense or perception of them. If we enquire of those whose office it is to attend the sick and the dying, we shall find, that, except in a very few acute cases, attended with convulsions, people expire quietly, and without the smallest indication of pain. Even when dreadful agonies seem so attend the afflicted, the spectators are rather terrified than the patients tormented; who, having recovered, after the most violent convulsions, possess not the smallest idea of what had passed, or even what they had suffered.

The greatest number of mankind die, therefore, without feeling the fatal stroke; and of the few who retain their senses to the last, there is hardly one, perhaps, who does not entertain the hope of recovery. Nature, for the happiness of man, has rendered this principle more powerful than reason. A person dying of a disorder which he already knows to be incurable, by repeated instances in others, and is now assured that it is so by the tears of his friends, and by the countenance or departure of the physician, is still buoyed up with the idea of getting over it; the opinion of others he considers as a groundless alarm; the hour of dissolution comes; and while every thing else is, as it were dead, hope is still alive and vigorous.

A sick man will say that he feels himself dying; that he is convinced he cannot recover; but if any person, from zeal, or indiscretion, shall tell him that his end is actually at hand, his countenance instantly changes, and betrays all the marks of surprize and uneasiness. He now seems not to believe, what he had been endeavouring to impress upon others; he had only some doubt, some uneasiness, about his situation; but his hopes were far greater than his fears; and but for the gloomy assiduity, the parade of woe, which generally surrounds a death-bed, and too often embitters the last moments, he would be insensible of his approaching dissolution.

By no means is death so dreadful, therefore, as we suppose it to be. It is a spectre which terrifies us at a distance, but disappears when we approach it more closely. Our conceptions of it are formed by prejudice, and dressed up by fancy. We consider it not only as a misfortune greater than any other, but as one accompanied by the most excruciating anguish. Death, it is said, must be terrible, since it is sufficient to separate the soul from the body; the pain must also be of considerable duration, since time is measured by the succession of our ideas; one minute of pain, in which these ideas succeed each other with a rapidity proportioned to the agony we suffer, must appear longer than a whole age, in which they flow in their usual gentleness and tranquillity. In such philosophy, what an abuse of reason! But for the consequences of it, hardly would it deserve to have its futility exposed. As by such arguments, however, weak minds are deceived, and the aspect of death rendered a thousand times more hideous than it possibly can be; to point out the erroneous principles may be of advantage.

When the soul is originally united to our body, do we experience any extraordinary joy, which delights and transports us? Most certainly not. What reason then can we have to suppose that the separation of the soul from that body may not be effected without pain? From what cause should such pain arise? Shall we fix its residence in the soul, or in the body? Pain of the mind can only be produced by thought, and that of the body is proportioned to its strength or weakness. In the instant of death, the body must be in its weakest state, and therefore if it does experience pain, it must be in a very trifling degree.

Let us now suppose a violent death; that for example, of a man whose head is carried off by a cannon-ball. Can the pain he suffers last longer than a moment? Has he, in the interval of that moment, a succession of ideas so rapid, that he can imagine the pangs he feels are equal to an hour, a day, an age? These points we shall endeavour to discuss.

I own the succession of our ideas is, in reality, the only natural measure of time; and that, in proportion as they flow with more or less uniformity, they appear of longer or shorter duration. But in this measure there is an unit, or fixed point, which is neither arbitrary nor indefinite, but determined by Nature, and correspondent to our organization. Between two ideas which succeed each other, there must be an interval that separates them; however quick one thought may be, a little time is required before it can be followed by another, no succession being possible in an indivisible instant. The same observation holds with respect to the sensations of the body. A transition from pain to pleasure, or even from one pain to another, requires a certain interval. This interval, by which our thoughts and sensations are necessarily separated, is the unit I mention; and it can neither be extremely long, nor extremely short; it must even be nearly upon an equality in its duration, as it depends upon the nature of the mind, and the organization of the body, whose movements can have but one certain degree of celerity. In the same individual, therefore, there can be no succession of ideas so rapid, or so slow, as to produce that enormous difference of duration, by which the pain of a minute is converted into that of an hour, a day, or a century.

A very acute pain, of however short continuance, tends to produce either a swoon, or death. As our organs have only a certain degree of strength, they cannot resist above a certain degree of pain. If that becomes excessive, it ceases, because the body being incapable of supporting it, is still less capable to transmit it to the mind, with which it can hold no correspondence, but by the action of these organs. Here this action ceases, and therefore, all internal sensation must necessarily cease also.

What has already been advanced, is perhaps amply sufficient to evince, that, at the instant of death, the pain is neither excessive nor of long duration; but in order to dispel all fear from the bosom of timidity itself, we shall add a few words more upon the subject. Though excessive pains admit of no reflection, yet signs, at least, of it have been observed in the very moment of a violent death. When Charles XII. received, at Frederickshall, the blow which terminated his exploits and existence, he clapped his hand upon his sword.

Since it excluded not reflection, this mortal pang could not, therefore, be excessive. The brave warrior found himself attacked; he reflected that he ought to defend himself; and thence, it is evident, he felt no more than what he might have suffered from an ordinary blow. That this action was nothing more than the result of a mechanical impulse it would be absurd to assert, as it has been evidently shewn, in our description of man, that the most precipitate movements of the passions depend upon reflection, and are nothing more than effects of an habitual exertion of the mind.

If I have rather enlarged on this topic it is only that I might destroy a prejudice so repugnant to the happiness of man. To this prejudice many have fallen victims; and I have myself known several, of the female sex in particular, who, from the very dread of death, have died in reality. Such terrible alarms seem, indeed, to be particular to those whom Nature or education have endowed with superior sensibility, as the gross of mankind look forward to death, if not with indifference at least without terror.

In viewing things as they are consists the spirit of true philosophy. With this philosophy our internal sensations would always correspond, were they not perverted by the illusions of imagination, and by the unfortunate habit of fabricating phantoms of excessive pains and of pleasure. Nothing appears terrible nor charming but what is at distance. To obtain a certain knowledge of either we must have the resolution, or the wisdom, to take a close and particular view of them, and all their extraordinary circumstances will disappear.

If there be any thing necessary to confirm what has been said concerning the gradual cessation of life, we might find it in the uncertainty of the signs of death. By consulting the writers on this subject, and particularly Winslow and Bruhier, we shall be convinced, that between life and death the shade is often so undistinguishable that all the powers of medical art are insufficient to determine upon it. According to them, "the colour of the face, the warmth of the body, the suppleness of the joints, are but equivocal signs of life; and that the paleness of the complexion, the coldness of the body, the stiffness of the extremities, the cessation of all motion, and the total insensibility of the parts, are signs to the full as equivocal of death." It is also the same with regard to the cessation of the pulse, and of respiration, which are sometimes so effectually kept under, that it is impossible to obtain the smallest perception of either. By carrying a mirror, or candle, to the mouth of a person supposed to be dead, people expect to find whether he breathes or not; but in this experiment there is little certainty; the mirror is often sullied after death has taken place, and remains unclouded while the person is still alive. Neither do burning nor scarifying, noises in the ears, nor pungent spirits applied to the nostrils, give indubitable proofs of the discontinuance of life; many are the instances of persons who have undergone all such trials without shewing any signs of life, and yet, to the astonishment of the spectators, recovered afterwards, without the smallest assistance.

Nothing can be more evident than that life, in some cases, has a near resemblance to death, and therefore that we ought to be extremely cautious of renouncing, and committing too hastily to the grave, the bodies of our fellow-creatures. Neither ten, twenty, nor twenty-four hours are sufficient to distinguish real from apparent death; and there are instances of persons who have been alive in the grave at the end of the second, and even the third day. Why suffer to be interred with precipitation those persons whose lives we ardently wished to prolong? Why, though all men are equally interested in the abolition of it, does the practice still subsist? On the authority of the most able physicians, it incontestably appears, "that the body, though living, is sometimes so far deprived of all vital function, as to have every external appearance of death; that, if in the space of three days, or seventy two hours, no sign of life appears, and on the contrary the body exhales a cadaverous smell, there is an infallible proof of actual death; and that then, though on no account till then, the interment can with safety take place."

Hereafter we shall have occasion to speak of the usages of different nations with respect to obsequies, interments, and embalments. The greatest part, even of the most savage people, pay more attention than we to their deceased friends. What with us is nothing more than a ceremony, they consider as an essential duty. Far superior is the respect which they pay to their dead: they clothe them, they speak to them, they recite their exploits, they extol their virtues; while we, who pique ourselves on our sensibility, with hardly an appearance of humanity, forsake and fly from them, we neither desire to see, nor have courage nor inclination to speak to them, and even avoid every place which may recall their idea to our minds. Than savages themselves, then, do we, in this respect, discover either more indifference or more weakness.

Having thus given a history of life, and of death, as they relate to the individual, let us now consider them both, as they affect the whole species. Man dies at every age; and though in general the duration of his life is longer than that of most animals, yet it is more uncertain and more variable.

Of late years attempts have been made to ascertain the degrees of such variations, and to establish, by different observations, some certainty as to the mortality of men at different ages. Were such observations sufficiently exact and numerous they would be admirably calculated to give a knowledge of the number of people, their increase, the consumption of provisions, and of a number of other important objects. Many writers of distinguished abilities, and, among others, Halley and Simpson, have given tables of the mortality of the human species; but as their labours have been confined to an examination of the bills of mortality in a few parishes of London, and other large cities, their researches, however accurate, seem, in my opinion, to give a very imperfect idea of the mortality of mankind in general.

In order to give a complete table of this nature it is necessary to scrutinise not only the parish-registers of such towns as London and Paris, where there is a perpetual ingress of strangers and egress of natives, but also those of different country places; that, by comparing the deaths which happen in the one with the deaths which happen in the other, a general conclusion may be formed. M. Dupré, of St. Maur, a member of the French academy, executed this project upon twelve different parishes in the country of France, and, three in Paris. Having obtained his permission to publish the tables he has drawn up on this occasion, I do it with the greater pleasure, as they are the only ones from which the probabilities of human life in general can with any certainty be established.

YEARS OF LIFE.

PARISHES.	deaths.	1	2	3	4
CLEMONT	1391	578	73	36	29
BRINON	1141	441	75	31	27
JOUY	588	231	43	11	13
LESTIOU	223	89	16	9	7
VANDEUVRE	672	156	58	18	19
ST. AGIL	954	359	64	30	21
THURY	262	103	31	8	4
ST. AMANT	748	170	61	24	11
MONTIGNY	833	346	57	19	25
VIELENEUVE	131	14	3	5	1
GOUSSAINVILLE	1615	565	184	63	38
IVRY	2247	686	298	96	61
Total Deaths	10805				
Division of 10805 deaths into the years they happened	}	3738	963	350	256
Deaths before the end of the 1st, 2d, 3d, &c. years.	}	3738	4701	5051	5307

Number of persons entered into their 1st, 2d, 3d, &c. years.	} 10805	7067	6104	5754
Sᴛ. Aɴᴅʀᴇ, Pᴀʀɪs,	1728	201	122	94	82

St. Aɴᴅʀᴇ, Pᴀʀɪs, 1728 201 122 94 82
St. Hɪᴘᴘᴏʟʏᴛᴜs, 2516 754 361 127 64
St. Nɪᴄᴏʟᴀs, 8945 1761 932 414 298
Total Deaths 13189

Division of the 13189 deaths into the years they happened.> } 2716 1415 635 444

Deaths before the end of the 1st, 2d, 3d, &c. years. } 2716 4131 4766 5210

Number of persons who entered into the 1st, 2d, &c. years. } 1318910473 9058 8423

Division of the 23994 deaths in the 3 parishes of Paris and the 12 villages. } 6454 2378 985 700

Deaths before the end of the 1st, 2d, years, &c. out of the 23994 } 6454 8832 9817 10517

Number of persons entered into their 1st and 2d years, &c. }2399417540151621 4177

YEARS OF LIFE.

5	6	7	8	9	10	11	12
16	16	14	10	8	4	6	5
10	16	9	9	8	5	2	12
5	8	4	6	1	0	3	0
1	4	3	1	1	1	0	1
10	11	8	10	3	2	1	3
20	11	4	7	2	7	3	3
3	2	2	2	1	2	0	0
12	15	3	6	8	6	4	4
16	21	9	7	5	5	2	4
1	0	0	0	0	0	0	1
34	21	17	15	12	8	5	5
50	29	34	26	13	19	9	6
178	154	107	99	62	59	35	44

5485 5639 5746 5845 5907 5966 6001 6045
5498 5320 5166 5059 4960 4898 4839 4804
50 35 28 14 8 7 3 9
60 55 25 16 20 8 9 9
221 162 147 111 64 40 34 38
331 252 200 141 92 55 46 56
5541 5793 5993 6134 6226 6281 6327 6383
7979 7648 7396 7196 7055 6963 6908 6862
509 406 307 240 154 114 8 100
11026 11432 11639 11979 12133 12247 12328 12428
12477 12968 12562 12255 12015 11861 11747 11666

YEARS OF LIFE.

13	14	15	16	17	18	19	20
6	5	5	6	6	10	3	13
2	6	4	5	9	4	5	14
3	3	1	6	4	4	3	5
0	1	1	1	1	0	0	0
3	4	5	9	3	3	4	7
3	3	5	2	7	8	5	6
0	0	1	0	1	1	1	1
2	5	1	5	3	6	1	4
4	2	4	2	2	3	3	5
0	0	1	0	2	4	0	1
9	5	5	2	5	10	9	10
4	4	8	7	4	14	10	12
36	38	41	42	47	67	44	78
6081	6119	6160	6202	6249	6316	6360	6438
4760	4724	4686	4645	4603	4556	4480	4445
6	7	10	13	13	11	10	7
6	7	6	5	7	9	7	3
25	21	33	37	37	28	44	53
37	35	49	55	57	487	61	63
6420	6455	6504	6559	6616	6664	6725	6788
6806	6769	6734	6685	6630	6573	6525	6464
73	73	90	97	104	115	105	141
12501	12574	12664	12761	12865	12980	13085	13226
11566	11493	11420	11330	11233	11129	11014	19009

YEARS OF LIFE.

21	22	23	24	25	26	27	28
8	9	10	7	22	9	13	10
8	14	7	11	24	9	7	13
2	4	4	4	5	2	2	3
0	0	3	0	1	1	1	3
4	6	8	6	22	3	5	10
6	4	6	3	11	10	4	9
1	3	1	1	2	2	0	5
7	6	6	4	5	4	4	3
4	3	10	8	7	3	3	3
1	4	1	0	1	0	2	1
6	10	5	6	11	9	9	8
6	15	10	9	10	14	5	9
51	80	68	62	121	66	55	77
6480	6569	6637	6699	6820	6886	6941	7018
4367	4316	4236	4168	4106	3985	3919	3864
9	17	11	9	9	8	17	13
2	8	7	9	10	13	10	10
31	56	48	41	59	47	53	51
42	81	66	59	78	68	80	74
6830	6911	6977	7036	7114	7182	7262	7336
6401	6359	6278	6212	6153	6075	6007	5927
93	161	134	121	199	134	135	151
13319	13480	13614	13735	13934	14068	14203	14354
10768	10675	10514	10380	10259	10060	9926	9793

YEARS OF LIFE.

29	30	31	32	33	34	35	36
7	24	4	13	14	8	17	12
6	28	6	15	3	4	20	8
4	8	2	5	4	3	13	6
1	1	4	4	3	1	6	4
1	28	2	9	1	3	17	5
2	16	8	7	2	5	18	9
2	2	0	3	1	0	7	0
3	8	2	8	6	5	7	4
0	6	1	10	3	4	8	4

1	2	1	2	1	0	6	5
10	10	4	14	6	7	8	8
5	13	8	11	18	10	19	12
42	146	42	101	62	50	146	77
7060	7206	7248	7349	7411	7461	7607	7684
3787	3745	3599	3557	3456	3394	3344	3198
11	21	6	10	17	15	21	14
9	7	9	12	13	13	16	21
34	63	25	57	41	54	82	75
54	91	40	79	71	82	119	110
7390	7481	7521	7600	7671	7753	7872	7982
5853	5799	5708	5668	5589	5518	5436	5317
96	237	82	180	153	132	205	187
14450	14687	14769	14949	15082	15214	15479	15666
9640	9544	9307	9245	9045	8912	8770	8515

YEARS OF LIFE.

37	38	39	40	41	42	43	44
16	15	3	41	4	10	10	6
8	8	6	37	6	8	3	6
7	4	1	20	0	3	0	4
4	1	1	4	0	2	2	0
5	4	0	41	1	3	2	2
4	5	1	22	2	8	7	3
1	2	2	4	1	3	1	4
5	5	3	20	1	6	2	4
1	2	0	8	3	6	5	4
0	5	0	7	0	3	1	0
5	2	7	14	10	11	4	5
13	23	3	27	7	19	7	14
71	76	27	245	35	82	44	52
7755	7831	7858	8103	8138	8220	8264	8316
3121	3050	2974	2947	2702	2667	2585	2541
8	12	4	26	5	19	12	10
15	13	10	24	4	18	14	9
58	59	46	109	37	73	58	45
81	84	60	159	46	110	84	64
8063	8147	8207	8366	8412	8522	8606	8670

5207	5126	5042	4982	4823	4777	4667	4583
158	160	87	404	81	192	128	116
15818	15978	16065	16469	16550	16742	16870	16986
8328	8176	8016	7929	7525	7444	7252	7124

YEARS OF LIFE.

45	46	47	48	49	50	51	52
20	5	8	5	6	31	0	5
11	5	6	9	0	23	1	3
13	3	4	2	0	20	2	3
3	3	0	3	3	5	1	1
14	5	3	1	0	31	0	2
14	1	3	3	0	24	3	9
3	0	0	0	0	3	0	0
13	3	4	6	0	23	1	4
13	6	1	6	1	10	2	5
2	1	2	3	0	7	2	1
11	9	5	12	6	15	4	9
22	10	7	12	6	24	6	14
139	51	43	62	22	216	22	56
8455	8506	8549	8611	8633	8849	8871	8927
2489	2350	2299	2256	2194	2172	1956	1934
24	21	9	13	10	24	7	18
33	14	13	15	21	20	10	19
111	54	47	68	50	120	40	59
168	89	69	96	72	164	57	96
8838	8927	8996	9092	9164	9328	9385	9481
4519	4351	4262	4193	4097	4025	3861	3804
307	140	112	158	94	380	79	152
17293	17433	17545	17703	17797	18177	18256	19408
7008	6701	6561	6449	6291	6197	5817	5738

YEARS OF LIFE.

53	54	55	56	57	58	59	60
5	5	14	5	5	4	4	52
3	2	10	6	2	3	0	24
2	5	7	4	5	2	0	20
0	0	2	2	0	3	0	2
1	1	13	1	1	2	0	35
2	2	14	3	5	3	3	22
1	1	4	0	1	3	1	6
4	4	6	5	4	7	2	27
2	5	10	3	4	9	2	13
0	1	0	3	3	2	1	4
5	9	6	10	10	10	3	24
13	9	29	12	13	13	3	40
38	41	111	54	51	61	19	269
8365	9009	9120	9174	9225	9286	9305	9574
1878	1840	1796	1685	1631	1580	1519	1500
8	10	19	11	15	17	11	46
6	10	25	9	15	18	12	35
49	46	125	56	48	86	48	184
63	66	169	76	78	121	71	265
9544	9610	9779	9855	9933	10054	10125	10390
3708	3645	3579	3410	3334	3256	3135	3064
101	110	280	130	129	182	90	534
18509	18619	18899	19029	19158	19340	19430	19964
5586	5485	5375	5095	4965	4836	4654	4564

YEARS OF LIFE.

61	62	63	64	65	66	67	68
2	6	5	2	5	5	3	4
1	3	4	7	7	6	3	6
0	5	2	4	5	2	1	1
0	0	1	0	3	1	1	0
0	0	1	1	5	3	0	2
3	2	7	5	7	3	6	5
0	3	2	2	2	1	3	1
0	4	3	4	12	7	5	6

3	7	5	5	7	6	2	5
3	0	1	1	2	3	0	1
6	9	7	6	13	17	13	15
3	12	12	11	14	21	5	23
21	51	50	48	82	75	42	69
9595	9646	9696	9744	9826	9401	9943	10012
1231	1210	1159	1109	1061	979	904	862
11	21	19	17	20	27	21	25
7	28	21	23	25	19	12	20
42	77	71	73	95	95	67	115
60	126	111	113	140	141	100	160
20450	10576	10687	10800	10940	11081	11181	11341
2799	2739	2613	2501	4389	2249	2108	2008
81	177	161	161	122	216	142	229
20045	20222	20383	20544	20766	20982	21124	21353
4030	3949	3772	3611	3450	3228	3012	2870

YEARS OF LIFE.

69	70	71	72	73	74	75	76
1	11	1	3	1	3	5	1
0	6	2	12	2	0	4	2
1	3	1	2	0	1	1	0
1	0	0	2	0	0	0	0
1	9	1	4	0	0	3	0
2	19	1	11	5	5	8	0
0	7	0	2	1	0	0	0
6	18	3	10	2	2	18	2
1	9	2	8	3	2	9	1
0	4	0	3	0	0	0	0
5	16	8	22	12	12	16	6
7	31	6	21	11	19	24	12
25	133	25	100	37	44	88	24
10037	10170	10195	10295	10332	10376	10464	10488
793	768	935	610	510	473	429	341
9	36	9	25	14	19	20	16
15	35	10	28	5	15	23	11
50	177	64	118	53	90	127	63
72	248	83	171	72	124	170	90

11413	11661	11744	11915	11987	12111	12281	12371
1848	1776	1528	1445	1274	1202	1078	908
97	381	108	271	109	168	258	114
21450	21831	21939	22210	22319	22487	22745	22859
2641	2544	2160	2155	1784	1675	1507	1249

YEARS OF LIFE.

77	78	79	80	81	82	83	84
1	2	2	6	0	0	0	3
0	3	0	3	1	0	0	0
0	0	0	2	0	0	0	0
0	0	0	1	0	0	0	0
1	0	0	7	0	0	0	0
3	4	0	6	0	0	0	0
1	0	0	3	0	0	0	0
4	4	2	17	1	3	1	3
4	2	0	5	1	4	1	1
2	1	1	1	3	0	0	0
6	8	1	17	6	9	5	7
11	14	9	19	7	14	4	7
33	38	15	89	16	30	11	21
10521	10559	10574	10663	10679	10709	10720	10741
317	284	246	231	142	126	96	85
10	25	8	17	4	10	8	7
18	15	8	18	4	5	16	4
59	69	80	121	32	41	37	25
87	109	46	156	40	56	61	36
12458	12567	12613	12769	12809	12865	12962	12962
818	731	622	576	420	380	324	263
120	147	61	245	50	86	72	57
22979	23126	23187	23432	23488	23574	23646	23703
1835	1015	868	807	562	506	426	348

YEARS OF LIFE.

85	86	87	88	89	90	91	92
0	1	0	0	1	0	0	0
0	0	0	0	0	0	0	0
0	0	0	1	0	0	0	0

1	0	0	0	0	0	0	0
0	0	1	1	0	0	0	0
0	0	0	0	0	2	0	0
0	0	0	0	0	0	0	0
4	0	1	2	0	4	1	1
0	0	0	0	0	1	0	0
0	0	0	0	1	0	0	0
2	4	4	2	2	0	0	0
5	4	4	3	1	2	0	2
12	9	8	9	5	9	1	3
10753	10762	10770	10779	10784	10793	10794	10797
64	52	43	35	26	21	12	11
3	7	4	5	2	4	0	2
10	4	1	4	2	2	2	2
35	19	20	25	24	17	5	9
48	30	25	34	8	23	7	13
13010	15040	13065	13099	16017	13130	13137	13150
227	179	149	124	90	82	59	52
50	39	33	43	13	32	8	16
23763	23802	22835	22878	23891	23923	23931	23947
291	231	192	159	116	103	71	63

YEARS OF LIFE.

93	94	95	96	97	98	99	100
0	0	0	0	0	0	0	0
0	0	0	0	0	0	0	0
0	8	0	0	0	0	0	0
0	0	0	0	0	0	0	0
0	0	0	0	0	0	0	0
0	0	0	0	0	0	0	1
0	0	0	0	0	0	0	0
0	0	2	1	0	3	0	0
0	0	0	0	0	0	0	0
0	0	0	0	0	0	0	0
0	0	0	0	0	0	0	0
0	0	1	0	0	0	0	0
0	0	3	1	0	3	0	1
10797	10797	10800	10801	10801	10804	10804	10805

8	8	8	4	4	4	1	1
1	2	0	1	1	0	0	0
1	1	2	1	0	1	0	0
5	4	5	2	1	4	1	4
7	7	7	4	2	5	1	4
13157	13164	13171	13175	13177	13182	13183	13187
39	32	25	18	14	12	7	6
7	7	10	5	2	8	1	5
23954	23961	23971	23976	23978	23986	23987	23992
47	40	33	23	18	16	8	7

From these tables many useful conclusions might be drawn. But I shall only consider those which respect the probabilities of the duration of life. It is observable, that in the columns opposite the years 10, 20, 30, 40, 50, 60, 70, and other round numbers as 25, 35, &c. the deaths in the country parishes are more numerous than in in the preceding or subsequent columns. The cause of this seeming inconsistency arises from the generality of country people being ignorant of their exact age, and therefore if they die at 58 or 59 in the parish register it is entered 60; and so of other round numbers. From this irregularity the inconvenience is not great, as it may easily be corrected by the manner in which the numbers succeed each other in the Tables.

By the tables in the country parishes it appears, that almost one half of the children die before the age of four years, and by the Paris table not before 16; which great difference; certainly arises from the children being sent into the country to nurse, and consequently increases the number of deaths there in infancy. As likely to come at the truth, I have blended the two tables, and from thence calculated the probabilities of the duration of life as follows:

TABLE *of the* PROBABILITIES *of the* DURATION *of* HUMAN LIFE.

Age	Duration of Life.		Age	Duration of Life.		Age	Duration of Life.	
Yrs.	Yrs.	Mths.	Yrs.	Yrs.	Mths.	Yrs.	Yrs.	Mths.
0	8	0	29	28	6	58	12	3
1	33	0	30	28	0	59	11	8
2	38	0	31	27	6	60	11	1
3	40	0	32	26	11	61	10	6
4	41	0	33	26	3	62	10	0
5	41	6	34	25	7	63	9	6
6	42	0	35	25	0	64	9	0
7	42	3	36	24	5	65	8	6

8	41	6	37	23	10	66	8	0
9	40	10	38	23	3	67	7	6
10	40	2	39	22	8	68	7	0
11	39	6	40	22	1	69	6	7
12	38	9	41	21	6	70	6	2
13	38	1	42	20	11	71	5	3
14	37	5	43	20	4	72	5	4
15	36	9	44	19	9	73	5	0
16	36	0	45	19	3	74	4	9
17	35	4	46	18	9	75	4	6
18	34	8	47	18	2	76	4	3
19	34	0	48	17	8	77	4	1
20	33	5	49	17	2	73	3	11
21	32	11	50	16	7	79	3	9
22	32	4	51	16	0	80	3	7
23	31	10	52	15	6	81	3	5
24	31	3	53	15	0	82	3	3
25	30	9	54	14	6	83	3	2
26	30	2	55	14	0	84	3	1
27	29	7	56	13	5	85	3	0
28	29	0	57	12	10			

By this table it appears, that an infant newly born has an equal chance of living eight years; that an infant of one will live 33 years longer; that a child of two will live 38 years longer; that a man of 20 will live 33 years and five months longer; that a man of 30 will live 28 years longer; and so proportionally of every other age.

It is also to be observed, first, that seven years is the age at which the longest duration of life is to be expected, since there is then an equal chance of living 42 years and three months longer; secondly that at the age of 12 one fourth of our existence is gone, as we cannot in reason expect above 38 or 39 years more; thirdly, that we have enjoyed one half of our existence at the age of 28, as we can reckon upon only 28 years more; and lastly, that by the age of 50 three fourths of life are passed, the remaining probability being only for 16 or 17 years.

But these physical truths, however mortifying, may be compensated by moral considerations. A man ought to consider as nothing the first fifteen years of his life. Every thing that happens in that long interval of time is effaced from the memory, or has at least so little connection with the views and objects Which afterwards occupy our thoughts that it gives us no concern.

Neither, indeed, have we the game succession of ideas, nor, it maybe said, the same existence. In a moral sense we do not begin to live till we have begun to regulate our thoughts, to direct them towards futurity, and to assume to ourselves a kind of consistency of character conformable to that state which has some relation to what we shall afterwards become. By considering the duration of life in this, the only real point of view, we shall find, that at the age of 25 we have passed but one fourth part of our life; at the age of 38 one half; and that, at the age of 56, there is one fourth of life still remains.

CHAPTER VI.

OF THE SENSE OF SEEING.

Having described the parts of which the human body consists, let us now proceed to examine its principal organs; the expansion of the senses, and their several functions; and at the same time, point out the errors to which, through them, we are in some measure subjected by Nature.

The eyes seem to be formed very early in the human embryo. In the chicken also, of all the double organs they are the soonest produced. I have observed in the eggs of several sorts of birds, and in those of lizards, that the eyes were more large, and early in their expansion, than any other parts of a two-fold growth. Though, in viviparous animals, and particularly in man, they are, at first, by no means so large in proportion as in the oviparous, yet they obtain their due formation sooner than any other parts of the body. It is the same with the organ of hearing; the small bones of the ear are entirely formed before any of the other bones have acquired any part of their growth or solidity. Hence it is evident, that the parts of the body, which are furnished with the greatest quantity of nerves, as the ears and eyes, are those which first appear, and which are the soonest brought to perfection.

If we examine the eyes of an infant, a few hours after its birth, we shall discern that it cannot make the smallest use of them; the organ not having acquired a sufficient consistency, the rays of light strike but confusedly upon the retina. Before the sixth week, children turn their eyes indiscriminately upon every object, without appearing to be affected by any, but at about this time they begin to fix them upon the most brilliant colours, and seem peculiarly desirous of turning them towards the light; this exercise does not give any exact notion of objects, but strengthens the eye, and qualifies it for future vision.

The first great error in the sense of seeing, is the inverted representation of objects upon the retina, and, till the sense of feeling has served to undeceive it, the child actually beholds every thing upside down. The second error in early vision is, that every object appears double; from the same object being formed distinctly upon each eye. This illusion like the other, can only be corrected by children from their being in the practice of handling different objects, and from which practice alone it is that they learn things are neither inverted nor double, and custom induces them to believe they see objects in the position the touch represents them to the mind; and therefore, were we denied the sense of feeling, that of seeing would not only deceive us as to the situation, but as to the number of every object around us.

We may easily be convinced that objects appear inverted, (which arises from the structure of the eye) by admitting the light to pass into a darkened room through a small aperture, when the images of the objects without will be represented upon the wall in an inverted position; for, as all the rays which issue from their different points cannot enter the hole in the same extent and position which they had in leaving the object, unless the aperture was as large as the object itself; as every part of the object sends forth its image on all sides; as the rays which from those images flow from all points of the object, as from so many centres, those only can pass through the small aperture which come in opposite directions. Thus the hole becomes a centre for the entire object, through which the rays from the upper, as well as from the lower parts of it, pass in converging directions; and, of consequence, they must cross each other at this centre, and thus represent the objects upon the wall, in an inverted position.

That we, in reality, see all objects double, is also evident; for example, if we hold up a finger, and look with the right eye at an object, it will appear against one particular part of the room, shutting that and looking with the left, it will seem to be on a different part, and if we open both eyes, the object will appear to be placed between the two extremes. But the truth is, the image of the object is formed in both eyes, one of which appears to the right, and the other to the left; and it is from the habit of touching that we suppose we see but one image placed between them both. From which it is clear that we see all objects double, although our imagination forms them single; and that, in fact, we see things where they are not, notwithstanding we have a pretty exact idea of their situation and position; and thus it is that till the sense of feeling has corrected the errors of sight, if instead of two eyes, we had an hundred, we should still fancy the objects single, although they were multiplied an hundred times.

In each eye, therefore, is formed a separate image of every object; and when the two images strike the correspondent parts of the retina, that is, the parts which are always affected at the same time, the object appears single: but, when the images strike the parts of the retina, which are not usually affected together, then it appears double, because we are not habitual to this unusual sensation, and are then somewhat in the situation of infants just beginning to exert the faculty of vision.

M. Chesselden relates the case of a man, who, in consequence of a blow on the head, became squint-eyed, and saw objects double for a long time: but who was at length enabled, by slow and gradual steps, to see them singly as he had formerly done, notwithstanding the squinting remained. Is not this a proof, still more evident, that in reality we see things double, and that it is by habit alone we conceive them to be single? Should it be asked why children require less time, in order to see things single, than persons more advanced in years, whose eyes may have been affected by accident? it might be answered, that the sensations of children, being unopposed by any contradictory habit, these errors are rectified with ease; but that persons who have for many years seen objects single, because they affected the two correspondent parts of the retina, and who now see them double, labour under the disadvantage of having a contrary habit to oppose, and must therefore be a considerable time before it is entirely obliterated.

By the sense of seeing we can form no idea of distances; without aided by the touch, every object would appear to be within our eyes; and an infant, that is as yet a stranger to the sense of feeling, must conceive that every thing it sees exists within itself. The objects only appear to be more or less bulky as they approach to, or recede from the eye; insomuch, that a a fly near the eye will appear larger than an ox at a distance. It is experience alone that can rectify this mistake; and it is by constantly measuring with the hand, and removing from one place to another, that children obtain ideas of distance and magnitude. They have no conception of size but from the extreme rays reflected from the object, of course every thing near appears large, and those at a distance small. The last man in a file of soldiers appears much more diminutive than the one who is nearest to us. We do not, however, perceive this difference, but continue to think him of equal stature; for the number of objects we have seen thus lessened by distance, and found by repeated experience to be of the natural size when we come closer, instantly correct the sense, and therefore we perceive every object nearly in its natural proportion, unless when we observe them in such situations as have not allowed us sufficient experience to correct the illusions of the eye. If, for example, we view men upon the ground, from a lofty tower, or look up to any object upon the top of a steeple, as we have not been in the habit of correcting the sense in that position, they appear to us exceedingly diminished, much more so than if we saw them at the same distance in an horizontal direction.

Though a small degree of reflection may serve to convince us of the truth of these positions, yet it may not be amiss to corroborate them by facts which cannot be disputed. M. Chesselden, having couched for a cataract a lad of thirteen years of age, who had from his birth been blind, and thus communicated to him the sense of seeing, was at great pains to mark the progress of his visual powers; his observations were afterwards published in the Philosophical Transactions. This youth was not absolutely and entirely blind: Like every other person, whose vision is obstructed by a cataract, he could distinguish day from night and even black from white, but of the figure of bodies he had no idea. At first the operation was performed only upon one of his eyes, and when he saw for the first time, so far was he from judging of distances, that he supposed (as he himself expressed it) every thing he saw touched his eyes, in the same manner as every thing he felt touched his skin. The objects that pleased him most were those whose surfaces were plain and the figures regular, though he could in no degree judge of their different forms, or assign why some were more agreeable to him than others. His ideas of colours during his former dark state were so imperfect, that when he saw them in reality he could hardly be persuaded they were the same. When such objects were shewn him as he had been formerly familiar with by the touch, he beheld them with earnestness, in order to know them again, but as he had too many to retain at once the greatest number were forgotten, and for one thing which he knew, after seeing it, there were a thousand, according to his own declaration, of which he no longer possessed the smallest remembrance. He was very much surprised to find that those persons, and those things, which he had loved best, were not the most pleasing to his sight; nor could he help testifying his disappointment in finding his parents less handsome than he had conceived them to be. Before he could distinguish that pictures resembled solid bodies above two months elapsed; till then he only considered them as surfaces diversified by a variety of colours; but when he began to perceive that these shadings actually represented human beings, he expected also to find their inequalities; and great was his surprise to find smooth and even what he had supposed a very unequal surface; and he inquired whether the deception existed in feeling or seeing. He was then shewn a miniature portrait of his father, which was contained in his mother's watch-case, and though he readily perceived the resemblance, yet he expressed his amazement how so large a face could be comprised in so small a compass; to him it appeared as strange as that a pint vessel should contain a bushel. At first he could bear but a very small quantity of light, and every object appeared larger than the life; but in proportion as he observed objects that were in reality large, he conceived the others to be equally diminished. Beyond the limits of what he saw he had no conception of any thing. He knew that the apartment he occupied was only a part of the house, and yet he could not imagine how the latter should be larger than the former. Before the operation he formed no great expectations of the pleasure he should receive from the new sense he was promised, excepting that thereby he might be enabled to read and write. He said among other things, that he could enjoy no greater delight from walking in the garden, because there he already walked at his ease, and was acquainted with every part of it. He also remarked that his blindness gave him one advantage over the rest of mankind, namely, that of being able to walk in the night with more confidence and security. No sooner, however, had he began to enjoy his new sense than he was transported beyond measure; he declared that every new object was a new source of delight, and that his pleasure was so great he had not language to express it. About a year after, he was carried to Epsom, where there is a beautiful and extensive prospect; with this he seemed greatly charmed; and the landscape before him he called a new method of seeing. He was couched in the other eye a year after the former, and the success was equally great. Every object appeared larger when he looked at it with the second eye to what it did with the other; and when he looked at any thing with both eyes it appeared twice as large as when he saw but with one, though he did not see double, or at least he shewed no marks from which any such conclusion might be drawn.

Mr. Chesselden instances several other persons who were in the same situation with this lad, and on whom he performed the same operation; and he assures us, that on first obtaining the use of their eyes they expressed their perceptions in the same manner, though less minutely; and that he particularly observed of them all, that as they had never had any occasion to move their eyes while deprived of sight, they were exceedingly embarrassed in learning how to direct them to the objects they wished to observe.

As from particular circumstances we cannot from a just idea of distance, and as we cannot judge of the magnitude of objects but by the largeness of the angle, or rather the image, which they form in our eyes, we are necessarily deceived as to the size of such objects. Every man knows how liable we are, in travelling by night, to mistake a bush which is at hand for a tree at a distance, or a tree at a distance for a bush which is at hand. In like manner, if we cannot distinguish objects by their figure we cannot judge of distance or size. In this case a fly, passing with rapidity before our eyes, will appear to be a bird at a considerable distance; and an horse standing in the middle of a plain will appear no bigger than a sheep till we have discovered that it is a horse, and then we shall recognize it to be as large as life.

Whenever, therefore, we find ourselves benighted in an unknown place, where upon account of the darkness no judgment is to be formed of distance, or figures of the objects that may present themselves, we are every moment in danger of being misled with respect to our ideas of such objects. Hence proceeds that internal fear and dread which most men experience from the obscurity of night, and of those strange and hideous spectres and gigantic figures which so many persons tell us they have seen. Though such figures, it is commonly asserted, exist solely in the imagination, yet they may appear literally to the eye, and be in every respect seen as described to us; for when we reflect that whenever we cannot judge of an unknown object but by the angle which it forms in the eye, this object is magnified in proportion to its propinquity; and that if it appears at the distance of twenty or thirty paces to be only a few feet high, when advanced within a short space of it, it will seem to be of considerable magnitude. At this the spectator must naturally be astonished and terrified, till he approaches and knows it by feeling; for in the very instant that he has an actual perception of what it is, the tremendous form it assumed to the eye will diminish, and it will appear in no other than its real and absolute form. If, on the other hand, he is afraid to approach it, and flies from the spot with precipitation, the only idea he can have of it will be that of the image which had been formed in his eye; the image of a figure he had seen, gigantic in its size, and horrible in its form. The prejudice with respect to spectres, therefore, originates from Nature, and depend not, as some philosophers have supposed, solely upon the imagination.

When we cannot form an idea of distance, by the knowledge of the intermediate space between us and any particular object, we endeavour to distinguish the form of that object, in order to judge of its size; but when we cannot perfectly distinguish the figures, and at the same time behold a number of objects, whose forms are correspondent, we conceive those which are most brilliant are most proximate, and those most obscure are most remote; a notion which is not unoften the source of very singular mistakes. In a multitude of objects disposed in a right line, as the lamps upon the road from Versailles to Paris, of which, as we cannot judge of the proximity or remoteness but by the quantity of light they transmit to the eye, it often happens that when examined at the distance of the eighth of a league, we see all the lamps situated on the right hand instead of the left, on which they are in reality situated. This fallacious appearance is produced from the above-mentioned cause, for as the spectator has no evidence of the distance he is from the lamps, but by the quantity of light they emit, so he conceives that the most brilliant lamps are those which are the first and the nearest to him. Now if some of the first lamps happen to be dull and obscure, and any one of the others particularly bright, that one would appear to be first and the rest behind, whatever was their real situation; and this seeming transposition would be solely owing to the supposed change of their situation from the left hand to the right; for to conceive to be before what is actually behind in a long file, is to see on the right what is situated on the left, or on the left what is situated on the right.

We may fairly consider sight as a species of touching, though very different from what we commonly understand by that sense; for in order to exercise the latter we must be near the object, whereas we can touch with the eye as far as the light the object contains will make an impression, or its figure form an angle therein. This angle, when the object is viewed at the greatest distance, is about the 3436th part of its diameter, therefore an object of a foot square is not visible beyond 3436 feet, or a man of five feet high at a greater distance than 17180 feet. But the extent of vision is in some measure influenced by the light which surrounds us, and we should be enabled to see any object in the night at 100 times greater distance than in the day, provided it was equally illuminated; thus, for instance, we can perceive a lighted candle at full two leagues in the night, supposing the diameter of the luminary to be one inch, whereas in the day we should not be able to discern it beyond the proportion of the above ratio; and as this is a circumstance which attends all objects when viewed at those different periods, we may conclude that one principal reason for our not being able to discern things at a greater distance, is the brilliancy of the light which fills up the intermediate space, and so destroys the reflected rays from those still more distant objects. When we are surrounded with strength of light the objects near make a forcible impression on the retina of the eye, and obliterate those far off, which are weak and faint; and, on the contrary, if we view a luminous body in the night, even at a considerable distance, that becomes perfectly visible, while those which are near are scarcely discernible. From these reasons it is, that a man at the bottom of a deep pit can see the stars, or, by employing a long tube in a dark room, may obtain some effects from the telescope in the middle of the day. From this it is evident, that if bodies were furnished with more strength of light they would be visible at greater distances, although the angle was not increased, for a small candle, which burns bright, is seen much farther off than a flambeau that is dim. Of these facts, relative to the influence of light, we have a still stronger proof in the variation between a microscope and telescope, both of them instruments of the same kind, increasing the visible angles of objects, whether they be really minute or rendered so by distance, and yet the latter does not magnify beyond a thousand times, whereas the former will exceed a million, and this difference plainly arises solely from the degree of light, for could the distant object be additionally illuminated, telescopes would have the same effect upon distant objects as microscopes have upon small bodies. But it is only by comparing the size of the angle formed in the retina of the eye, the degree of light which illuminates the adjacent and intermediate objects, and the strength of light which proceeds from, or is reflected by the object itself, that we can conclude upon the distance at which any particular body will be visible.

The power of seeing objects at a distance is very rarely equal in both eyes. When this inequality is great, the person so circumstanced generally shuts that eye with which he sees the least, and employs the other with all its power, and which is one cause of squinting. The object does not appear doubly distinct, by both eyes being placed upon it although they are equally strong, but has frequently been proved not to exceed a 13th part more than if beheld with one; and this is supposed to arise from the two optic nerves uniting near the place they came out of the skull and then separating by an obtuse angle before they enter the eyes; but as the motion made by the impression of objects cannot pass to the brain without passing this united part, the two motions must therefore be combined, and, consequently, cannot act with that force as though they were distinct; but from repeated experiments seem to bear the proportion above stated.

There are many reasons to suppose that short-sighted persons see objects larger than others; and it is a certain truth that they see them less. I am myself short-sighted, and my left-eye is stronger than my right. A thousand times have I experienced, upon looking at any object, as the letters of a book, that they appear least to the weakest eye; and that, when I place the book so that the letters appear double, the images of the left-eye, are greater than those of the right. Several others, I have examined, who were in similar circumstances, and I have always found, that the eye which saw every object best, saw it also largest. This may be ascribed to particular habits; for near-sighted people being accustomed to approach close to the object, and to view but a small part of it at a time, they acquire a small standard for magnitude, and when the whole of the object is seen, it necessarily appears smaller to them than to others, whose vision is more enlarged.

There have been many instances of persons becoming short-sighted on a sudden, therefore attributing it to the roundness or prominence of the eye is by no means certain. Mr. Smith, in his Optics, speaks of a young man that became short-sighted as he quitted a cold bath, and who was under the necessity of using a concave glass all his life after; and it cannot be supposed that the vitreous humours were instantly inflated so as to cause this difference in vision. Short-sightedness may arise from the position of the various parts of the eye, especially the retina, from a less degree of sensibility in the retina, or the smallness of the pupil. In the two first cases a concave glass may be used to advantage, but yet objects will not be seen so far, or so distinct, through these glasses as others will perceive with the eye alone, for as short-sighted persons see objects in a diminished form, the concave glass diminishes them still farther.

Infants having their eyes smaller than those of adults, must of consequence, see objects smaller also. For as the image formed on the back of the eye must be large, as the eye is capacious, so infants, having it not so great, cannot have so large a picture of the object. This may likewise be a reason, why they are unable to see so distinctly, or at such distances, as persons who have attained the years of maturity, for as objects appear less they must sooner become invisible.

Old people see bodies close to them very indistinctly, but bodies at a great distance from them with more precision, than young ones. This may happen from an alteration in the coats, or perhaps the humours of the eye; and not, as is supposed, entirely from their diminution. The cornea, for instance, may become too rigid to adapt itself, and take a proper convexity for seeing near objects, as a flatness must be occasioned by drying that will be sufficient of itself to render their eyes more calculated for distant vision. Although clear and distinct are frequently confounded by writers on optics, yet they are very different; for we may be said, for instance, to clearly see a tower, as soon as we get a view of it, but we must approach near enough to distinguish its component parts before we see it distinctly. Men in years see clearly, but not distinctly; they can discern large bodies at a distance, but cannot distinguish small objects, as the characters in a book, without the help of magnifying glasses. On the contrary, short-sighted people see small objects distinctly, but need the aid of concave glasses to reduce large ones. Much light is also necessary for clear sight, while a small quantity is sufficient for distinct vision.

When an object is extremely brilliant, or we fix our eyes too long upon the same object, the organ is hurt and fatigued, vision becomes indistinct, and the image of the object, having made too violent an impression, appears painted on every thing we look at, and mixes with every object that occurs. How dangerous the looking upon bright and luminous objects is to the sight, is evident from the effect it has on the inhabitants of countries which are covered for the greatest part of the year with snow; and travellers, who cross those countries, are obliged to cover their eyes with crape. In the sandy plains of Africa, the reflection of the light is so strong, that it is impossible for the eye to sustain the effects of it. Such persons therefore, as write, or read for any continuance, should chase a moderate light, for though it may seem insufficient at first, yet the eye will gradually become accustomed to the shade; and at any rate, it will be less injured by too little light than by too much.

CHAPTER VII.

OF THE SENSE OF HEARING.

As the sense of hearing, as well as that of seeing, gives us perceptions of remote objects, so it is subject to similar errors, and may deceive us, when we cannot rectify by the touch, the ideas which it excites. It communicates no distinct intelligence of the distance from whence a sounding body is heard: a great noise far off, and a small one near, produce the same sensation, and, unless we receive aid from some other sense, we can never distinctly tell whether the sound be a great or a small one. It is not till we have, by experience, become acquainted with any particular sound that we can judge of the distance from whence we hear it; but if, for example, we hear the sound of a bell, we are at no great loss to determine its distance, any more than we are of that of a cannon from the report, judging in both cases from similar sounds, which we have been previously acquainted with.

Every body that strikes against another produces a sound which is simple in bodies non-elastic, but is often repeated in such as are elastic. If we strike a bell, a single blow produces a sound, which is repeated while the sonorous body continues to vibrate. These undulations succeed each other so fast, that the ear supposes them one continued sound; whereas, in reality, they form many. A circumstance of this kind happened to myself, for lying on the bed half asleep, I distinctly counted five strokes of the hammer upon the bell of the clock, and rising immediately found it was but the hour of one, and was convinced by examining the machinery that it had struck no more. A person, therefore, who should for the first time, hear the toll of a bell, would very probably be able to distinguish these breaks of sound; and, in fact, we can readily ourselves perceive remission in sounds.

Sounding bodies are of two kinds; those unelastic ones, which being struck, return but a single sound; and those more elastic returning a succession of sounds, which uniting together form a tone. This tone may be considered as a number of sounds produced one after the other by the same body, as we find in a bell, which continues to sound for some time after it is struck. A continuing tone may be also produced from a non-elastic body, by repeating the blow quick and often, as when we beat a drum, or draw a bow along the string of a fiddle.

Considering the subject in this light, we shall find the number of blows or quickness of repetition will have no effect in altering the tone, but only make it more even or more distinct, whereas if we increase the force of the blow by striking the body with double the weight, this will produce a tone twice as loud as the former. From hence we may infer, that all bodies give a louder and graver tone, not in proportion to the number of times they are struck, but to the force that strikes them. And if this be so, those philosophers who make the tone of a sonorous body, a bell, or the string of an harpsichord, for instance, to depend upon the number only of its vibrations, and not the force, have mistaken what is only an effect for a cause. A bell, or an elastic string, can only be considered as a drum beaten; and the frequency of the blows can make no alteration whatsoever in the tone. The largest bells, and the longest and thickest strings, have the most forcible vibrations; and, therefore, their tones will be more loud and more grave in proportion to the size and weight of the body with which they are struck.

If we strike a body incapable of vibration with a double force, or a double mass of matter, it will produce a sound doubly grave. Music has been said, by the ancients, to have been first invented from the blows of different hammers on an anvil. Suppose then we strike an anvil with a hammer of one pound weight, and then with a hammer of two pounds, it is plain that the latter will produce a sound twice as grave as the former. But if we strike with a two pound hammer, and then with a three pound, the last will produce a sound only one third more grave than the former. If we strike with a three, and then with a four, it will likewise follow that the latter will be a quarter part more grave than the former. Now, in the comparing between all those sounds, it is obvious that the difference between one and two is more easily perceived than between two and three, three and four, or any numbers succeeding in the same proportion. The succession of sounds will be, therefore, pleasing in proportion to the ease with which they may be distinguished. That sound which is double the former, or in other words, the octave to the preceding tone, will be the most pleasing harmony. The next to that, which is as two to three, will be most agreeable. And thus universally, those sounds whose differences may be most easily compared are the most agreeable.

It is most certain that the cause of pleasure in all our senses originates from the justness of proportion, and that disproportion never creates a pleasing sensation. The lad whom Mr. Chesselden restored to sights was at first most delighted with those objects which were regular and smooth on the surface; from this it is plain that the ideas we entertain of beauty from the eye originates from regularity and proportion; it is the same with the sense of feeling, smooth, round, and uniform bodies are more pleasing than those which are rough and irregular; why should not therefore the same preference be given by the ear to the proportion of sounds?

Sound has, in common with light, the property of being extensively diffused; and also admits of reflection. The laws of this reflection, it is true, are less understood: all we know is, that sound is reflected by hard bodies, and that their being hollow, sometimes increases the reverberation. A wall or a mountain sometimes reflects sounds so distinct that we are almost induced to suppose it proceeds from them rather than from an opposite quarter. Vaults and hollow rocks also produce distinct echoes.

The internal part of the ear is particularly formed for reflecting sounds, and may, in some measure, be compared to the cavern of a rock. In this cavity sounds are repeated, and by that means conveyed to the membranous part of the lamina, which being an expansion of the auditory nerves transmits them to the mind. The internal cavity of the ear, which is fashioned out in the temporal bone, like a cavern cut into a rock, seems to be fitted for the purposes of echoing sound with the greatest precision.

One of the most common complaints in old age is deafness, which probably proceeds from the rigidity of the nerves in the labyrinth of the ear, augmenting as we advance in years, and when the membranous part of the lamina becomes ossified deafness is the consequence, and is in that case incurable. It sometimes happens from a stoppage of the wax, but it may then be relieved by art. In order to know whether the defect be an internal or art external one, let the deaf person put a repeating watch into his mouth, and if he hears it strike, he may be assured that his disorder proceeds from an external cause, and may be, in some measure, relieved.

It often happens, that people with bad voices, and unmusical ears, hear better with one ear than the other, and suspecting there might be some analogy between the ears and eyes, as those who squint have more strength in one eye than the other, I made several experiments, and always found their defect in judging properly of sounds proceeded from the inequality of their ears, and their receiving by both at the same time unequal sensations, and those persons who hear false also sing false, without knowing it. They also frequently deceive themselves with regard to the side from whence the sound comes, generally supposing the noise to come on the part of the best ear. This, however, is only applicable to those who are born with a defect in the hearing.

Such as are hard of hearing reap the same advantage from the trumpet made for this purpose that short-sighted persons do from concave glasses. As the sight is affected with age so is the hearing, and equally requires the assistance of art. Trumpets for assisting hearing might be easily enlarged, so as to increase sounds, in the same manner that the telescope does bodies; but they could be used to advantage only in places of solitude and stillness, as the neighbouring sounds would mix with the more distant ones, and the whole would produce in the ear nothing but tumult and confusion.

Hearing is a much more necessary sense to man than to any other animal. In the latter it is only a warning against danger, or an encouragement to mutual assistance. In man, it is the source of most of his pleasures, and without it the rest of his senses would be of little benefit. A man born deaf must necessarily be dumb, and his whole sphere of knowledge must be bounded by sensual objects. We shall here notice a singular instance of a young man, who, born deaf, at the age of 24 suddenly acquired the faculty of hearing. The account, which is given in the Memoirs of the Academy of Sciences, 1703, page 18, is in substance as follows:

"A young man, of the town of Chartres, aged about 24, the son of a tradesman, who had been deaf and dumb from his birth, began to speak of a sudden, to the utter astonishment of the whole town. He gave his friends to understand, that for three or four months before, he had heard the sound of the bells, and was greatly surprised at this new and unknown sensation. After some time a kind of water issued from his left ear, and he then heard perfectly well with both. During these three months he listened attentively to all he heard, and accustomed himself to speak softly the words pronounced by others. He laboured hard in perfecting himself in the pronunciation, and in the ideas attached to every sound. At length, supposing himself qualified to break silence, he declared that he could speak, though as yet but imperfectly. Soon after some able divines questioned him concerning his ideas of his past state, and principally with respect to God, his soul, the moral beauty of virtue and deformity of vice. Of these, however, he did not appear to have the slightest conception. He had gone to mass indeed with his parents, had learned to sign himself with the cross, to kneel down, and to assume all the external signs of devotion; but he did all this without comprehending the intention or the cause. He had no idea even of death, but led a life of pure animal instinct, and though entirely taken up with sensual objects, and such as were present, he yet did not seem to have made any reflections upon them. The young man was not, however, in want of understanding, but the understanding of a man deprived of all intercourse with society is so very confined, that the mind is, in some measure, totally under the control of its immediate sensations."

It is possible, nevertheless, to communicate ideas to deaf men, and even to give them precise notions of general subjects, by means of signs, and by writing. A person born deaf, may be taught to read, to write, and even by the motion of the lips to understand what is said to him; a plain proof how much the senses resemble, and may supply the defects of each other.

On this subject it may not be improper to quote a fact, of which I was myself a witness. One M. Pereire, a native of Portugal, who had made it his particular study to teach persons born deaf and dumb, brought to my house a young man who was thus unhappily circumstanced. He was at the age of nineteen, in the month of July, 1746, when M. Pereire undertook to teach him to speak and read. More than four months had not elapsed, when he was capable of pronouncing syllables and words; and in the space of ten months, he perfectly understood, and could, with tolerable distinctness, pronounce about thirteen hundred different words. This education, so favourably begun, was interrupted for nine months by the absence of the master; who then found him far less intelligent than he had left him. His pronunciation was vitiated, and of the words he had learned most of, he retained not the smallest remembrance. M. Pereire accordingly renewed his instructions in the month of February, 1748; and from that time he never left him till June 1749. At one of the meetings of the French Academy this young man was brought them, and had several questions proposed to him in writing. To these his answers, whether written or verbal, were highly satisfactory. His pronunciation, indeed, was slow, and the sound of his voice was harsh; but at these defects there is little cause to wonder, as it is by imitation alone that our organs are enabled to form precise, soft, and well-articulated sounds, and, as this young man was deaf, he could not be expected to imitate what he did not hear; but which harshness, by the assiduity and skill of his master, might, however, in some degree, be corrected afterwards.

In the above case, the expedition of the master, and the progress of the pupil, who indeed seemed to be no wise deficient in point of natural ability and understanding, are an ample proof, that persons born deaf and dumb may, by art, be brought to converse with other men; and I am persuaded that, had this young man been instructed so early as at the age of seven or eight, he would have attained as great a number of ideas as mankind possess in general.

CHAPTER VIII.

OF THE SENSES IN GENERAL.

The animal body is composed of different matters, of which some are insensible, as the bones, the fat, the blood, &c. and others, as the membranes and the nerves, appear to be active substances, on which depend the action of every member. The nerves are the immediate organs of the mind, but which may be said to diversify from a difference in disposition, insomuch, that according to their position, arrangement, and quality, they transmit to the mind different kinds of sentiment, which have been distinguished by the name of sensations, and which appear, in effect, to have no resemblance to each other. Nevertheless, if we consider that all external senses are only nervous membranes, differently placed and disposed; that the nerves are the general organs of feeling, and that in the animal body, no other substance is possessed of this property, we shall be led to believe that the senses, having all one common principle, and the nerves proceeding from the same substance, though in various forms, the sensations which result from them are not so essentially different as they at first appear.

The eye ought to be regarded as an expansion of the optic nerve, whose position being more exterior than that of any other nerve, has the most quick and the most delicate sensation. It will be moved, therefore, by the smallest particles of matter, as those of light; and will consequently give us sensations of distant bodies, provided they produce or reflect those small particles. The ear is not placed so exteriorly as the eye, and in which there not being so great an expansion of nerves, will not be possessed of the like degree of sensibility, nor will it be affected by particles more gross, as those which form sounds, and will give us sensations of such distant objects as can put those particles in motion. As they are much grosser than those of light, and have less quickness, they cannot extend themselves so far; and consequently the ear will not give us sensations of objects so distant as those which the eye communicates. The membrane, which is the seat of smell, being still less furnished with nerves than the ear, it will only give us sensations of particles of matter which are more gross and less remote, such as the odour from bodies, which may be said to be the essential oils which exhale and float in the air, as light bodies swim upon the water. As the nerves are also in less quantity, and more divided over the tongue, and palate, and the odoriferous parts are not strong enough to affect them, the oily or saline parts must detach themselves from other bodies, and lodge upon the tongue to produce the sensation of taste. This sense differs materially from that of smelling, because the last brings to us sensations of things at a certain distance, but the former requires a kind of contact, which operates by the means of the fusion of certain parts of matter, such as salts, oils, &c. In short, as the nerves are minutely divided, and as the skin affords them but a very thin covering, no particles of matter so small as those which form light, sound, or odours, can affect them; and the sense of feeling gives us no sensation of distant objects, but of those only whose contact is immediate.

It appears, therefore, that the difference between our senses is occasioned by the more or less exterior position of the nerves, and of their greater or smaller quantity in the different organs. It is for this reason that a nerve, when irritated by a stroke, or uncovered by a wound, gives us often the sensation of light, without the assistance, of the eye; and from the same cause we often experience sensations of sound, though the ear be not affected by any thing exterior.

When the particles of luminous or sonorous matters are re-united in great quantities, they form a kind of solid body, that produces different kinds of sensations, which appear not to have any relation with the first. The particles which compose light being collected in great quantities, affect not only the eyes but also the nervous parts of the skin, and produce the sensation of heat, which is a sentiment, different from the first, though originating from the same cause. Heat, then, is a sensation arising from a contact with light, which acts as a solid body, or as a mass of matter in motion. The action of light, like other matters in motion, is evident when we expose, light bodies to the focus of a burning glass; the action of the light communicates before even it heats them, a motion by which they are disturbed and displaced. Heat, then, acts as solid bodies act upon each other, since it is capable of displacing light matters, and communicating to them a movement of impulsion.

The like happens when the sonorous particles are collected in great quantities; they produce sensible agitation, which is very different from the action of sound upon the ear. Any violent explosion, as a loud clap of thunder, shakes us, and communicates a kind of trembling to all the neighbouring bodies. Sound then also acts as a solid body, for it is not the agitation of the air which causes this tremulous motion, since even at that time we do not remark that it is accompanied with the wind; besides, however strong the wind may be, it never produces such violent agitations. It is by this action of the sonorous particles that a cord in vibration sets the next in motion; and we ourselves feel, when the noise is violent, a kind of fluttering very different from the sensation of sound by the ear, although it be an effect of the same cause.

All the difference in our sensations are produced by the greater or smaller number, and by the more or less exterior position of the nerves, which is the cause that some of our senses, as the eye, ear, and smell, may be affected by the small particles which exhale from particular bodies; others, as tasting and feeling, require actual contact, or more gross emanations, so as to form a solid mass; and it is this feeling which gives us the sensation of solidity, or fluidity, and of the heat of bodies.

A fluid differs from a solid, because it has not any particles gross enough to admit us to grasp it on different sides at one time. The particles which compose fluids cannot touch each other but at one point, or so few points, that no part can have any considerable adliesion with another. Solid bodies, reduced even into an impalpable powder, do not absolutely lose their solidity, because the parts, touching each other by many sides, preserve a degree of cohesion; and this is the reason why we can make them up in masses, and squeeze them together.

The sense of feeling is spread over the whole body, but employs itself differently in different parts. The sensation which results from feeling is excited by the contact of some foreign body to that of our own. If we apply a foreign body against the breast or shoulder we shall feel it, but without having a single idea of its form, because the breast or shoulder touches but one side only. It is the same with respect to all other parts which cannot bend themselves round or embrace at one time many parts of foreign bodies. Those parts of our body, which, like the hand, are divided into many flexible and moveable parts, and can apply themselves at one time upon different sides of a foreign body, are those only which can give us the ideas of their form and size.

It is not, therefore, because there are a greater quantity of nervous tufts at the extremity of the fingers than in any other part of the body, that the hand is, in effect, the principal organ of feeling, but merely because it is divided into many parts all moveable, all flexible, all acting at the same time, and are all obedient to the will; and which alone gives us distinct ideas of the figure and form of bodies. Feeling is no more than a contact of superficies, and the superficies of the hand are greater, in proportion, than that of any other part of the human body, because there is not any one which is so greatly divided. This advantage, when added to those derived from the flexibility of the fingers, suffices to render this part the most perfect organ to give us the exact and precise ideas of the form of bodies, and, if the hand had twenty fingers, it is not to be doubted but that the sense of feeling would be infinitely more perfect; and if we should suppose that it were divided into an infinity of parts we should have, even in the very moment of the touch, exact and precise ideas of the figure and difference of bodies, however small. If, on the contrary, the hand were without fingers, we should have but very imperfect and confused knowledge of the objects which surround us.

Animals which have hands appear to be the most acute; apes do things so resembling the mechanical actions of man that they seem to be actuated by the same sensations; but those animals which are deprived of hands having not any part divided and flexible enough to be able to twist round the superficies of bodies, they cannot have any precise notion either of the form or size of them. It is for this reason that we often see them frightened at objects which they ought to be the best acquainted with. The principal organ of their feeling is the muzzle, because it is divided in two parts by the mouth, and because the tongue serves them for touching bodies, and turning them, which they do over and over again, before they take them between their teeth.

It may also be conjectured, that animals, which, as the scuttle-fish, the polypus, and many insects, have a great number of arms or paws, which they can unite and join, may also have an advantage over others, in knowing how to chuse what is most agreeable to them. Fishes, therefore, whose bodies are covered with scales, ought to be the most stupid of all animals, for they cannot have any knowledge of the form of bodies; and their sense of feeling must be very obtuse, since they cannot feel but through the scales. Thus all animals, whose bodies have no divided extremities, as arms, legs, paws, &c. will have much less sense of feeling than others. Serpents, however, are less stupid than fishes, because, although they have no extremities, and are covered with a hard and scaly coat, they have the faculty of bending round foreign bodies, and by that means obtaining some conception of their form and magnitude.

The two great obstacles to the exercise of the sense of feeling then are, first, the uniformity of the figure of the body of the animal, or the defect of the different divided and flexible parts; and secondly, the cloathing of the skin, whether with hair, feathers, scales, shells, &c. The more this cloathing is hard and solid, the less the sentiment of feeling will be; and the finer and more delicate the skin, the sense of feeling will be the more quick and exquisite. Women, among other advantages over men, have their skin more fine, and the sense of feeling more delicate.

The fœtus in the womb of the mother, has a very delicate skin; it must therefore feel every exterior impression in the most acute manner; but as it swims in a liquid, and as liquids break the action of all the causes which may occasion any shock, it can but very seldom be injured, and never without some violent shock be received by the mother. Although the sense of feeling depends, in a great measure upon the fineness of the skin, yet, as it can have but little exercise in the fœtus state, so can it have but little sensation arising from feeling.

In a new-born infant, the hands remain as useless as in the fœtus, because, by swaddling they are not permitted to make use of them, till the end of six or seven weeks; by this absurd custom, we retard the unfolding of this important sense on which all our knowledge depends; and therefore we should act more wisely, were we to allow the infant the free use of its hands the moment of its birth, as it would then sooner acquire ideas of the form of things; and who knows how far our first ideas have an influence over our subsequent ones? One man, perhaps, possesses more ingenuity, or capacity than another, merely because in his earliest infancy he was allowed to make a greater and readier use of this sense. As soon as children are indulged with the liberty of their hands, they endeavour to touch whatever is presented to them. They take pleasure in handling every thing they are capable of grasping; they seem as if desirous to find out the form of bodies, by feeling them on every side; and they amuse or instruct themselves in this manner with new objects. And which predilection for novelty remains our favourite amusement through life.

It is by feeling alone that we can attain any complete and certain intelligence, and it is by that alone, all the other senses are prevented from being perpetual sources of illusion and error. But in what manner is this important sense developed? In what manner are our first ideas attained? Have we not forgot every thing that passed during the cloud of infancy? How shall we trace our thoughts back to their origin? Even in attempting thus to trace them, is there not presumption? There is, and were the object in view of less importance, with justice might it be stigmatized, but as the mind cannot be employed in a more noble research, every effort may surely be exerted in so important a contemplation.

Let us suppose, then, a man newly brought into existence, whose body and organs were perfectly formed, but who, awaking amidst the productions of Nature, is an utter stranger to himself and every thing he perceives. Of a man thus circumstanced what would be the first emotions, the first sensations, the first opinions? Were he himself to give us a detail of his conceptions at this period, how would he express them? Might it not be in some measure as follows? And here let us suppose such a man to speak for himself.

"Well do I recollect that joyful, anxious moment, when I first became conscious of my own existence; I knew not what I was, where I was, nor from whence I came. On opening my eyes, what an addition to my surprise! The light of day, the azure vault of heaven, the verdure of the earth, the transparency of the waters, all employed, all animated my spirits, and filled me with inexpressible delight.

"At first, I imagined that all those objects were within me, and formed a part of myself. Impressed with this idea, I turned my eyes toward the sun, whose splendour instantly dazzled and overpowered me. Involuntarily I closed my eye-lids, though not without a slight sensation of pain; and, during this short interval of darkness, I imagined that I was about to sink into nothing.

"Full of affliction and astonishment at this great change, I was roused by a variety of sounds. The whistling of the breezes, and the melody of birds, formed a concert, of which the soft impression pervaded the inmost recesses of my soul. I continued to listen, and was persuaded, that this music was actually within me.

"So much was I engrossed with this new kind of existence, that I entirely forgot the light part of my being, which I had known the first, till again I opened my eyes. What joy to find myself once more in possession of so many brilliant objects! The present pleasure surpassed the former, and for a time suspended the charming effect of sound.

"I turned my eyes upon a thousand different objects, I soon found that I could lose and restore them at pleasure; and with a repetition of this new power I continued to amuse myself.

"I began to see without emotion, and to hear without confusion, when a light breeze, communicated a new sensation of pleasures by wafting its perfumes to my nostrils, and excited in me a kind of additional self-love.

"Occupied by these different sensations, and impelled by the various pleasures of my new existence, I instantly arose, and was transported by perceiving that I moved along, as if by some unknown, some hidden power.

"Hardly had I advanced one step, when the novelty of my situation rendered me immoveable. My surprise returned; for I supposed that all the objects around me were in motion, and the whole creation seemed once more to be in disorder.

"I carried my hand to my head, I touched my forehead, I felt my whole frame. Then I found my hand to be the principal organ of my existence. All its informations were so distinct, so perfect, and so superior to what I had experienced from the other senses, that I employed myself for some time in repeating its enjoyments. Every part of my body, which I touched with my hand, seemed to touch my hand in turn, and actually gave back sensation for sensation.

"It was not long before I perceived that this faculty of feeling was expanded over my whole frame, and I began to discover the limits of my existence, which at first I had supposed of an immense extent, and diffused over all the objects I saw.

"Upon casting my eyes upon my body, I conceived it to be of a size so enormous, that all other objects seemed to be, in comparison, as so many luminous particles. I gazed upon my person with pleasure. I examined the formation of my hand, and all its motions; and my hand appeared to be more or less large, in proportion as it was more or less distant from my eyes. On bringing it very near, it concealed, I found, almost every other object from my sight.

"I began to suspect there was some fallacy in the sensation I experienced from the eye, because as I perceived my hand was only a small part, I could not conceive how it should appear so large; I therefore resolved to depend for information upon the touch, which as yet had never deceived me. This precaution was highly serviceable. I renewed my motions, and walked with my face turned toward the heavens. Happening to strike lightly against a palm-tree, I was dismayed, and laid my hand, though not without fear, upon this object, and found it to be a being distinct from myself, because it did not return double sensation as my own body had done. Now it was that, for the first time, I perceived there was something external, something which did not form an actual part of my own existence.

"From this new discovery I concluded that I ought to form my opinion with respect to external objects, in the same manner as I had done with respect to the parts of my body. I resolved, therefore, to feel whatever I saw, and vainly attempted to touch the sun, I stretched forth my arm and found nothing but an airy vacuum. Every effort I made, as each object appeared to me equally near, led me from one fit of surprize into another, nor was it till after an infinite number of trials that I was enabled to use the eye as a guide to the hand, and that I perceived there were some objects more remote from me than others.

"Amazed and mortified at the uncertainty of my state, and the endless delusions to which I seemed subjected, the more I reflected the more I was fatigued and oppressed with thought; I seated myself beneath a tree loaded with delicious fruit, within my reach. On stretching forth my arm, and gently touching it, the fruit instantly separated from the branch; I seized it, and being able to grasp in my hand an entire substance, which formed no part of myself, appeared of great importance. When I held it up its weight, though in itself trivial, seemed like an animated impulse, in conquering which I found another and a greater pleasure.

"I held the fruit near my eye, and I considered its form and its colours. Its fragrance prompted me to carry it near my lips, and with eagerness did I inhale that fragrance. The perfume envited my sense of tasting, which I found to be superior to that of smelling. What savour, what novelty of sensation, did I now experience. Nothing could be more exquisite. What before had been pleasure was how heightened into luxury. The power of tasting gave me the idea of possession. I imagined that the substance of this fruit had become a part of my own, and that I was empowered to transform things without me at will.

"Charmed at the idea of this new power, and incited by the sensations I had already experienced, I continued to pluck the fruit and to eat. At length, however, an agreeable languor stealing upon my senses, my limbs became heavy, and my soul seemed to lose its activity. My sensations, no longer vivid and distinct, presented to me only feeble and irregular images. In the instant, as it were, my eyes became useless, closed, and my head, no longer borne up by the strength of the muscles, sunk back, and found a support upon the verdant turf beneath me.

"To every thing around me I was now lost and insensible. Of my very existence I retained not the smallest sensation. How long I continued thus asleep I know not, for as yet I had not formed the smallest idea of time. My awaking appeared like a second birth, and I only felt that my existence had experienced a certain interruption. This short annihilation produced in me a sensation of fear, and I began to conclude that I was not to exist for ever.

"In this state of doubt and perplexity I also began to suspect that sleep had robbed me of some part of my late powers, when turning around, in order to resolve my doubts, with what astonishment did I behold another form similar to my own? I took it for another self; and I imagined that, far from having lost any thing during my late state of annihilation, my existence was in reality doubled.

"Over this new being I carried my hand, and found, with rapture and astonishment, that it was not a part of myself, but something more; something more charming, something more glorious! nor could I help supposing that my existence was about to be transfused entirely into this, as it were, second part of my being. New ideas and new passions now arose, took possession of my soul, and excited my curiosity. By the touch of my hand I found her to be animated; expression and vivacity darted from her eyes and impressed my soul, and love served to complete that happiness which was begun in the individual, and every sense was gratified in its full variety."

CHAPTER IX.

OF THE VARIETIES IN THE HUMAN SPECIES.

Every thing which we have hitherto advanced relates to man as an individual. The history of the species requires a separate detail, of which the principal facts can only be derived from the varieties that are found in the inhabitants of different regions. Of the varieties, the first and the most remarkable is the colour, the second is the form and size, and the third is the disposition. Considered in its full extent, each of these objects might afford materials for a volume. Our remarks, however, shall be general, and confined to such points as have been established on undoubted testimony.

In examining the surface of the earth, and beginning our inquiries from the north, we find in Lapland, and in the northern parts of Tartary, a race of small-sized men, whose figure is uncouth, and whose physiognomy is as wild as their manners are unpolished. Though they seem to be of a degenerate species they yet are numerous, and the countries they occupy are extensive.

The Danish, Swedish, and Muscovite Laplanders, the inhabitants of Nova-Zembla, the Borandians, the Samoiedes, the Ostiacks of the old continent, the Greenlanders, and the savages to the north of the Esquimaux Indians, of the new continent, appear to be of one common race, which has been extended and multiplied along the coasts of the northern seas, in deserts and climates, considered as uninhabitable by every other nation. These people have broad faces and flat noses; their eyes are of a yellowish brown, inclining to black, their eye-lids are drawn toward the temples, their cheek-bones are extremely prominent, their mouths are large, the lower part of their countenances is narrow, their lips thick and turned outward; their voices are shrill, with heads bulky, hair black and straight, and skin of a tawny colour. They are small in stature, and though meagre, they are yet of a squat form. In general their size is about four feet, and the tallest exceed not four feet and a half. Among these people, if there is any difference to be found, it depends on the greater or less degree of deformity. The Borandians, for example, are still less than the Laplanders. The white of their eye is of a darker yellow, and they are also more tawny; and their legs, instead of being slender, like those of the latter, are thick and bulky. The Samoiedes are more squat than the Laplanders; their heads are larger, their noses longer, their complexion more dark, their legs shorter, their hair longer, and their beards more scanty. The Greenlanders have the most tawny skin, its colour being that of a deep olive, and it is even said that some of them are as black as those of Ethiopia. Throughout them all it is to be observed, the women are as unseemly as the men; and so nearly do they resemble each other, that at first it is not easy to distinguish them. The women of Greenland are very small, but well proportioned; their hair is more black, and their skin softer, than those of the Samoiede women: their breasts are of such length that children are able to receive the nipple, which is of a jet black, over the mother's shoulder. Some travellers say they have no hair but upon the head, and that they are not subject to the periodical complaints common to the sex. Their visage is large, their eyes small, black, and lively, and their feet and hands are short. In every other respect the Samoiede and the Greenland women are similar. The savages north of the Esquimaux, and even in the northern parts of Newfoundland, bear a resemblance to the Greenlanders; their eyes, it is true, are larger, but, like them, they are of small stature, have flat noses, and large and broad faces.

Nor is it alone in deformity, in diminutiveness, and in the colour of the hair and eyes, that these nations resemble each other, but also in their inclinations and manners. Incivility, superstition, and ignorance, are alike conspicuous in them all.

The Danish Laplanders have a large black cat, which they make a confidant in all their secrets, a counsellor in all their difficulties, and whom they consult on all occasions. Among the Swedish Laplanders, there is in every family a drum, for the purpose of consulting the devil; and though they are robust and nimble, they are yet so timid and dastardly, that no inducement can bring them into the field of battle. Gustavus Adolphus undertook, but undertook in vain, to form a regiment of Laplanders. Indeed there is reason to suppose that they cannot live but in their own country, and in their own manner. In travelling over the ice and snow, they use skates made of fur, which are in length about two ells, and half a foot broad, and which are raised and pointed before, and fastened to the foot by straps of leather. With these they make such dispatch on the snow, that they easily overtake the swiftest animals. They also use a pole, pointed with iron at one end, and rounded at the other. This pole serves to push them along, to direct their course, to keep them from falling, to stop the impetuosity of their career, and to kill what game they overtake. With their skates they descend the steepest precipices, and scale the most craggy mountains; nor are the women less skilful in such exercises than the men. They are all accustomed to the bow and arrow; and it is asserted, that the Muscovite Laplanders launch a javelin with so much dexterity, that at the distance of thirty paces they are sure to hit a mark no larger than a silver crown, and with such force, that it will transfix a human body. They hunt the ermine, the fox, the lynx, and the martin, whose skins they barter for brandy and tobacco. Their food consists principally of dried fish, and the flesh of the bear and rein-deer. Of the bones of fishes, pounded and mixed with the tender bark of the pine or birch-tree, is their bread composed. Their drink is either train-oil or brandy and when deprived of these, their favourite beverage is water, in which juniper-berries have been infused.

Examined in a moral sense, the Laplanders have few virtues, and all the vices of ignorance. Immersed in superstition and idolatry, of a Supreme Being they have no conception; nor is it easy to determine which is most conspicuous, the grossness of their understandings, or the barbarity of their manners, being equally destitute of courage and shame. Boys and girls, mothers and sons, brothers and sisters, bathe together naked, without being in the smallest degree ashamed. When they come out of their baths, which are warm, they immediately go into the rivers. It is the custom among all these people to offer their wives and daughters to strangers, and are much offended if the offer is not accepted.

In winter, the Laplanders, clothe themselves with the skin of the rein-deer, and in summer with the skins of birds. To the uses of linen they are utter strangers. The women of Nova-Zembla have the nose and ears pierced, and ornament them with pendants of blue stone; and to add a lustre to their charms, they form blue streaks upon their forehead and chin. The men wear no hair on the head, and cut their beards round. The Greenland women dress themselves with the skin of the dog-fish: they also paint their faces with blue and yellow, and wear pendants in their ears. They all live underground, or in huts almost so, covered with the bark of trees, or the bones of fishes. Some of them form subterraneous trenches, from one hut to another, by which, during the winter months, they can enjoy the society of their neighbours without going out. A continued series of darkness for several months obliges them to illuminate their dreary abodes with lamps, in which they burn the same train oil they use as drink. In summer they have scarcely more comfort than in winter, being obliged to live perpetually in a thick smoke, which is the only device they have contrived for the destruction of gnats, which are perhaps more numerous in these regions of frost, than in those of the most scorching heat. Under all these hardships they are subject to few diseases, and they live to a prodigious age. So vigorous indeed are the old men, that they are hardly to be distinguished from the young. The only infirmity they experience is that of blindness, which is very common among them. Perpetually dazzled by the strong reflection of the snow in winter, and enveloped in clouds of smoke in summer, few when advanced in years are found to retain the use of their eyes.

As all the different tribes or nations, therefore, resemble each other in form, in shape, in colour, in manners, and even in oddity of customs, they are undoubtedly of the same race of men. The practice of offering their women to strangers, and of being pleased when they are thought worthy of caresses, may proceed from a consciousness of their own deformity as well as that of their women. In appearance, the woman, whom a stranger has accepted, they afterwards respect for her superior beauty. At any rate it is certain, although remote from each other, and separated by a great sea, the custom is general in all the above countries. We even meet with it among the Crim Tartars, the Calmucks, and among several other nations of Siberia and of Tartary, where personal deformity is almost as conspicuous as in those of the North. In all the neighbouring nations, on the other hand, as in China, and in Persia[C], where the women are remarkable for beauty, the men are also remarkable for jealousy.

[C] La Boulai tells us, that in order to prevent all cause of jealousy, when the women of Schach die, the place of their interment is industriously kept secret, in like manner as the ancient Egyptians delayed the embalment of their wives for several days after their decease, that the surgeons might have no temptation.

In examining the different nations adjacent to this extensive territory, which the Laplanders occupy, we find they have no affinity. Alone are they resembled by the Ostiacks and the Tongusians, whose situation is to the south and south-east of the Samoiedes. The Samoiedes and Borandians bear no resemblance to the Russians; nor do the Laplanders to the Fins, the Goths, the Danes, or the Norwegians. The Greenlanders are likewise entirely different from the savages of Canada, who are tall and well proportioned, and though the tribes differ from each other, they do more so from the Laplanders. The Ostiacks, however, seem to be a less ugly and taller branch of the Samoiedes. They live on raw fish or flesh, and for drink they prefer blood to water. Like the Laplanders and the Samoiedes they are immersed in idolatry; nor are they known to have any fixed abode. In fine, they appear to form a shade between the race of Laplanders and the Tartarians; or rather, indeed, may it be said that the Laplanders, the Samoiedes, the Borandians, the Nova-Zemblians, and perhaps the Greenlanders, and the savages to the north of the Esquimaux Indians, are Tartars reduced to the lowest point of degeneracy; that the Ostiacks are less degenerated than the Tongusians, who though to the full as ugly, are yet more sizeable and shapely. The Samoiedes and Laplanders live in the latitude of 68 or 69, the Ostiacks and the Tongusians in that of 60. The Tartars, who are situated along the Wolga, in the latitude of 55, are gross, stupid, and beastly; like the Tongusians, they have hardly any idea of religion, nor will they receive for their wives any women until they have had an intercourse with other men.

The Tartars occupy the greatest part of Asia, and in fact extend from Russia to Kamtschatka, a space in length from 11 to 1200 leagues and from 700 to 750 in breadth; a circumference twenty times larger than the whole kingdom of France. The Tartars terminate China, the kingdoms of Boutan and Alva, and the empires of Mogul and Persia, even to the Caspian Sea, on the north and west. They spread along the Wolga, and over the west coast of the Caspian Sea, even to Daghestan. They have penetrated to the north coast of the Black Sea, and formed settlements in the Crimea, and in the neighbourhood of Moldavia and the Ukraine. All these people have the upper part of their face very large and wrinkled even while yet in their youth. Their noses are short and flat, their eyes little, and sunk in their head; their cheek-bones are high; the lower part of their face is narrow; their chin is long and prominent; their teeth are long and straggling; their eye-brows are so large as to cover the eyes; their eye-lids are thick; the face broad and flat; their complexion tawny, their hair black; they have but little beard, which is disposed like the Chinese; they have thick thighs and short legs, and though but of middling stature, they are remarkably strong and robust. The ugliest of them are the Calmucks, in whose appearance there seems to be something frightful. They are all wanderers and vagabonds; and their only shelter is that of tents, made of hair or skins. Their food is horse-flesh, and flesh of other animals, either raw or a little softened by being between the horse and the saddle. They eat also fish dried in the sun. Their most common drink is mare's milk, fermented, with millet ground into meal. They all have the head shaved, except a tuft of hair on the top, which they let grow sufficiently long to form into tresses on each side of the face. The women, who are as ugly as the men, wear their hair, which they bind up with bits of copper, and other ornaments of the same nature.

The majority of these tribes are alike strangers to religion, morality, and decency. They are robbers by profession; and those of Daghestan, who live in the neighbourhood of civilized countries, sustain a great traffic of slaves, whom they carry off by forte, and afterwards sell to the Turks and the Persians. Their wealth consists chiefly of horses, which are more numerous, perhaps, in Tartary than in any other part of the world. They live in the same place with their horses, and are continually employed in training, dressing, and exercising them, whom they reduce to such implicit obedience, that they actually appear to understand, as it were, the intention of their riders.

To attain a knowledge of the particular differences which subsist in the race of Tartars, we have only to compare the descriptions that travellers have given of their different tribes. The Calmucks, who are situated in the neighbourhood of the Caspian Sea, between the Muscovites and the great Tartars, are, according to Tavernier, robust, but the most ugly and the most deformed of all human beings. Their faces are so flat and so broad that their eyes, which are uncommonly small, are from five to six inches asunder; and their noses so flat that two holes are barely perceivable instead of nostrils. Next to the Calmucks, the natives of Daghestan rank in the class of deformity. The little Tartars, or the Tartars of Nogai, who dwell near the Black Sea, are less ugly than the Calmucks, though their faces are broad, their eyes small, and in their figures there is a great resemblance. From their intermixture with the Circassians, the Moldavians, and other neighbouring nations, it is probable that this race have lost much of their original ugliness. The Tartars of Siberia have, like the Calmucks, broad faces, short flat noses, and small eyes; and though their language is different, yet they bear so strong a resemblance to each other, that they can only be considered as the same people. The further we advance eastward we find the features of the Tartars are gradually softened, but the characteristics essential to the race still remain. The Mongou Tartars, according to Palafox, who conquered China, and who were the most polished, though they are the least deformed, yet, like all the other tribes, their eyes are small, faces broad and flat, scanty beards, either black or red; their noses compressed and short, and their complexions tawny.

The people of Thibet, and the other southern provinces of Tartary, are also of a more agreeable aspect. Mr. Sanchez, formerly first physician to the Russian army, a gentleman distinguished by his abilities, has obligingly communicated to me in writing the remarks he had made in the course of his travels through Tartary.

In the years 1735, 1736, and 1737, he visited the Ukraine, the banks of the Don to the sea of Zabach, and the confines of Cuban to Asoph. He traversed the deserts between the countries of the Crimea and Backmut; he went among the Calmucks, who wander about without any fixed habitation, from the kingdom of Casan to the banks of the Don; as also the Crimea and Nogai-Tartars, who wander between the Crimea and the Ukraine, and likewise the Kergissi and Tcheremissi-Tartars, who are situated to the north of Astracan, between the latitude of 50 and 60. These according to him are more diminutive and squat, less active and more corpulent; their eyes are black, complexions tawny, and their faces larger and broader than those we have mentioned. He adds, that among these Tartars, he saw numbers of men and women who had no resemblance to them, but were as white as the people of Poland. They have many slaves among them, brought from among the Russians and Poles; and as their religion admits a number of wives and concubines; and as their Sultans, and Murzas or nobles, prefer the women of Georgia and Circassia for their wives, the children produced from such alliances are less ugly, and more fair than from connections among themselves. There is even a whole tribe of Tartars, called Kabardinski-Tartars, who are remarkable for their beauty. Of these Mr. Sanchez saw *three hundred* on horseback, who were going to enter into the service of Russia; and he declares that he never saw men of a more noble and manly figure; their complexions were fair, fresh and ruddy; their eyes were large and black, and they were tall and well proportioned. He was assured by the Lieutenant-general of Serapikin, who had made a long residence at Kabarda, that the women were equally handsome; but this tribe, so different from all the Tartars around them, came originally from the Ukraine, and removed to Kabarda about the beginning of the last century.

Though the Tartar blood is intermixed, on one side with that of the Chinese, and on the other with that of the Oriental Russians, yet there is sufficient characteristics of the race remaining to suppose them of one common stock. Among the Muscovites are numbers, whose form of visage and body bear a strong resemblance to those of the Tartars. The Chinese are totally different in their dispositions, manners, and customs. The Tartars are naturally fierce, warlike, and addicted to the chace, inured to fatigue, fond of independence, and to a degree of brutality uncivilized. Altogether opposite are the manners of the Chinese; they are effeminate, pacific, indolent, superstitious, slavish, and full of ceremony and compliment. In their features, and form, however, there is so striking a resemblance, as to leave a doubt whether they did not spring from the same race.

Some travellers tell us, that the Chinese are large and fat, their limbs well formed, their faces broad and round, their eyes small, eye-brows large, their eye-lids turned upwards, and their noses short and flat; that upon the chin they have very little beard, and upon each lip not more than seven or eight tufts of hair. Those who inhabit the southern provinces are more brown and tawny than those in the northern; that in colour they resemble the natives of Mauritania, or the more swarthy Spaniards; but those in the middle provinces are as fair as the Germans.

According to Dampier and others, the Chinese are not all fat and bulky, but they consider being so as an ornament to the human figure. In speaking of the island of St. John, on the coast of China, the former says, that the inhabitants are tall, erect, and little encumbered with fat; that their countenances are long, and their foreheads high; their eyes little, their nose tolerably large, and raised in the middle; their mouths of a moderate size, their lips rather thin, their complexion ash-colour, and their hair black; that they have naturally little beard, and even that they pluck out, leaving only a few hairs upon the chin and upper lip.

According to Le Gentil, the Chinese have nothing disagreeable in their countenance, especially in the northern provinces. In the southern ones, when necessarily much exposed to the sun, they are swarthy. That in general their eyes are small and of an oval form, their nose short, their bodies thick, and their stature of a middling height; he assures us that the women do every thing in their power to make their eyes appear little and oblong, that for this purpose it is a constant practice with young girls, instructed by their mothers, forcibly to extend their eye-lids. This, with the addition of a flat nose, ears long, large, open, and pendent, is accounted complete beauty. He adds, their complexion is delicate, their lips of a fine vermilion, their mouths well proportioned, their hair very black, but that chewing beetle blackens their teeth, and by the use of paint they so greatly injure their skin, that before the age of thirty they have all the appearance of old age.

Palafox assures us that the Chinese are more fair than the oriental Tartars; that they have also less beards, but that in every other respect their visages are nearly the same. It is very uncommon, he says, to see blue eyes either in China or in the Philippine islands; and when seen, it is in Europeans, or in those of European parents.

Inigo de Biervillas asserts, that the women of China are better made than the men. Of the latter, he says, their visages are large and complexions rather yellow; their noses broad, and generally compressed, and their bodies are of a thickness greatly resembling that of a Hollander. The women, on the contrary, though they are generally rather fat than otherwise, are however of a free and easy shape; their complexion and skin are admirable; and their eyes are incomparably fine; but from the great pains taken to compress it in their infancy, there are few to be seen of whose nose the shape is even tolerable.

All the Dutch travellers allow that the Chinese have in general broad faces, small eyes, flat noses, and hardly any beard; that the natives of Canton, and the whole of the southern coast, are as tawny as the inhabitants of Fez, in Africa, but that those of the interior provinces are mostly fair. Now if we compare the descriptions we have already given, from the above authors, of the Chinese and Tartars, hardly will a doubt remain that, although they differ a little in stature and countenance, they originate from one stock, and that the points in which they differ proceed entirely either from the climate, or the mixture of races. Chardin says, "the size of the little Tartars is commonly smaller than the Europeans by four inches, and they are thicker in the same proportion. Their complexion is of the colour of copper; their faces are flat, large, and square; their noses compressed, and their eyes are little. Now these are exactly the features of the inhabitants of China; for I have found, after the most minute investigation, that there is the same conformation of face and body throughout the nations to the east and north of the Caspian Sea, and to the east of the peninsula of Malacca. From this circumstance I was inclined to believe that, however different they may appear either in their complexion or manners, they proceed from one stock, for difference of colour depends entirely upon the quality of the climate and the food; and difference in manners is determined by the nature of the soil, and by the greater or less degree of opulence."

Father Parennin, who lived long in China, and whose observations are so accurate and so minute, tells us, that the western neighbours of the Chinese, from Thibet northward to Chamo, differ from the Chinese in manners, language, physiognomy, and external conformation; that they are a people rude, ignorant, and slothful, charges that cannot be laid to the Chinese; and that when any of these Tartars go to Pekin, and the Chinese are asked the reason of this difference, they answer, that it proceeds from the water and the soil; in other words, that it is the nature of the country which produces this change upon the bodies and dispositions of the inhabitants. He adds, that this remark seems to be more applicable with respect to China than to any other country he ever saw; that following the emperor northward into Tartary, to the latitude of 48, he found Chinese from Nanquin who had settled there, whose children had become actual Mongous, being bow-legged, with their heads sunk into their shoulders, and a countenance which created disgust.

So strongly do the Japanese resemble the Chinese, that we can hardly scruple to rank them in the same class. Living in a more southern climate they are more yellow or more brown. In general their stature is short, their face, as well as nose, broad and flat, their eyes small, their hair black, and their beard little more than perceptible. They are haughty, fond of war, full of dexterity and vigour, civil and obliging, smooth-tongued, and courteous, but fickle and vain. With astonishing patience they sustain hunger, thirst, cold, heat, fatigue, and all the other hardships of life. Their ceremonies, or rather grimaces, in eating, are numerous and uncouth. They are laborious skilful artificers, and, in a word, their dispositions, manners, and customs are the same as the Chinese.

One singular custom which they have in common, is, so to contract the feet of the women, that they are hardly able to support themselves. Some travellers mention, that in China, when a girl has passed her third year, they bend the foot in such a manner that the toes are made to come under the sole; that they apply to it a strong water, which burns away the flesh; and then they wrap them up in a number of bandages. They add, that the women feel the pain of this operation all their lives; that they walk with great difficulty; and that their gait is to the last degree ungraceful. Other travellers say that they only compress the foot with so much violence as to prevent its growth; but they unanimously allow, that every woman of condition, and even every handsome woman must have a foot small enough to enter with ease the slipper of a child of six years old.

The Japanese, and the Chinese, we may therefore conclude, proceed from the same stock, that for their civilization we must recur to a very distant part of antiquity, and that they differ more from the Tartars in their manners than their figure. To this civilization, the excellence of the soil, the mildness of the climate, and their vicinity to the sea, have perhaps greatly contributed; while the Tartars, from their inland situation, and being separated from other nations by high mountains, have remained wanderers over their vast deserts, which are situated under a climate to the last degree inclement, especially towards the north. The country of Jesso, which is to the north of Japan, and of which, from its situation, the climate might be expected to be temperate, is however cold, barren, and mountainous, and its inhabitants are altogether different from those of China and Japan. They are ignorant and brutal, without manners, and without arts. Their bodies are short and thick; their hair long, their eyes black, their foreheads flat; and their complexions, though yellow, are rather less so than that of the Japanese. Over their bodies, and even the face, they have much hair; they live like savages, and their food consists of the oily parts of whales and other fishes. They are to the last degree indolent and slovenly; their children go almost naked; nor have their women devised any external ornament beyond that of painting their eye-brows and lips of a blue colour. The sole occupation and pleasure of the men are hunting and fishing; and though they have some customs similar to the Japanese, as that of quavering when they sing, yet in general they bear a much more striking resemblance to the northern Tartars, or to the Samoiedes, than to the Japanese.

In examining nations adjacent to China, on the south and west, we find that the Cochin-Chinese, who inhabit a mountainous region to the southward of China, are more tawny and more ugly than the Chinese; and that the Tonquinese, whose country is more fertile, and whose climate is more mild, are in every respect proportionally more handsome.

According to Dampier, the Tonquinese are of a middling height; and though their complexion is tawny, their skin is so delicate and smooth, that the smallest change is perceptible in their countenance, when they happen either to grow pale, or to redden; a circumstance in which they differ from all other Indians. In common their visage is flat and oval; their nose and lips are thick; and they use every art, in order to render their teeth as black as possible.

These nations, therefore, differ but little from the Chinese. They resemble the natives of the southern provinces in colour; if they are more tawny, it is because they live in a warmer climate; and though their faces are less flat, and their noses less contracted, we yet cannot help considering them as a people of the same origin.

Thus it is also with the natives of Siam, of Pegu, of Aracan, of Laos, &c. Of all these the features have a considerable resemblance to those of the Chinese; and though they differ from them in colour, yet their affinity to the Chinese is greater than to the other Indians. The size of the Siamese, says Loubère, is rather small, their bodies are well proportioned, their faces are large, and their cheek-bones prominent, their forehead is suddenly contracted, and terminates in a point like the chin; their eyes are small and oblique; the white of the eye is somewhat yellow; their cheeks are hollow, from the elevation of the cheek-bones; their mouths are large, their lips thick, their teeth black, their complexion is coarse, and of a brown colour mixed with red, or, according to some travellers, of an ash colour, to which the continual sultriness of the air contributes as much as the birth; their nose is short and rounded at the point; their ears are large, and the bigger they are the more they are held in estimation.

This taste for long ears is highly prevalent in the east; in different places different arts are used to render them so, and in some they draw them down almost to the shoulders. As for the Siamese, however, their ears are naturally larger than ours; their hair is thick, black, and straight; and both sexes wear it so short, that it does not descend lower than the ear. They anoint their lips with a kind of perfumed pomatum, which makes them appear very pale; they have little beard, and that they pluck out by the roots; nor is it customary with them to pare their nails.

Struys says, that the Siamese women wear pendants in their ears of such mass and weight, that the holes become so large the thumb may be put through them. He adds, that the complexion of both sexes is tawny; that though not tall, they are shapely; and that the Siamese are in general a mild and a civilized people.

According to Father Tachard, the Siamese are exceedingly alert, and have among them tumblers, &c. not less expert and skilful than those in Europe. He says, that the custom they have of blackening the teeth, proceeds from an idea that it is not becoming in man to have teeth white like the brute creation; that it is for this reason they begrime them with black varnish, and then abstain from meat for several days, that it may thoroughly adhere.

The inhabitants of the kingdom of Pegu and Aracan are more black, yet bear a strong resemblance both to the Siamese and the Chinese. Those of Aracan put great value upon a forehead large and flat, and to render them so, they apply a plate of lead to the forehead of their children the minute they are born. Their nostrils are large, their eyes are small and lively, and their ears are of such length as to hang over their shoulders. They feed without disgust on mice, rats, serpents, and fish, however corrupted. Their women are tolerably fair, and their ears are as long as those of the men. The people of Achen, who are situated further north than those of Aracan, have also flat visages, and an olive-coloured skin; they allow their boys to go quite naked, and their girls have only a slight plate of silver to conceal what Nature dictates.

None of these nations differ much from the Chinese, and all resemble the Tartars in the smallness of their eyes, the largeness of their visage, and the olive colour of their skin. In proceeding southward the features begin to change more sensibly. The inhabitants of Malacca, and of the island of Sumatra, are black, diminutive, lively, and well proportioned. Though naked from the middle upward, a little kind of scarf excepted, which they wear sometimes over the right and sometimes over the left shoulder, their aspect is fierce. They are naturally brave, and even formidable when they have swallowed a certain quantity of opium, which intoxicates them with a kind of fury.

According to Dampier, the inhabitants of Sumatra and Malacca are of the same race; they speak nearly the same language, and they have the same bold and haughty disposition. They are of a middling stature, their visage long, their eyes black, their noses of a moderate size, their lips thin, and their teeth are blackened.

In the island of Pugniatan, or Pissagan, within 16 leagues of Sumatra, the natives are tall, and of a yellow complexion, like the Brazilians; their hair is long, and they go completely naked. Those of the Nicobar islands, which lie northward of Sumatra, are of a tawny or yellowish colour, and they also go naked. In speaking of these last islanders, Dampier says, that they are tall and well proportioned; that their visage is long, their hair black and straight, and their noses of a moderate size; that the women have no eye-brows, which it is probable they do not suffer to grow. In Sombreo, an island north of the Nicobar islands, the inhabitants are very black, and they paint their faces with green, yellow, and other colours.

These natives of Malacca, of Sumatra, and of the little adjacent islands, though different from each other, are much more so from the Chinese and the Tartars, and seem to have sprung from another race. The inhabitants of Java, nevertheless, have not the smallest resemblance to those of Sumatra and Malacca, while to the Chinese (the colour alone excepted, which, like the Malaccas, is red mixed with black) they seem to be intimately related. Pigafetta describes them as a people not unlike the Brazilians. Their complexion, says he, is coarse, and their bodies are square and muscular, though in size they are neither very tall nor very short; their visage is flat, their cheeks flabby, their eyes small, their eye-brows inclined to the temples, and their beards thin and short. Father Tachard says, that the people of Java are well made and robust; that they are lively and resolute; and that the extreme heat of the climate obliges them to go almost naked. From other descriptions it appears, that the inhabitants of Java are neither black nor white, but of a purplish red, and that they are mild, familiar and courteous.

Legat informs us, that the women of Java, who are not exposed to the rays of the sun, are less tawny than the men, that their countenance is comely, their breasts prominent and shapely, their complexions beautiful, though brown; their hands delicate, their hair soft, their eyes brilliant, their smile agreeable, and that numbers of them dance with elegance and spirit.

Of the Dutch travellers, the generality allow, that the natives of this island are robust, well proportioned, nervous, and full of muscular vigour; that their visage is flat, their check-bones broad and prominent, their eye-lids large, their eyes small, their hair long, and their complexion tawny; that they have little beard; that they wear their hair and their nails very long; and that in order to beautify their teeth, they polish them with files. In a little island fronting that of Java, the women are tawny, their eyes small, their mouths large, their noses flat, and their hair long and black.

From all these accounts we may infer, that the inhabitants of Java greatly resemble the Tartars and Chinese; while those of Malacca, Sumatra, and of the neighbouring little islands differ from them equally in the features of the face, and in the form of the body. This may have very naturally happened; for the peninsula of Malacca, the islands of Sumatra and Java, as well as all the other islands of the Indian Archipelago, must have been peopled by the nations of the neighbouring continents, and even by the Europeans, who have had settlements there for these three hundred years. This must have occasioned a very great variety in the inhabitants both in the features and colour, and in the form of the body and proportion of the limbs. In the island of Java, for example, there is a people called the *Chacrelas*, who are altogether different, not only from the natives of the island, but even from all the other Indians. The Chacrelas are white and fair, and their eyes are so weak that, incapable of supporting the light of the sun, they go about with them lowered and almost closed till night, when their vision becomes more strong.

According to Pyrard, all the inhabitants of the Malacca islands are similar to those of Sumatra and Java in manners, mode of living, habits, language, and colour. According to Maldeslo, the men are rather black than tawny, and the women are more fair. They have all, he says, black hair, large eyes, eye-brows and eye-lids, and bodies vigorous and robust. They are also nimble and active; and though their hair very soon becomes grey, they yet live to a great age. Each island, he further remarks, has its particular language; nor can it be doubted but that they have been peopled by different nations. The inhabitants of Borneo and of Baly, he adds, are rather black than tawny; but according to other travellers, they are only brown like the other Indians. Carreri says, that the inhabitants of Ternate are of the same colour as those of Malacca, which is a little darker than those of Philippine islands; that their countenances are comely; that the men are more shapely than the women, and that both bestow particular care upon their hair.

The Dutch travellers tell us, that the natives of the Island of Banda are remarkable for longevity; that they have seen one man at the age of 130, and numbers on the verge of that period; that in general they are indolent and inactive; and that while the men amuse themselves in sauntering abroad, the women are subjected to all the offices of labour at home. Dampier observes, that the original natives of the island of Timor, which is one of those most adjacent to New Holland, are a middling size, and of an erect form; that their limbs are slender, their visages long, their hair black and bristly, and their skin exceedingly black; that they are alert and dexterous, but superlatively indolent and slothful. He adds, however, that the inhabitants of the Bay of Laphno are, for the most part, tawny or copper-coloured.

In turning northward we find Manilla, and the other Philippine islands, of which the inhabitants are perhaps more intermixed than those of any other region in the universe, by the alliances they have formed with the Spaniards, the Indians, the Chinese, the Malabars, the blacks, &c. The negroes, who live in the rocks and woods of Manilla, differ entirely from the other inhabitants; of some the hair is short and frizly, like the negroes of Angola, and of others it is long. Their colour consists of various shades of black. According to Gemelli Carreri, there are some among them who, like the islanders mentioned by Ptolemy, have tails of the length of four or five inches. This traveller adds, that he has been assured, by Jesuits of undoubted testimony, that in the island of Mindoro, which is not far from Manilla, there is a race of men called *Manghians*, who have all tails of that length, and that some of these men had even embraced the Catholic faith; that they are of an olive colour, and have long hair.

Dampier says, that the inhabitants of the island of Mindanao, which is one of the principal and most southerly of the Philippines, are of a middling height, that their limbs are small, their bodies erect, their heads small, their visages oval, their foreheads flat, their eyes black and small, their noses short, their mouths moderate, their lips thin and red, their teeth black, their hair black and smooth, and their skin tawny, but of a brighter yellow than many of the other Indians; that in point of complexion the women have the advantage of the men; that they are also more shapely, and have features tolerably regular; that the men are in general ingenious and alert, but slothful, and addicted to thievery.

Northward of Manilla is the island of Formosa, situated at no great distance from the coast of Fokien, in China, but the natives bear no resemblance to the Chinese. According to Struys, the Formosans are of small stature, particularly those who inhabit the mountains, and that they have broad faces. The women have large coarse breasts, and a beard like the men; their ears, naturally long, they render still more so by thick shells, which they wear as pendants; their hair is black and long, and their complexions are of different degrees of yellow. Though averse to labour, they are yet admirably skilled in the use of the javelin and bow; they are excellent swimmers, and run with incredible swiftness. Struys declares, that in this island he actually saw a man with a tail above a foot long, covered with reddish hair, not unlike that of an ox, and that this man assured him, if it was a blemish to have a tail, it proceeded from the climate, for all the natives of the southern part of the island had tails like himself.

I know not what credit we ought to give to this relation of Struys, for if the fact be true, it must at least be exaggerated; it differs from what other travellers have said with respect to these men with tails, and even from the account of Ptolemy, and from that of Mark Paul, the latter of whom, in his geographical description, says, that in the kingdom of Lambry there are mountaineers who have tails of the length of the hand. Struys seems to rest upon the authority of Mark Paul, as Gemelli Carreri does upon that of Ptolemy, though the tail he mentions to have seen is widely different in its dimensions from those of the blacks of Manilla, the inhabitants of Lambry, and other places, as described by other writers.

The editor of the description of the island of Formosa, from the memoirs of Psalmanazar, makes no mention of a people so very extraordinary; but says, that though the climate is exceedingly hot, the women, those especially who are not exposed to the rays of the sun, are exceedingly fair and beautiful; that with certain lotions they take particular care to preserve their complexion; that they are equally attentive to the beauty of their teeth, and instead of rendering them black, like the Japanese and Chinese, they use every effort to keep them white; that the men are not tall, but thick and strong; that they are commonly vigorous, indefatigable, skilful in war, and dexterous in manual exercises.

In their accounts of the natives of Formosa, the Dutch travellers differ from all those we have yet mentioned. Mandelslo, as well as the writers of the collection of voyages, which paved the way for the establishment of the Dutch East-India Company, informs us that these islanders are taller than the Europeans; that the colour of their skin is of a dark brown; that their bodies are hairy; and that the women are low in stature, but robust, fat, and tolerably well proportioned.

In few writers respecting this island do we find any mention of men with tails; and of the form and features of the natives, authors differ also prodigiously. With respect to one fact they seem, however, to agree, though it is not perhaps less extraordinary, namely, that the women are not allowed to bear children before the age of 35, though allowed to marry long before that period. In speaking of this custom, Rechteren thus expresses himself: "After the women are married, they must not become mothers till they have completed their 35th or 37th year. When they happen to be pregnant before that time, their priestesses trample upon their bellies with their feet, and thus occasion a miscarriage, as painful and dangerous, if not more so than the natural labour. To bring a child into the world previous to the age prescribed, would be not only a disgrace but an enormous crime. I have seen women who had suffered 16 of these forced miscarriages, and were only allowed to bring into the world their 17th child."

The Mariana-islands, or the Ladrones, which are the most remote from the eastern coast, are inhabited by a people rude and uncivilized. Father Gobien says that, till the arrival of the Europeans, they had never seen fire; and that nothing could exceed their astonishment when, on the arrival of Magellan, they first beheld it. Their complexion is tawny, though less brown than that of the natives of the Philippines; in strength and robustness they surpass the Europeans. They are tall and well proportioned; and though they feed solely on roots, fruits, and fish, they are very corpulent, which however, does not check their nimbleness and activity. They live to a great age; nor is it uncommon to find among them persons who, strangers to sickness, have already reached their 100th year.

Carreri says, that the natives of these islands are of a gigantic figure, corpulent, and so strong that they can raise a weight of 500 pounds upon their shoulders. In general their hair is frizly, their noses thick, their eyes are large, and their colour like that of the Indians. The natives of Guan, one of these islands, have long black hair, large noses, thick lips, white teeth, long visages, and fierce aspects. They are also exceedingly robust; and it is said they do not in height measure less than seven feet.

Southward of the Mariana-islands, and eastward of the Malaccas, we find the country of the Papous, and New Guinea, which seem to be the most southern regions. Argensola tells us, that the Papous are as black as the Caffres, that their hair is frizly, and their countenance meagre and disagreeable. In this country, nevertheless, there are people as fair as the Germans; but their eyes are exceedingly weak and delicate. According to Le Maire, they are not only very black, but also savage and brutal; they wear rings in their ears and nostrils, and sometimes also in the partition of the nose; they likewise wear bracelets of mother-of-pearl above the elbows and on the wrists, and cover their heads with a cap made of the bark of a tree painted with several colours. They are well proportioned, have a sufficiency of beard; their teeth are black, as is also the hair, which, though frizly, is not so woolly as that of the negroes. They run very fast, and their weapons consist of clubs, spears, and sabres, made of hard wood, the use of iron being unknown to them. They also employ their teeth as weapons, and bite like dogs; beetle and pimento mixed with chalk make part of their food. The women are of hideous aspect; their breasts hang down to the navel; their bellies are extremely prominent; their arms and limbs are small; and in their visages they resemble so many apes.

Dampier says, that the natives of the island of Sabala, in New Guinea, are a class of tawny Indians, with long black hair, and whose manners are not much different from those of Mindanao, and the other oriental islands; but besides them, it is also peopled by negroes, with short woolly hair. Speaking of another island, which he calls *Garret-Denys*, he says, that the natives are black, vigorous, and well shaped; that their heads are large and round; that their hair, which they cut in different fashions, and tinge with different colours, as red, white, and yellow, is short and frizly; that their faces are large and round, and their noses thick and flat; that nevertheless their physiognomy would not be absolutely disagreeable, did they not thrust a kind of peg, about one inch thick and four inches long, across the nostrils, so that both ends may touch the cheek-bones; and that they pierce their ears with similar pegs.

According to the same author, the natives of the coast of New Holland, which is in the latitude of 16, and to the south of the island of Timor, are of all mankind perhaps the most miserable, and the most upon a level with the brutes. They are tall, erect, and thin; their limbs are long and slender; their heads are large; their foreheads round, and their eye-brows thick. Their eye-lids are always half shut; a habit they contract in their infancy to save their eyes from the gnats, and as they never open their eyes, they cannot see at a distance without raising their head, as if looking at something over their heads. Their noses and lips are thick, and their mouths large. They pull out, it would seem, the two front teeth of the upper jaw; for in neither sex, nor at any age, are they ever found to possess these teeth. They have no beard; their visage is long, nor does it contain one pleasing feature. Their hair is short, black, and frizly, like that of the negroes; and their skin is as black as those of Guinea. Their whole cloathing consists of a bit of the bark of a tree fastened round the middle. They have no houses, and they sleep on the bare ground, without any covering. They associate, men, women, and children, promiscuously, in troops, to the number of 20 or 30. Their only food is a small fish, which they catch by forming reservoirs in little arms of the sea, and to every kind of grain or bread they are utter strangers.

The natives of another part of New Holland, in the 22d or 23d degree of south latitude, seem to be of the same race as those We have now described; they are ugly to an extreme; their eyes have the same defect as those of the others; their skin is black, their hair frizly, and their bodies tall and slender.

From these descriptions it appears, that the islands and coasts of the Indian ocean are peopled by men widely different from each other. The natives of Malacca, of Sumatra, and of the Nicobar islands, appear to derive their origin from those of the peninsula of Indus, and those of Java from the Chinese, the white men excepted, who go by the name of Chacrelas, and who must have sprung from the Europeans. The natives of the Malacca islands seem also in general to have originated from the Indians in the peninsula; but those of the island of Timor, which is near to New Holland, are almost similar to the people of that country. Those of Formosa, and the Mariana islands, resemble each other in size, vigour, and features, and seem to form a race distinct from that of every other people around them. The Papus, and other nations in the neighbourhood of New Guinea, are real blacks, and resemble those of Africa, though at a prodigious distance from that continent, and separated from it by a space of 2,200 leagues of sea. The natives of New Holland resemble the Hottentots. But before we draw any conclusions from all these relations and differences, it is necessary to pursue our enquiries with respect to the different nations of Asia and Africa.

The Moguls, and other nations of the peninsula of India, are not unlike the Europeans in shape and in features; but they differ more or less from them in colour. The Moguls are olive, though in the Indian language the word *Mogul* signifies *White*. The women are extremely delicate, and they bathe themselves very often: they are of an olive colour as well as the men; and, what is opposite to the women in Europe, their legs and thighs are long, and their bodies are short. Tavernier says, that after passing Lahor, and the kingdom of Cashmire, the women have naturally no hair on any part of the body, and the men have hardly any beard. According to Thevenot, the Mogul women are very fruitful, though exceedingly chaste, and suffer so little from the pains of child-birth, that they are often abroad the day following. He adds, that in the kingdom of Decan they are allowed to marry, the male by his tenth, and the female by her eighth year; and at that age they not unoften have children; but the women who become mothers so soon usually cease bearing before they arrive at 30, and by that period they appear wrinkled, and marked with all the deformities of age. It is not an uncommon practice among them to have their skins pricked in the shape of flowers, and by painting them with the juices of plants, they perfectly resemble them.

The natives of Bengal are more yellow than the Moguls. In disposition also they differ totally; their women, instead of being chaste, of all the Indian women are the most lascivious. In this country they carry on a great traffic of slaves, male and female. They also make numbers of eunuchs. They are comely and well-shaped, are fond of commerce, and have much mildness in their manners.

The natives of the coast of Coromandel are more black than the people of Bengal; they are also less civilized, and in general go nearly naked. Those of the coast of Malabar are still more black; their hair is black also, straight, and long, and are of the same size with the Europeans. Even in their towns men, women, and children, bathe promiscuously in public basons. Their women wear rings in their noses; they are married at the age of eight, and though black, or at least of a very deep brown, they yet are comely and well proportioned.

The customs of the different Indian nations are all very singular, if not whimsical. The Banians eat nothing which has had life in it; they are even afraid to kill the smallest reptile, however offensive to them; they throw rice and beans into their rivers as food for the fishes, and grains of different kinds upon the earth for the birds and insects. When they meet a hunter, or a fisher, they earnestly beg of him to desist; if deaf to their entreaties, they offer him money for his gun, or his nets, and when no persuasion nor offer will avail, they trouble the water to frighten away the fishes, and cry with all their strength to put the birds and other game to flight.

The Naires of Calicut form a class of nobles, whose sole profession is that of arms. These men are handsome, and of a comely aspect, though of an olive colour, and though they lengthen their ears to such a pitch as to make them fall over their shoulders, and sometimes lower, they are tall, hardy, courageous, and highly expert in military exercise. These Naires are allowed no more than one wife, but the women may have as many husbands as they please. Father Tachard says, that they sometimes have not fewer than ten, whom they consider as so many slaves, subjected by their beauty. This privilege is annexed to nobility, from which the women of condition derive to themselves every possible advantage. Those of inferior rank are allowed but one husband, but they comfort themselves under this restraint by the caresses of strangers, with whom they carry on their illicit amours, in defiance of their husbands, who dare not even speak to them upon the subject. The mothers prostitute their daughters in their early infancy. The nobles, or Naires, seem to be of a race different from the lower order, for the latter, men as well as women, are more ugly, yellow, unshapely, and more diminutive. Among the Naires there are some whose legs are as thick as the body of another man. This deformity they have from their birth, and not from any particular malady; and nevertheless they are exceedingly active. This race of men with thick legs have not increased much either among the Naires or any other classes of Indians; they are, however, in other places, and especially in Ceylon, where they are said to be the race of St. Thomas.

The natives of Ceylon are not unlike those of the coast of Malabar. They are less black, but their ears are as large, and descend as low. They are of a mild aspect, and naturally nimble, alert, and lively. Their hair which is very black, the men wear short; the common people go almost naked; and the women, according to a custom pretty general in India, have their bosoms uncovered. In Ceylon there is a species of savages, who are called *Bedas*; they occupy a small district on the north part of the island, and seem to be of a peculiar race. The spot they inhabit is entirely covered with wood, amidst which they conceal themselves so closely that it is with great difficulty they are discovered. Their complexion is fair, and sometimes red, like that of the

Europeans. Their language has not the smallest affinity to that of any of the other Indians. They have no villages nor houses, nor hold any intercourse with the rest of mankind. Their weapons are bows and arrows, with which they kill a great number of boars, stags, and other animals; they never dress their meat, but sweeten it with honey, which they possess in great abundance. We are strangers to the origin of this tribe, which is far from being numerous, and of which every family lives separate. It appears that the Bedas of Ceylon, as well as the Chacrelas of Java, who are both fair and few in number, are of European extraction. It is possible that some European men and women might have formerly been deserted in these islands, or thrown upon then by shipwreck, and that for fear of being maltreated by the natives, they and their descendants have remained in the woods, and in the mountainous parts of the country, where, habituated to a savage life, they might at length consider it as preferable.

It is supposed that the natives of the Maldivia islands are descended from those of Ceylon, yet they bear no resemblance, the latter being black and badly formed; the former shapely, and, their olive colour excepted, little different from the Europeans. Besides they are a people composed of all nations. Those of the northern parts are more civilized than those of the southern. The women, notwithstanding their olive colour are handsome; and some of them are as fair as those of Europe. Their hair is universally black: this they consider as a beauty; and they studiously render it of that colour, by keeping the heads of their boys and girls constantly shaved every eight days till the age of eight or nine years. Another beauty is to have the hair very long, and very thick; and for this purpose they anoint their head and body with a perfumed oil. These islanders love exercise, and are industrious artists; they are superstitious and greatly addicted to women; and though the women are particularly cautious of exposing their bosoms, they are yet exceeding debauched, and lavish of their favours.

The natives of Cambaia are of an ash-colour; and those bordering on the sea the most swarthy. In their accounts of Guzarat, the Dutch tell us, that the natives are all of yellow shades; that they are of the same size as the Europeans; that the women who are rarely exposed to the sun, are fairer than the men; and that some of them are little more swarthy than the Portuguese. Mandelslo says, that the people of Guzarat are all of a colour more or less tawny or olive, according to the climate in which they are situated; that the men are strong and shapely, have large faces and black eyes; that the women are small but well proportioned, that they wear their hair long, also pegs in their nostrils, and large pendants in their ears. Few of them are deformed; some have a more clear complexion than others, yet they have all black straight hair. The ancient inhabitants of Guzarat are easily distinguished from the others by their colour, which is much more black, and by their being more stupid and barbarous.

Goa is the chief Portuguese settlement in the Indies, and though it may have lost much of its former splendor, it is still, however, a rich and a commercial city. Here, at one time, more slaves were sold than in any other part of the world; and where the most beautiful women and girls, from all parts of Asia, became the property of the highest bidder. These slaves were of all colours, and were skilled in music, as well as in the arts of sewing and embroidery. The Indians were chiefly captivated with the Caffre girls from Mosambique, who are all black. "It is remarkable, says Pyrard, that the sweat of the Indian men or women has no disagreeable smell; whereas of the negroes of Africa, the stench, when they are in any degree over-heated, is insupportable. He adds, that the Indian women are fond of the European men, and that they prefer them to the white men of the Indies."

The Persians are neighbours to the Moguls, and bear a considerable likeness to them; those especially who occupy the southern parts of Persia. The natives of Ormus, and of the provinces of Bascia and Balascia, are very brown and tawny; those of Chesmur, and the other provinces, in which the heat is less intense than in Ormus, are more fair; and those of the northern provinces are tolerably white. The women who inhabit the islands of the Persian gulph, are, according to the Dutch travellers, brown or yellow, and not in the least agreeable. They have several modes and customs similar to those of the Indian women, as having a hole formed through the cartilage of the nose, for the admission of a ring, and through the skin of the nose, immediately below the eyes, for that of a gold wire. Indeed this custom of piercing the nose, in order to embellish it with rings and other trinkets, has extended much farther than the gulph of Persia. Many of the women in Arabia have an incision made through their nostrils for the same purpose; and with this people it is an act of gallantry for the husband to salute his wife through those rings, which are sometimes so large as to encompass the whole mouth.

Xenophon, in speaking of the Persians, says, that they were generally fat and gross; Marcellinus, on the contrary, says, that in his time they were meagre and thin. Olearius adds, that they are to this day what the last mentioned author describes, that they are full of strength and vigour, and that their complexion is olive-coloured, their hair black, and their noses aquiline.

That the Persian blood is naturally gross, says Chardin, is evident from the Guebres, who are a remnant of the ancient Persians, and who are ugly, ill shaped, and coarse skinned. It is evident also from the inhabitants of the provinces nearest to India, who, as they never form any alliances but among each other, are little less deformed than the Guebres. Throughout the rest of the kingdom the Persian blood has become highly refined, by intermixtures with the Georgians and Circassians, two nations the most remarkable for the beauty of the inhabitants of any in the world. Thus in Persia there is hardly a man of distinction whose mother came not from Georgia or Circassia; and even the king himself is commonly, by the mother's side, sprung from a native of one or other of these countries. As it is many years since this mixture first took place, the Persian women, though still inferior in beauty to the Georgian, have become very handsome. The men are commonly tall, erect, fresh-coloured, and vigorous; their air is graceful, and their appearance engaging. The mildness of their climate, and the sobriety in which they are brought up, contribute much to their personal beauty. This they in no degree inherit from their fathers, for without the above mixture the men of rank in Persia would be extremely ugly and deformed, being descendants of the Tartars. The Persians, on the contrary, are polished and ingenious; their imagination is lively, quick, and fertile; though fond of arts and sciences, they are yet ambitious of warlike honours; they are proud and very fond of praise; have much familiarity in their tempers; they are amorous and voluptuous, luxuriant, and prodigal, and are alike unacquainted with economy and commerce.

Though in general tolerably sober, they are immoderate devourers of fruit; and nothing is more common than to see one man eat twelve pounds of melons. Some will eat three or four times that quantity, and by over-indulging their appetite for fruit, numbers lose their lives.

Fine women of every colour are common in Persia, as they are brought thither by merchants, selected on account of their beauty. The white women come from Poland, from Muscovy, from Circassia, from Georgia, and from the frontiers of Great Tartary, the tawny ones from the territories of the Great Mogul, the kingdom of Golconda and Visapore; and the black ones from the coast of the Red Sea.

Among the inferior classes of women a strange superstition prevails. Such as are barren imagine that they have only to pass under the suspended body of a gibbeted criminal to become fruitful; the influence of a male corpse, and that even from a distance, will communicate to them fecundity. When this expedient fails, they go into the canals which flow from the public baths, when they know a number of men are bathing. Should the latter supposed specific prove alike ineffectual as the former, their last resource is to swallow that part of the prepuce which is cut off in the operation of circumcision; and this they deem a sovereign remedy against sterility.

The inhabitants of Persia, of Turkey, of Arabia, of Egypt, and of all Barbary, may be considered as one and the same people, who, in the time of

Mahomet and his successors, invaded immense territories, extended their dominions, and became exceedingly intermixed with the original natives of all those countries. The Persians, the Turks, and the Moors, are to a certain degree civilized; but the Arabs, have for the most part remained in a state of lawless independence. They live like the Tartars, without law, without government, and almost without society: theft, robbery, and violence, are authorized by their chiefs; they glory in their vices, and pay no respect to virtue; and all human institutions they despise, excepting such as are founded upon fanaticism and superstition.

They are inured to labour, and to which they habituate their horses, allowing them refreshment but once in twenty-four hours. Their horses are necessarily meagre, but are excellent coursers, and seem indefatigable.

In general the Arabs live miserably: they have neither bread nor wine, nor do they take the trouble to cultivate the earth. Instead of bread, they use wild grain, mixed and kneaded with the milk of their camels, sheep, and goats. These they conduct in flocks from place to place, till they find a spot of sufficient herbage for them. On this spot they erect their tents, and live with their wives and children till the herbage is consumed, when they decamp and proceed in search of more.

However hard may be their mode of living, and simple their food, yet the Arabs are robust and stout; they are of a tolerable size and rather handsome. As the generality of them go naked, or with the slight covering of a wretched shirt, their skins are much scorched by the heat of the sun. Those of the coasts of Arabia-Felix, and of the island of Scotora, are more diminutive; their complexion is either ash-coloured or tawny; and in form they resemble the Abyssinians.

The Arabs paint their arms, lips, and different parts of their body, of a deep blue, which they penetrate into the flesh by means of a kind of needle contrived on purpose, and it can never be effaced. This custom is also common among the negroes who traffic with the Mahometans. Some of the young girls among the Arabs paint various devices on their bodies, of a blue colour, which is done by vitriol on the point of a lancet, and this they consider as an embellishment to their beauty.

La Boulaye says, that the Arabian women of the Desert paint their hands, lips, and chin, of a blue colour; that in their noses they mostly have gold or silver rings, of three inches in diameter; that though born fair, they yet lose all their complexion by being constantly exposed to the sun; that the young girls are very agreeable, and immoderately fond of singing; that their songs are not melancholy and plaintive like those of the Turks and Persians, but more strange, they raise their voices as much as possible, and articulate with prodigious velocity.

"The Arabian princesses and ladies," says another traveller, ""are very beautiful, and being always sheltered from the sun, are very fair. The women of the inferior classes are not only naturally tawny, but are rendered much more so by the sun, and are of a disagreeable figure. They prick their lips with needles, and cover them with gunpowder, mixed with ox-gall, by which the lips are rendered blue and livid ever after. In like manner they prick the cheeks, and each side of the mouth and chin. They draw a line of black along the eye-lids, as also on the outward corner of each eye, that it may appear more expanded, for large and prominent eyes are considered the principal beauty of the Eastern women. To express the beauty of women, the Arabs say, "She has the eyes of the antelope." To this animal they always compare their mistresses; and black eyes, or the eyes of the antelope, never fail to be the burden of their love songs. Than the antelope nothing can be more beautiful; and it particularly discovers a certain innocent fear, which bears a strong resemblance to the natural modesty and timidity of a young woman. The ladies, and women newly married, blacken the eye-brows, and make them unite on the middle of their forehead; they also prick their arms and hands, and form upon them figures of animals, flowers, &c. They also paint their nails of a reddish colour. The men paint the tails of their horses with this colour. The women wear rings in their ears, and bracelets upon their arms and legs."

To this account it may be added, that the Arabs are all jealous of their wives, and that, whether they obtain them by purchase or carry them away by force, they treat them with, mildness and even with respect.

The Egyptians, though they live so near the Arabians, have the same religion, and are governed by the same laws, yet they are very different in their manners and customs. In all the towns and villages along the Nile, for example, we meet with girls set apart for the embraces of travellers, without any obligation to pay for such indulgence. For this purpose they have houses always full of these girls; and when a rich man finds himself dying, as an act of pious charity he disburses a sum of money to provide damsels and an edifice of this kind. When any of these girls have a male child, the mother is obliged to rear him till the age of three or four, after which she carries him to the patron of the house, or his heir, who employs him as one of his slaves. The girls, however, remain with the mother, and when of a proper age they supply her place.

The Egyptian women are very brown, their eyes ate lively, their stature rather low, their mode of dress by no means agreeable, and their conversation very tiresome. They are remarkable for bearing a number of children; and some travellers pretend, that the fertility occasioned by the inundation of the Nile is not confined to the earth, but to the human and animal creation. They add, that by drinking of the Nile, or by bathing in it, the first two months after its overflow, which are those of July and August, the women generally conceive; that in April and May they are as generally delivered, and that cows almost always bring forth two calves, a ewe two lambs, &c.

To reconcile this benign influence of the Nile with the troublesome disorders occasioned by it would be difficult. Granger says, that in Egypt the air is unwholesome; that the eyes are peculiarly subject to diseases so inveterate, that many lose their sight; that in this country there are more blind people than in any other; and that during the increase of the Nile the generality of the inhabitants are afflicted with obstinate dysenteries, occasioned by the water being then strongly impregnated with saline particles.

Though the women of Egypt are commonly small, yet the men are of a good height. Both, generally speaking, are of an olive colour, and the more we remove from Cairo the more tawny we find the natives, till we come to the confines of Nubia, where they are nearly as black as the Nubians themselves.

The greatest defects of the Egyptians are, idleness and cowardice. They do nothing the whole day but drink coffee, smoke tobacco, sleep, or chatter in the streets. They are extremely ignorant, yet are full of the most ridiculous vanity. Though they cannot deny they have lost that nobleness they once possessed, their skill in sciences and in arms, their history, and even their language; and that from an illustrious nation they have degenerated into a people dastardly and enslaved, they yet scruple not to despise all other nations, and to take offence at advising them to send their children to Europe, to acquire a knowledge of the arts and sciences.

Of a distinct origin are the numerous natives that inhabit the coasts of the Mediterranean, between Egypt and the western ocean, as well as the extensive territories from Barbary to Mount Atlas. The Arabs, Vandals, Spaniards, and, more anciently, the Romans and the Egyptians, peopled these regions with men very different from each other. The inhabitants of the mountains of Arras, for example, have an aspect and complexion very different from those of their neighbours; their skin, far from being tawny, is fair and ruddy; and their hair is of a deep yellow, while that of the adjacent nations is black; circumstances which have led Dr. Shaw to suppose them the descendants of the Vandals, who, on their expulsion, might have settled in some parts of these mountains.

The women of the kingdom of Tripoli, though so near to those of Egypt, have yet no resemblance to them. The former are tall; and they even consider length of stature as an essential article of beauty. Like the Arabian women they mark their cheeks and chin; and as in Turkey they so highly esteem red hair, they even paint that of their children with vermilion.

In general the Moorish women affect to wear their hair down to their heels, and those whose hair is less in length, use false locks; and they all adorn their tresses with ribbons. The hair of the eye-lids they tinge with the dust of black lead; and the dark colour which this gives to the eyes they esteem a singular beauty. In this circumstance, indeed they differ not from the women of ancient Greece and Rome.

Most part of the Moorish women would pass for handsome even in Europe. The skin of their children is exceedingly fair and delicate; and though the boys, by being exposed to the sun, soon grow swarthy, yet the girls, who are kept more at home, retain their beauty till the age of 30, when they commonly cease to have children. At this premature sterility they have less cause to repine, as they are often mothers at the age of 11, and grandmothers at that of 22; and living as long as European women, they commonly see several generations.

In reading Marmol's description of these different nations, it is evident that the inhabitants of the mountains of Barbary are fair, and those of the sea-coasts and plains are very brown and tawny. He says expressly, that the inhabitants of Capex, a city of Tunis, are poor people exceedingly black; that those who dwell on the river Dara, in the kingdom of Morocco, are very tawny; and that the inhabitants of Zarhou, and of the mountains of Fez, on the side of Mount Atlas, are white. He adds, that the latter are so little affected by cold, that even in frost and snow their dress is very slight; and through the whole year they go with the head uncovered. The Numidians, he says, are rather tawny than black; the women are tolerably fair, and even lusty, though the men are meagre; but that the inhabitants of Guaden, at the extremity of Numidia, and on the frontiers of Senegal, are rather black that tawny; that, on the other hand, in the province of Dara, the women are beautiful and fresh-coloured; and that throughout the whole regions negro-slaves of both sexes are numerous.

The difference then is not great among the nations that dwell between the 20th, 30th, or 35th degree north latitude, in the old continent; that is, from the Mogul empire to Barbary, and even from the Ganges to the western coasts of Morocco, if we except the varieties occasioned by the mixture with more northern nations, by which some of these vast countries have been conquered and peopled. In this territory, the extent of which is not less than 2000 leagues, the inhabitants are in general brown and tawny, yet well made, and tolerably handsome.

If we next examine those who live in climates more temperate we shall find that the people northward of Mogul and Persia, the Armenians, Turks, Georgians, Mingrelians Circassians, Greeks, and the Europeans at large, are the most fair and handsome in the world; and that however remote Cashmire may be from Spain, or Circassia from France, yet situated nearly at the same distance from the equator, the resemblance between the natives is singularly striking.

The people of Cashmire, says Bernier, are celebrated for beauty; they are as well made as the Europeans; they have nothing of the Tartar visages; nor have they that flat nose, and those pig's eyes we met with among their neighbours. The women are particularly handsome; and it is very common for strangers, on coming to the court of Mogul, to provide themselves with wives from Cashmire, in order to have children that may pass for true Moguls.

The natives of Georgia are of a more refined extraction than those of Cashmire. In the whole of that country we find not an ugly face; and the women enjoy from Nature graces superior to those of any other race. They are tall and well-shaped; their waist is exceedingly delicate, and their faces are truly charming. The men are also very handsome; and, from their natural ingenuity, were it not counteracted by a wretched education, which renders them ignorant and vicious, they might successfully cultivate the arts and sciences. In no country whatever, perhaps, are libertinism and drunkenness carried to so great a pitch as in Georgia. Chardin says, that even the clergy are exceedingly addicted to wine; that, in the character of slaves, they retain a number of concubines, and that at this custom, as being general and even authorised, no person takes offence. He adds, that the prefect of the Capuchins assured him, that the Patriarch of Georgia publicly declares, that he who, at the grand festivals, as those of Easter and Christmas, does not get drunk, is unworthy to be called a Christian, and ought to be excommunicated. With all their vices the Georgians are a civil and humane people, little subject to passion, but irreconcileable enemies when provoked, and have conceived an antipathy.

"The women of Circassia," says Struys, "are also exceedingly fair and beautiful. Their complexion has the finest tints, their forehead is large and smooth, and, without the aid of art, their eye-brows are so delicate, that they appear as curved threads of silk. Their eyes are large, expressive, and full of fire; their noses finely shaped, and their lips perfect vermilion; their mouths are small, and constantly expressive of smiles, and their chins form the termination of a perfect oval. Their necks and breasts are admirably formed; their stature is tall, and the shape of their body easy; their skin is white as snow, and their hair of the most beautiful black. They wear a little black stuff cap, over which is fastened a roller of the same colour; but, what is truly ridiculous, the widows, instead of this roller, wear the bladder of an ox, or a cow, blown out as much as possible, which disfigures them amazingly. In summer the inferior classes wear nothing but a shift, which is open down to the middle, and is generally blue, yellow, or red. Though tolerably familiar with strangers, they are faithful to their husbands, who are by no means jealous of them."

Tavernier says also, that the women of Comania and Circassia are, like those of Georgia, very shapely and beautiful; that they retain the freshness of their complexion till the age of 45 or 50; that they are all very industrious, and often employed in the most servile offices. In marriage these people possess an uncommon degree of liberty. If the husband is not contented with his wife, and he makes his complaint first, the lord of the district sends for the wife, orders her to be sold, and provides the husband with another. If the woman complains first, her husband is taken from her, and she is left at her freedom.

The Mingrelians are said to be as beautiful, and as well shaped as the Georgians or Circassians; and, indeed, they all seem to be of the same race. The women of Mingrelia, says Chardin, are very handsome, have a majestic air, their faces and forms are admirable, and have a look so engaging as to attract every beholder. Those who are less handsome, or advanced in years, daub their eye-brows, cheeks, forehead, nose, and chin, with paint; the rest only paint the eye-brows. They bestow every possible attention to their dress, which is similar to that of the Persians. They are lively, civil, and obliging, yet full of perfidy, and there is no wickedness they will not put in practice, in order to obtain, to preserve, or get rid of a lover. The men have likewise many bad qualities. They are all bred up to thievery, which they make a business and amusement. With infinite satisfaction do they relate the different depredations they have committed, for which they are extolled, and derive their greatest glory. In Mingrelia, falsehood, robbery, and murder, they call good actions; whoredom, bigamy, and incest, virtuous habits. The husbands are little disturbed with jealousy; and when he detects his wife in the actual embraces of her gallant, he has only a right to demand a pig from him, which is his only atonement, his only revenge; and the pig they generally eat between them. They pretend it is a very good and laudable custom to have a number of wives and concubines, because they can have a greater increase of children, whom they can sell for gold, or exchange for goods or provisions. The Mingrelian slaves are not very dear. A man from the age of 25 to 40 is purchased for 15 crowns, and if older for eight or ten, a handsome girl, from 13 to 18 for 20 crowns; a woman for 12 crowns; and a child for three or four.

The Turks, who purchase a vast number of these slaves, are so intermixed with Armenians, Georgians, Turcomans, Arabs, Egyptians, and even

Europeans, it is hardly possible to distinguish the real natives of Asia Minor, Syria, and the rest of Turkey. The Turkish men are generally robust, and tolerably well made, and it is rare to find a deformed person among them. The women are also commonly beautiful, and free from blemishes; they are very fair, because they seldom stir from home, and never without being veiled.

According to Belon, there is not a woman in Asia whose complexion is not fresh as a rose, whose skin is not fair, delicate, and smooth as velvet. Of the earth of China, diluted, they form a kind of ointment, with which they rub all over their bodies before they bathe. Some likewise paint their eye-brows black, while others eradicate the hairs with rusma, and paint themselves eye-brows in the form of a cresent, which are beautiful when viewed at a distance, but quite the reverse when examined more closely. This custom is very ancient. Among the Turks, he adds, neither men nor women wear hair on any part of the body, the head and chin excepted; that they use rusma mixed with quick lime, and diluted in water, which they apply before they go into the warm bath, and so soon as they begin to sweat in thus bathing the hair rubs off with the hand, and the skin remains soft and smooth, as if there had never been any upon it. He remarks further, that in Egypt there is a shrub called *Alcanna*, the leaves of which dried and powdered make a reddish yellow colour, which the women of Turkey use to colour their hair, hands, and feet. With this they also tinge the hair of their infants, and the manes of their horses. The Turkish women employ every art to add to their beauty, as do also the Persian, but the articles they use are different, as the men of the former prefer red, and those of the latter brown complexions.

It has been pretended that the Jews, who came originally from Syria, and Palestine, have the same brown complexion they had formerly. As Misson, however, justly observes, the Jews of Portugal alone are tawny. As they always marry with their own tribe, the complexion of the parents is transmitted to the child, and thus with little diminution preserved, even in the northern countries. The German Jews, those of Prague, for example, are not more swarthy than the other Germans.

The present natives of Judea resemble the other Turks, being only a little more brown than those of Constantinople, or on the coasts of the Black Sea, in like manner as the Arabians are more brown than the Syrians, from their situation being more southern.

It is the same with the Greeks. Those of the northern parts are more fair, while those of the southern islands, or provinces, are brown. Generally speaking, the Greek women are more handsome and vivacious than the Turks; they also enjoy a greater degree of liberty. Carreri says, the women of the island of Chio are fair, handsome, lively, and very familiar with the men; that the girls see strangers without restraint; and that they all have their necks uncovered. He likewise says, that the Greek women have the finest hair in the world, especially in the vicinage of Constantinople; but that those whose hair descends to the heels, have features less regular.

The Greeks consider large eyes, and elevated eye-brows, as a very great beauty in either sex; and we may remark in all busts and medals of ancient Greeks, the eyes are much larger than those of the ancient Romans.

The inhabitants of the Archipelago are excellent swimmers and divers. According to Thevenot, they are trained to the practice of bringing up goods which have been sunk into the sea; and that in the island of Samos, a young man has no chance of obtaining a wife, unless he can dive eight, and Dapper says twenty, fathoms. The latter adds, that in some of the islands, as in Nicaria, they have a strange custom of speaking to each other at a distance, and that their voices are so strong, that when a quarter of a league, nay even a whole league asunder, they maintain a conversation, though not without long intervals, as after a question is asked, the answer does not arrive for several seconds.

The Greeks, Neapolitans, Sicilians, Corsicans, Sardinians, and Spaniards, being situated nearly under the same line, are uniform in point of complexion. Those people are more swarthy than the English, French, Germans, Polanders, Moldavians, Circassians, and all the other inhabitants of the north of Europe, till we advance to Lapland; where, as already observed, we find another race of men. In travelling through Spain, we begin to perceive a difference of colour even at Bayonne. There the women have a complexion more brown, and eyes more brilliant.

The Spaniards are meagre, rather short, yet handsome. They are yellow and swarthy; but their eyes are beautiful, their teeth well ranged, and their features are regular. Their children are born fair and handsome; but as they grow up their complexion changes surprisingly; the air and sun render them yellow and tawny; nor is it difficult to distinguish a Spaniard from a native of any other country in Europe. In some provinces of Spain, as in the environs of the river Bidassoa, it is remarked, the inhabitants have ears of an immoderate size.

Black or brown hair begins to be rather unfrequent in England, Flanders, Holland, and in the northern provinces of Germany; nor is it hardly to be seen in Denmark, Sweden, or Roland. According to Linnæus, the Goths are tail, their hair smooth and white as silver, and the iris of their eye is bluish. The Finlanders are muscular and fleshy; the hair long, and of a yellowish white, and the iris of the eye is of a deep yellow.

In Sweden the women are exceedingly fruitful. Rudbeck says, that they commonly bear 8, 10, or 12 children, and not unoften 18, 20, 24, 28, and even 30. He adds, that the men often live to the age of 100, some to that of 140; that one Swede lived to 156 years, and another to 161.

This author is an enthusiast with regard to his country, and according to him, Sweden is the first country in the world. This fertility in the women does not imply a greater propensity to love. In cold climates the inhabitants are far more chaste than in warm; and though they produce more children in Sweden, the women are less amorous than those of Spain or Portugal. It is universally known, that the northern nations have to so great a degree overrun all Europe, that historians have distinguished the north by the appellation of *Officina Gentium.*

The author of the "Voyages Historiques de l'Europe," agrees with Rudbeck, that there are more instances of longevity in Sweden, than in any other European nation; and that he saw several persons who, he was assured, had passed the age of 150. This longevity he attributes to the salubrity of their climate; and of the people of Denmark he makes the same remark; the Danes, he adds, are tall, robust, and of a lively and florid complexion; that the women are likewise very fair, well made, and exceedingly prolific.

Before the reign of Czar Peter I. we are told, the Muscovites had not emerged from barbarism. Born in slavery, they were ignorant, brutal, cruel, without courage and without manners. Men and women bathed promiscuously in stoves heated to a degree intolerable to all persons but themselves; and on quitting this warm bath they plunged, like the Laplanders, into cold water. Their food was homely; and their favourite dishes were cucumbers or melons, brought from Astracan, which in summer they preserved in a mixture of water, flour, and salt. From ridiculous scruples they refrained from the use of several meats, particularly pigeons and veal. Yet even at this period of unrefinement, the women were skilled in the arts of colouring their checks, plucking out their eye-brows, and painting artificial ones. They also adorned themselves with pearls and jewels, and their garments were made of rich and valuable stuffs. From these circumstances does it not appear, that the barbarism of the Muscovites was near a close, and that their sovereign had less trouble in polishing them than some authors have endeavoured to insinuate? They are now a people civilized, commercial, studious Of the arts and sciences, fond of spectacles, and ingenious novelties.

Some authors have said that the air of Muscovy is so salutary, as to prevent its being visited with a pestilence. In the annals of the country, however, it is recorded, that in the year 1741, and during the six subsequent years, the Muscovites were dreadfully afflicted with a contagious distemper, insomuch that even the constitution of their descendants has been altered by it; few of the inhabitants attaining now the age of an 100, whereas before that period numbers lived much beyond it.

The Ingrians and Carelians, who inhabit the northern provinces of Muscovy, and are the original natives of the country round Petersburgh, are men of vigour and robust constitutions. Their complexion is generally fair; they resemble the Finlanders, and speak the same language, which has no affinity to that of any other European nation.

By this historical description of all the different inhabitants of Europe and Asia, it appears that the variation in their colour depends greatly, though not entirely, on the climates. There are many other causes, by which not only the colour, but even the form and features may be influenced; and among the principal may be reckoned the nature of the food, and the manners, or mode of living. A civilized people, who enjoy a life of ease and tranquillity, and who, by the superintendance of a well regulated government, are protected from the fear and oppression of misery, will, from these reasons alone, be more handsome and vigorous than those of a savage and careless nation, of which each individual, deriving no assistance from society, is obliged to provide for his own subsistence, to sustain alternately the excesses of hunger and the effects of unwholesome food; to be alternately exhausted with labour and lassitude; and to undergo the rigours of a severe climate, without being able to shelter himself from them; to act, in a word, more frequently like an animal than a man. In the supposition that two nations, thus differently circumstanced, were even to live in the same climate, there can be no doubt but that the savage people would be more ugly, tawny, diminutive, and more wrinkled, than those enjoying civilized society. Should the former possess any advantage, it would consist in the superior strength, or rather hardiness of the body. It might likewise happen that among the savage people there would be fewer instances of lameness or bodily deformities; for in a civilized state, where one individual contributes to the support of another, where the strong has no power over the weak, where the qualities of the body are less esteemed than those of the mind, men thus defective live and even multiply; but among a savage people, as each individual subsists and defends himself merely by his corporal strength and address, those who are unhappily born weak and defective, or who become sick or disabled, soon cease to form a part of their number.

We must then admit of three causes as jointly productive of the varieties which we have remarked in the different nations of the earth. First, the influence of the climate; secondly, the food; and thirdly, the manners; the two last having great dependence on the former. But before we lay down the reasons on which this opinion is founded, it is necessary to describe the people of Africa and America in the same manner as we have those of Europe and Asia.

The nations of the whole northern part of Africa, from the Mediterranean to the Tropic, we have already mentioned. All those beyond the Tropic, from the Red Sea to the Ocean, an extent of 100 or 150 leagues, are of the Moorish species, though so tawny that they appear almost black. The women are rather fairer than the men, and tolerably handsome. Among these Moors there is a vast number of mulattoes, who are of a black still more deep, their mothers being negro women, whom the Moors purchase, and by whom they have a number of children.

Beyond this territory, in the 17th or 18th degree of north latitude, we find the negroes of Senegal and Nubia, both on the coast of the western ocean and that of the Red Sea; and after them all the other nations of Africa, from the 18th degree north to the 18th degree south latitude, are perfectly black, the Ethiopians or Abyssinians excepted. The portion of the globe by Nature allotted to this race of men, therefore, contains an extent of ground, parallel to the equator, of about 900 leagues in breadth, and considerably more in length, especially northward of the equinoctial line. Beyond the 18th or 20th degree of south latitude the natives are no longer negroes, as will appear when we come to speak of the Caffres and Hottentots.

By confounding the Ethiopians with their neighbours the Nubians, who are nevertheless of a different race, we have been long in an error with respect to their colour and features. Marmol says, the Ethiopians are absolutely black, that they have large faces and flat noses, and in this description the Dutch travellers agree. The truth, however, is, that they differ from the Nubians both in colour and features. The skin of the Ethiopians is brown or olive-coloured, like that of the southern Arabs, from whom probably they derive their origin. They are tall, have regular features, strongly marked; their eyes are large and beautiful; their noses well proportioned; their lips thin, and their teeth white. The Nubians, on the contrary, have flat noses, thick and prominent lips, and their faces exceedingly black. These Nubians, as well as the Barberins, their western neighbours, are a species of negroes not unlike those of Senegal.

The Ethiopians are a people between barbarism and civilization. Their garments are of cotton or silk. Their houses are low, and of a bad construction; their lands are wretchedly neglected, owing to their nobles, who despise, maltreat, and plunder the citizens and common people. Each of these classes live separate from the other, and have their own villages or hamlets. Unprovided with salt, they purchase it for its weight in gold. So fond are they of raw meat that, at their feasts, the second course, which they consider as the most delicate, consists of flesh entirely so. Though they have vines they make no wine; and their usual beverage is a sour composition made with tamarinds. They use horses for travelling, and mules for carrying their merchandize. Of the arts or sciences they have little knowledge; their language is without rules; and their manner of writing, though their characters are more beautiful than those of the Arabians, is so imperfect, that, to write an epistle, they require several days. Their mode of salutation is something whimsical. Each takes the right hand of the other, and carries it to his mouth; this done, the saluter takes off the scarf of the person saluted, and fastens it round his own body, by which the latter is left half naked, few of the Ethiopians wearing any thing more than this scarf and a pair of cotton drawers.

In Admiral Drake's voyage round the world, he mentions a fact, which, however, extraordinary, appears not incredible. He says that on the frontiers of the deserts of Ethiopia there is a people called the *Acridophagi*, or *Locust-eaters*, who are black, meagre, exceedingly nimble, and very small. In the spring, by certain hot and westerly winds, an infinite number of locusts are blown into that country, on which, as they are unprovided with cattle or with fish, they are reduced to the necessity of subsisting. After collecting them in large quantities they salt them, and keep them for food throughout the year. This wretched nourishment produces singular effects: they hardly live to the age of 40, and when they approach that age winged insects engender under their skin, which at first creates a violent itching, and shortly multiply so prodigiously, that their whole flesh swarms with them. They begin by eating through the belly, then the breast, and continue their ravages till they eat all the flesh from the bones. Thus, by devouring insects are these men devoured by them in turn. Were this fact well authenticated it would afford a large field for reflection.

There are vast deserts in Ethiopia, as well as in that tract of land which extends to Cape Gardafu. This country, which may be considered as the eastern part of Ethiopia, is almost entirely uninhabited. To the south, Ethiopia is bounded by the Bediouns, and a few other nations who follow the law of Mahomet; a circumstance which corroborates the supposition, that the Ethiopians are of Arabian extraction; indeed they are only separated by the strait of Babel-Mandel; and therefore it is probable, that the Arabians had formerly invaded Ethiopia, and driven the natives northward into Nubia.

The Arabians have even extended themselves along the coast of Melinda, of which the inhabitants are of the Mahometan religion, and only a tawny complexion, The natives of Zanguebar, are not black; they generally speak Arabic, and their garments are made of cotton. This country, though under the torrid zone, is not excessively hot; and yet the hair of the natives is black and frizly like that of the Negroes. We find, on the whole of this coast, as well as at Mosambique and Madagascar, some white men, who, it is pretended came originally from China, and settled there, in the time that the Chinese navigated all the Eastern seas, in the same manner as they are now navigated by the Europeans. Whatever foundation there may be for this opinion, it is certain that the natives of this oriental coast of Africa are black, and that the tawny or white men we find there, have come from other countries. But, to form a just idea of the differences among these black nations, we should examine them more minutely.

In the first place, it is evident, from comparing the descriptions given by travellers, that there is as much variety in the race of blacks as in that of the whites; and that, like the latter, the former have their Tartars and their Circassians. Those of Guinea are extremely ugly, and have an insufferable stench; those of Sofala, and Mosambique, are handsome, and have no bad smell. It is necessary, then, to divide the blacks into different races; and in my opinion, they may be reduced to two principal ones, that of the Negroes, and that of the Caffres. In the first I comprehend the blacks of Nubia, Senegal, Cape de Verd, Gambia, Sierra-Leone, the Teeth and Gold Coasts, of the coast of Juda, Benin, Gabon, Loango, Congo, Angola, and of Benguela, till we come to Cape-Negro. In the second I place the inhabitants beyond Cape-Negro to the point of Africa, where they assume the name of Hottentots; as also all those of the eastern coast of Africa, such as those of the land of Natal, Sofala, Monomotapa, Mosambique, and of Melinda; the blacks of Madagascar, and the neighbouring islands, are likewise Caffres and not Negroes. These two races of black men resemble each other more in colour than in their features, hair, skin, or smell. In their manners and disposition there is also a prodigious difference.

When we come particularly to examine the different people of which these races are composed, we shall perceive as many varieties among the blacks as the whites; and all the shades from brown to black, as we have already remarked from brown to fair in the white races.

Let us begin, then, with the countries northward of Senegal, and, in proceeding along the coasts, take a view of all the different tribes which travellers have discovered and described. In the first place it is certain that the natives of the Canary islands are not Negroes; since from authentic information it appears, that the ancient inhabitants were tall, well-made, and of a becoming complexion; that the women were handsome, and had remarkable fine hair; and that those who occupied the southern parts were more of an olive colour than those in the northern. In the relation of his voyage to Lima, Duret remarks, that the ancient inhabitants of the island of

Teneriffe were tall and vigorous, though meagre and tawny, and that most of them had flat noses. Excepting the flat nose, therefore, these people had nothing in common with the Negroes. The natives of Africa in the same latitude with these islands, are Moors, and very tawny, but who belong, as well as the islanders, to the race of whites.

The inhabitants of Cape-Blanc are Moors, who follow the law of Mahomet, and who wander about, like the Arabians, in quest of pasture for their horses, camels, oxen, goats, and sheep. The Negroes, with whom they traffic, give them eight or ten slaves for a horse, and two or three for a camel. It is from these Moors, that we procure gum-arabic, which they dissolve in their milk. They scarcely ever eat any meat, and never destroy their cattle, unless dying of sickness, or old age.

The Moors are separated from the Negroes by the river Senegal; they live on the north-side, and are only tawny; but the Negroes who reside on the south, are absolutely black. The Moors lead an erratic life, while the Negroes occupy villages; the former are free and independent; the latter have tyrants who hold them in slavery; the Moors are short, meagre, of a disagreeable aspect, but ingenious and subtle; the Negroes are tall, bulky, and well made, but simple and stupid. The country inhabited by Moors is sandy and sterile, where verdue is to be seen in a very few places; that inhabited by the Negroes, is rich, abounding in pasturage, in millet, and in trees always green, though few bear any fruit fit for food.

In some places both to the north and south of the river we find a species of men called *Foulies*, who seem to form a shade between the Moors and Negroes, and whom, it is possible, are Mulattoes produced by a coalition of the two nations. These *Foulies* are not black like the Negroes, yet darker than the Moors; they are also more civilized than the former; they follow the laws of Mahomet, and are hospitable to strangers.

The islands of Cape de Verd are peopled with Mulattoes, descended from the Portuguese, who first settled there, and the original Negro-inhabitants. They are called *copper-coloured* Negroes, because, though they resemble the Negroes in their features, they are yet more of a yellow than black; they are well-made, ingenious, but intolerably indolent. By hunting and fishing they chiefly subsist, and they train up their dogs to hunt the wild goats. They freely resign their wives and daughters to the embraces of strangers for the smallest consideration. For pins and other trifles they will exchange parrots, porcelain shells, ambergris, &c.

The first Negroes we meet with are those on the south of the Senegal. These people, as well as those who occupy the different territories between this river and that of Gambia, are called *Jaloffs*. They are tall, very black, well proportioned, and their features are less harsh than those of the other Negroes; some of them, especially among the females, have features far from being irregular. They have the same ideas of beauty as the Europeans, considering fine eyes, a well formed nose, small mouth, and thin lips, as essential ingredients; in the ground of the picture alone do they differ from us; for, with them, the colour must be exceedingly black and glossy to render it complete; Their skin is soft and delicate, and, colour alone excepted, we find among them, women as handsome as in any other country of the world, they are usually very gay, lively, and amorous. They are very fond of white men whom they exert every assiduity to please, both to gratify themselves, and to obtain presents which may flatter their vanity. To their predilection for strangers the husbands make not the smallest opposition, (to whom indeed, they not only make a free offer of their wives, daughters, or sisters, but even construe it into a dishonour, if that offer is rejected) but undergo all the violent effects of jealousy, if they detect them with any of their own nation. These women are never without a pipe in their mouths, and their skin, when they undergo any extraordinary heat, has a disagreeable smell, though by no means so strong as that of other negroes. They are highly fond of leaping and dancing to the sound of a calabash, drum, or kettle; and all the movements of their dances are so many lascivious or indecent postures. They frequently bathe; and to render their teeth even, they polish them with files. The generality of the young women have figures of animals, flowers, &c. marked upon their skin.

While at work, or travelling, the Negro-women almost always carry their infants on their backs. To this custom some travellers ascribe the flat nose and big bellies among Negroes; since the mother, from necessarily giving sudden jerks, is apt to strike the nose of the child against her back; who, in order to avoid the blow, keeps its head back by pushing the belly forward. Their hair is black and woolly. In hair and in complexion, consists their principal difference from the rest of mankind; and, perhaps, there is a stronger resemblance between their features and those of the Europeans, than between the visage of a Tartar and that of a Frenchman.

Father du Tertre says expressly, that, if most negroes are flat-nosed, it is because the parents crush the noses of their children; that they also compress their lips, to render them thick; and that those who escape these operations their features are as comely as those of the Europeans. This remark, however, applies only to the negroes of Senegal, who, of all others, are the most beautiful. Among all other negroes, thick lips, broad and flat noses, appear formed as gifts by nature; and which are by them considered so much as beauties that every art is used upon the children who, at their birth, discover a deficiency in those ornaments.

The Negro women are very fruitful; in child-birth they experience little difficulty, and require not the smallest assistance; nor of its effects do they feel any consequence beyond the second day. As nurses and mothers they deserve great encomiums, being exceedingly tender of their children. They are more ingenious and alert than the men, and they even study to acquire the virtues of discretion and temperance. Father Jaric says, that to habituate themselves to eat and speak little, the Jaloff negro women put water into their mouths in the morning, and keep it there till the hour allotted for the first meal arrives.

The negroes of the island of Goree, and of the Cape de Verd coast, are, like those of Senegal, well made, and very black. So highly do they prize their colour, which is also glossy, that they despise those who are not the same as much as white men despise the tawny. They are strong and robust, but indolent and slothful, and cultivate neither corn, wine, nor fruit. Rarely do they eat meat; fish and millet are their chief sustenance. They eat no herbs, and because Europeans do, they compare them to horses. Of spirituous liquors they are fond to an excess, and for which they will sell their relations, children, and even themselves. They go almost naked, wearing only a small piece of calico, which descends from the waist to the middle of the thigh, and which, they say, is all that the heat of their climate will allow them to wear. Notwithstanding their poverty, and wretchedness of food, they are contented and cheerful. They also think their country is the finest in the world, and that, because they are the blackest, they are the most beautiful of men; and were it not that their women discover a fondness for white men they would deem them unworthy of their notice.

Though the negroes of Sierra Leona are less black than those of Senegal, they are not, however, as Struys asserts, of a reddish colour. The custom prevalent among them, as well as among the negroes of Guinea, of painting their bodies with red, and other colours, possibly misled that author. Among the latter the women are more debauched than at Senegal; prodigious numbers of them are common prostitutes, from which they incur not the smallest disgrace. Both sexes go with their heads uncovered, and their hair, which is very short, they shave or cut in various forms. In their ears they wear pendants, which weigh three or four ounces, made of teeth, horns, shells, wood, &c. Some have the upper lip, or nostrils, pierced, for the same purpose. They wear a kind of apron made of apes' skins and the bark of trees. They eat fish and flesh, but yams and bananas are their chief food. They have no passions but for women, and no inclinations but to remain idle and inactive. They live in wretched huts, frequently situated on dreary wilds, though in the neighbourhood of fertile and delightful spots. The roads from one place to another are commonly twice as long as they need be; they never attempt to curtail them, and even when told how in half the time they may reach any particular spot, they persist in mechanically following the beaten path. They never measure time, nor have the smallest idea of its value.

Though the negroes of Guinea are generally healthy, they seldom attain old age. A negro, at the age of 50, is a very old man. This contracted period of existence may, with great probability, be imputed to the premature intercourse between the sexes. The boys, in their tenderest years, are permitted to pursue every debauchery; and as for the girls, nothing in the whole country is so rare as to find one who remembers the period at which she ceased to be a virgin.

The inhabitants of the island of St. Thomas, of Annobona, &c. are negroes, similar to those of the neighbouring continent. Dispersed, however, by the Europeans, they are few in number, and those subjected to the bondage of their invaders. Both sexes, the covering of a kind of short apron excepted, go naked. Mandelslo says, that the Europeans, who settle on the island of St. Thomas, which is but one degree and a half from the equator, retain their white colour till the third generation; and he seems to insinuate that they afterwards become black: but that this change should be so suddenly effected seems by no means probable.

The negroes of the coasts of Juda and Arada are less black than those of Senegal, Guinea, and Congo. So fond are they of the flesh of dogs that they prefer it to all other viands; and, at their feasts, a roasted dog is always the first dish presented. This predilection for dog's-flesh is not peculiar to the Negroes, but common among the Tartars and savages of North America. The former, in some places, castrate their dogs, in order to make them fat, and more palatable.

According to Pigafetta, and Drake, who seems to have literally copied him, the negroes of Congo are black, though in a less degree than those of Senegal. Of the generality the hair is black and frizly, though of some it is red. They are of a middle stature; their eyes are either brown or of a sea-green colour; their lips are not so thick as those of the other negroes, and their features are not unlike those of the Europeans.

In some of the provinces of Congo the customs are truly singular. When, for example a person dies at Loango, they place the body upon a kind of amphitheatre, about six feet high, in a sitting posture, with the hands resting upon the knees; they deck it out in the most ornamental dress, and then light up fires before and behind it: as the clothes absorb the moisture they cover it with fresh ones, until the corpse is thoroughly dried, when, with much funeral ceremony they commit it to the earth. In the province of Malimba the husband is ennobled by the wife; and when the sovereign dies, and only leaves a single daughter, to her, provided she is marriageable, devolves the royal authority. The first thing she does is to travel over the whole of her kingdom.

On this occasion all her male subjects are obliged, previous to her arrival at each town and village, to form themselves into a line for her reception, and she selects one to pass the night with her. When returned from her journey she sends for the man who best pleased her and instantly marries him; after which the whole regal authority devolves to the husband. These facts M. de la Brosse communicated to me in his written remarks on what he saw most worthy of notice, during his voyage to the coast of Angola, in 1738; and of the vindictiveness of these negroes he adds the following anecdote:—"Every day (says he) did they demand brandy of us for the king and chief men of the place. Happening one day to refuse it them we had soon reason to repent; for several officers, both French and English, having gone a fishing up a small lake, they erected a tent for the purpose of enjoying the fruits of their pastime. While thus employed they were joined by seven or eight negroes, the chiefs of Loango, who, in the customary mode of salutation, presented to them their hands. These they had previously rubbed with a subtle poison, whose effect is instantaneous, when unhappily the persons to whom it is communicated takes any thing without first washing their hands; and so successful were they in their purpose, that no less than eight persons perished upon the spot."

As a cure for a pain of the head, or for any bodily pain whatever, these negroes make a slight wound upon the part affected, and through a small horn, with a narrow hole, they suck out the blood till they obtain relief.

The negroes of Senegal, Gambia, Cape de Verd, Angola, and Congo, are of a more beautiful black than those of Juda, Issigni, Arada, and of the circumjacent places. They are exceedingly black when in health, but when sick they become of a copper-colour.

"In our islands (says Father du Tertre in his history of the Antilles) the negroes of Angola are preferred to those of Cape de Verd, for bodily strength; but when heated, their stench is so strong, that the air whithersoever they pass is infected with it for above a quarter of an hour. The negroes of Cape de Verd smell not so strong, their skin likewise is more black and beautiful, their body is of a better shape, their features less harsh, they are much tidier, and in disposition more mild."

The negroes of Guinea are well qualified for the office of tillage, and other laborious employments; those of Senegal are less vigorous, yet are good domestic servants, and very ingenious. Father Charlevoix says, that of all negroes the Senegal ones are the most shapely, most tractable, and as domestic the most useful; that the Bambaras are the tallest, but they are all idle and knavish; that the Aradas best understand the culture of the earth; that the Congos are the smallest, but most expert swimmers; that the Nagos are the most humane, the Mondongos the most cruel; the Mimes the most resolute, the most capricious, and the most subject to despair; that the Creole-negroes, from whatever nation they derive their origin, inherit nothing from their parents but the spirit of servitude and colour; they are more ingenious, rational, and adroit, but more idle and debauched than those of Africa. He adds, that the understanding of the negroes is exceedingly contracted; that numbers of them seem to be even entirely stupid, and can never be made to count more than three; that they have no memory, and are as ignorant of what is past, as of what is to come; that the most sprightly ridicule the others with a tolerable grace; that they are full of dissimulation, and would sooner perish than divulge a secret; that they are commonly mild, humane, tractable, simple, credulous, and even superstitious; that they possess fidelity and courage, and might with proper discipline make a tolerable figure in the field.

If the negroes are deficient in genius, they are by no means so in their feelings; they are cheerful or melancholy, laborious or inactive, friendly or hostile, according to the manner in which they are treated. If properly fed, and well treated, they are contented, joyous, obliging, and on their very countenance we may read the satisfaction of their soul. If hardly dealt with their spirits forsake them, they droop with sorrow, and will die of melancholy. They are alike impressed with injuries and favours. To the authors of the one they are implacable enemies; while to those who use them well they imbibe an affection which makes them defy all danger and hazard to express their zeal and attachment. To their children, friends, and countrymen, they are naturally compassionate; the little they have they chearfully distribute among those who are in necessity, though otherwise than from that necessity they have not the smallest knowledge of them. That they have excellent hearts is evident, and in having those they have the seeds of every virtue. Their sufferings demand a tear. Are they not sufficiently wretched in being reduced to a state of slavery; in being obliged always to work without reaping the smallest fruits of their labour, without being abused, buffeted, and treated like brutes? Humanity revolts at those oppressions, which nothing but the thirst of gold could ever have introduced, and which would still, perhaps, produce an aggravated repetition, did not the law prescribe limits to the brutality of the master, and to the misery of his slave. Negroes are compelled to labour; and yet of the coarsest food they are sparingly supplied. Their unfeeling masters say, they can support hunger well; that what would serve an European for one meal is to them a sufficient subsistence for three days; however little they eat or sleep, they are alike hardy, alike capable of fatigue. How can men, in whom the smallest sentiment of humanity remains, adopt such maxims, and on such shallow foundations attempt to justify excesses to which nothing could ever have given birth but the most sordid avarice? But let us turn from the gloomy picture, and return to our subject.

Of the people who inhabit the coasts, or the interior parts of Africa, from

Cape Negro to Cape de Voltes, an extent of about 400 leagues, we know little more than that they are not so black as the other negroes, and that they much resemble their neighbours the Hottentots: the latter are a people well known, and few travellers have omitted speaking of them. They are not Negroes, but Caffres; and their skin would be only of a tawny hue did they not render it black with paint and grease.

M. Kolbe, though he has given so minute a description of the Hottentots, considers them, however, as Negroes. He assures us their hair is short, black, frizled, and woolly, and that not in a single instance did he ever perceive it long. But from this alone we are not authorised to consider them as real negroes. M. Kolbe himself says their colour is olive, and never black, though they take the utmost pains to render it so; nor, in the next place, can there be much certainty derived from the appearance of their hair, as they never either comb or wash it, but rub it daily with grease and soot in large quantities, which gives it the resemblance of a fleece of black sheep loaded with dirt; besides, they are in disposition different from the negroes. The latter are cleanly, sedentary, and easily subjected to slavery; the former, on the other hand, are frightfully filthy, unsettled, independent, and highly jealous of their liberty. These contrarieties are more than sufficient to confirm us in the opinion that the Hottentots are of a race distinct from that of the Negroes.

Gama, who first doubled the Cape of Good Hope, on his arrival in the bay of St. Helena, on the 4th of November, 1479, found the inhabitants black, short in stature, and ugly in aspect. He does not say, however, that they were naturally as black as the negroes, and doubtless they only appeared to him so black as he describes, from the grease and soot with which they are covered. The same traveller remarks, that in the articulation of their voice there was something similar to a sigh. Their habits were made of skins, and their weapons consisted of sticks hardened with the fire, and pointed with the horn of some animal. To the arts in use among the Negroes, the Hottentots, it is plain, are utter strangers.

The Dutch travellers say, that the Savages northward of the Cape are smaller than the Europeans; that their colour is a reddish brown; that they are very ugly, and take great pains to render themselves black; and their hair is like that of a man who has long hung in chains. They add, that the Hottentots are of the colour of the Mulattoes; that their visage is unshapely; that they are meagre, of a moderate height, and very nimble; and that their language resembles the clucking of turkey-cocks. Father Tachard says, that though they have commonly hair as cottony as the Negroes, there are numbers who have it long, and which floats upon their shoulders. He even asserts, that some of them are as white as Europeans, but that they begrime their skin with a mixture of grease and the powder of a certain black stone, and that the women are naturally fair, but they blacken themselves to please their husbands. Ovington says, that the Hottentots are more tawny than the other Indians; that no people bear so strong a resemblance to the Negroes in colour and features, but that they are less black, their hair is not so frizly, nor their nose so flat.

From all these testimonies it is evident that the Hottentots are not real negroes, but a people of the black race, approaching to the whites, as the Moors of the white race do to the black. These Hottentots, moreover, form a species of very extraordinary savages. The women, who are much smaller than the men, have a kind of excrescence, or hard skin, which grows over the os pubis, and descends to the middle of the thighs in the form of an apron. Thevenot says the same thing of the Egyptian women, but instead of allowing this skin to grow, they burn it off with hot irons. I doubt whether the remark is true with respect to the Egyptian women; but certain it is that all the female natives of the Cape are subject to this monstrous deformity, and which they expose to such persons as have the curiosity to see it. The men, though not by nature, are all demi-eunuchs, being, from an absurd custom, deprived of one of their testicles at about the age of eighteen years. M. Kolbe saw this operation performed upon a young Hottentot; and the circumstances with which the ceremony is accompanied are so singular as to merit a recital.

After having rubbed the young man with the fat of the entrails of sheep, which had been killed on purpose, they stretched him upon his back, and tied his hands and his feet, while three or four of his friends held him. Then the priest (for it is a religious ceremony) made an incision with a very sharp knife, look out the left testicle[D], and in its place deposited a ball of fat of the same size, which had been prepared with certain medicinal herbs. After sewing up the wound with the tendon of a sheep they untied the patient; but the priest before he left him rubbed his whole body with the hot fat of the sheep, or rather poured it on so plentifully, that when the fat cooled, it formed a kind of crust. This rubbing was so violent, that the young man, whose previous sufferings had been sufficiently great, was now covered with large drops of sweat, and began to smoke like a roasted capon. On this crust of grease the operator then made furrows with his nails, from one extremity to the other, and after making water in them, he renewed his frictions, and filled up the furrows with more grease. The instant the ceremony is concluded they leave the patient, in general more dead than alive, yet he is obliged to crawl in the best manner he can to a little hut, built for him on purpose, near the spot where the operation is performed. There he perishes or recovers without assistance or nourishment but the fat upon his skin, which he may lick if he pleases. At the expiration of two days he generally recovers. He is then allowed to appear abroad; and as a proof that his recovery is complete he must run and shew himself as nimble as a stag.

[D] Tavernier, in speaking of this strange custom, says that it is the right testicle which they cut off.

Though all the Hottentots have broad flat noses, yet they would not be so did not their mothers, considering a prominent nose as a deformity, flatten them immediately after their birth. Their lips are also thick, their teeth white, their eye-brows bushy, their heads large, their bodies meagre, and their limbs are slender. They seldom live longer than 40 years; and this short duration of life is doubtless caused by their being continually covered with filth, and living chiefly upon meat that is corrupted. As most travellers have already given very large accounts of these filthy people, I shall only add one fact, as related by Tavernier. The Dutch, he says, once took away a Hottentot girl, soon after her birth, and bringing her up among themselves, she became as white as any European. From this fact he presumes, that all the Hottentots would be tolerably fair, were it not for their custom of perpetually begriming themselves.

Along the coast of Africa beyond the Cape of Good Hope, we find the land of Natal, and a people very different from the Hottentots, being better made, less ugly, and naturally more black. Their visage is oval, their nose well proportioned, their teeth white, their aspect agreeable, and their hair by nature frizly. They are also fond of grease, and wear caps made of the fat of oxen. These caps are from eight to ten inches high, and they take much time to make them; for the fat must be well refined, which they apply by little and little, and so thoroughly intermix it with the hair that it never falls off. Kolbe says, that from their birth and without any precaution to render it so, their noses are flat; they also differ from the Hottentots in not stuttering, nor striking the palate with the tongue; that they have houses, cultivate the ground, and produce from it a kind of maize, or Turkish corn, of which they make beer, a drink unknown to the Hottentots.

After the land of Natal, we find the territories of Sofala and Monomotapa. The people of the former, according to Pigafetta, are black, but more tall and lusty than the other Caffres. It is in the environs of the kingdom of Sofala that this author places the Amazons; but nothing is more uncertain than what has been propagated with respect to these female warriors.

The natives of Monomotapa, the Dutch travellers inform us, are tall, well proportioned, black, and of good complexions. The young girls go naked, except a bit of calico about their middle; but so soon as they are married they put on garments. This people, notwithstanding their blackness, are different from the negroes, their features are neither so harsh nor so ugly; their bodies have no bad smell; and they are incapable of servitude or hard labour. Father

Charlevoix says, that some blacks from Monomotapa, and from Madagascar, have been seen in America; but that they could not be inured to labour, and that they soon died.

The natives of Madagascar and Mosambique are black, more or less. Those of Madagascar have the hair on the crown of their head less frizly than those of Mosambique. Neither of them are real negroes; and though those of the coast are enslaved by the Portuguese, yet those of the internal part of the continent are savage and jealous of their liberty. They all go absolutely naked; they feed on the flesh of elephants, and traffic with the ivory.

In Madagascar there are blacks and whites who, though very tawny, yet seem a distinct race of men. The hair of the first is black and frizly; that of the latter is less black, less frizly, and longer. The common opinion is, that these white men derive their origin from the Chinese. But, as Francis Cauche justly remarks, there is a greater probability that they are of European race; as in all he saw, there was not one who had either the flat face or flat nose, of the Chinese. He likewise says, that these white men are fairer than the Castillans; that their hair is very long; that the black men are not flat-nosed like those of the continent; and that their lips are thin. There are also in this island a number of persons of an olive or tawny colour, evidently produced by the intermixture of the blacks and whites. The same traveller observes, that the natives round the bay of St. Augustine are tawny; that they have no beard; that their hair is long and straight; that they are tall and well proportioned; and that they are all circumcised, though probably they never heard of the law of Mahomet, as they have neither temples, mosques, nor religion.

The French, who were the first who landed and settled upon the above island, found the white men we speak of; and they remarked, that the blacks paid great respect to them. Madagascar is exceedingly populous, and rich in pasturage and in cattle. Both sexes are highly debauched; nor is it a dishonour to a woman to be a prostitute. They are fond of singing, dancing, and pastimes in general. Though naturally very lazy, they have some knowledge of the mechanic arts. They have husbandmen, carpenters, potters, blacksmiths, and even goldsmiths; yet their houses are without accommodation, and they sleep upon mats; they eat flesh almost raw, and devour even the hides of their oxen after burning off the hair; they also eat the wax with the honey. The common people go almost naked; but the richer classes wear drawers, or short petticoats, of cotton and silk.

Those who inhabit the interior parts of Africa are not sufficiently known to be justly described. Those whom the Arabians call *Zingues*, are an almost savage race of black men. Marmol says, they multiply prodigiously, and would overrun all the neighbouring countries, were it not for certain hot winds, which from time to time occasion a great mortality amongthem.

It appears, then, from these facts, that the Negroes are blacks of a different species from the Caffres. From the descriptions we have given, it is also evident that the colour depends principally upon the climate, and that the peculiarity of the features depends greatly on the customs prevalent among different nations, such as flattening the nose, drawing back the eye-lids, plucking the hair out of the eye-brows, lengthening the ears, thickening the lips, flattening the visage, &c. No stronger proof can be adduced of the influence of climate upon colour, than finding under the same latitude, and at the distance of 1000 leagues, two nations so similar as those of Senegal and Nubia; and also that the Hottentots, who must have derived their origin from a black race, are whiter than any other Africans, because the climate in which they live is the coldest. Should there being a tawny race on one side the Senegal, and perfect blacks on the other, be stated as an objection, it is only necessary to recollect what has been already intimated concerning the effects of food, which must operate upon the colour, as well as upon the temperament of the body in general. An example may easily be had in the brute creation. The flesh of the hares, for instance, which live on plains and marshy places, is much more white than those which, though in the same neighbourhood, live on mountains and dry grounds. The colour of the flesh proceeds from that of the blood, and other humours of the body, of which the quality is necessarily influenced by the nature of the nourishment.

In all ages has the origin of black men formed a grand object of enquiry. The ancients, who hardly knew any but those of Nubia, considered them as forming the last shade of the tawny colour; and confounded them with the Ethiopians, and other African nations, who, though extremely brown, have more affinity to the white than to the black race. They concluded, that the differences of colour in men arose solely from the difference of climate, and that blackness was occasioned by a perpetual exposure to the violent heat of the sun. To this opinion, which seems probable, great objections arose, when it was known, that, in more southern climates, and even under the equator itself, as at Melinda, and at Mosambique, the generality of the inhabitants were not black but only very tawny; and when it was observed that black men, if transported into more temperate regions, lost nothing of their colour, but communicated it to their decendants. If we reflect on the migrations of different nations, and on the time which is necessary to render a change in the colour, we shall find no inconsistency in the opinion of the ancients. The real natives of that part of Africa are Nubians, who were originally black, and will perpetually remain so, while they inhabit the same climate, and do not mix with the whites. The Ethiopians, the Abyssinians, and even the natives of Melinda, derive their origin from the whites, yet as their religion and customs are the same with those of the Arabians, they resemble them in colour, though indeed more tawny than those of the southern parts. This even proves, that, in the same race of men, the greater or less degree of black depends on the heat of the climate. Many ages might perhaps elapse, before a white race would become altogether black; but there is a probability that, in time, a white people, transported from the north to the equator, would experience that change, especially if they were to change their manners, and to feed solely on the productions of the warm climate.

Of little weight is the objection which may be made to this opinion, from the difference of the features, for in the features of a negro, which have not been disfigured in his infancy, and the features of an European, there is less difference than between those of a Tartar and a Chinese, or of a Circassian and a Greek. As for the hair, its nature depends so greatly on that of the skin, that any differences which it produces ought to be considered as accidental, since we find in the same country, and in the same town, men whose hair is entirely different from one another. In France, for instance, we meet with men whose hair is as short and frizly as that of a negro; besides, so powerful is the influence of climate upon the colour of the hair, both of men and of animals, that, in the kingdoms of the north, black hair is seldom seen; and hares, squirrels, weasels, and many other animals, which, in countries less cold, are brown or grey, are there white, or nearly so. The difference produced by cold and heat, is so conspicuous, that in Sweden hares, and certain other animals, are grey during the summer, and white in winter.

But there is another circumstance more powerful, and, from the first view of it, indeed insuperable; namely, that in the New World there is not one true black to be seen, the natives being red, tawny, or copper-coloured. If blackness was the effect of heat the natives of the Antilles, Mexico, Santa-Fé, Guiana, the country of the Amazons, and Peru, would necessarily be so, since those countries of America are situated in the same latitude with Senegal, Guinea, and Angola, in Africa. In Brazil, Paraguay, and Chili, did the colour of men depend upon the climate, or the distance from the pole, we might expect to find men similar to the Caffres and Hottentots. But before we enter into a discussion of this subject, it is necessary that we should examine the different natives of America, as we shall then be more enabled to form just comparisons, and to draw general conclusions.

In the most northern parts of America we find a species of Laplanders similar to those of Europe, or to the Samoiedes of Asia, and though they are few in number yet they are diffused over a very considerable extent of country. Those who inhabit the lands of Davis's Straits are small, of an olive complexion, and their limbs short and thick. They are skilful fishers, and eat their fish and meat raw; their drink is pure water, or the blood of the dog-fish; they are very strong, and live to a great age. Here we see the figure, colour, and manners of the Laplanders; and, what is truly singular, as in the neighbourhood of the Laplanders of Europe, we meet with the Finlanders, who are white, comely, tall, and well made; so, adjacent to the Laplanders of America, we meet with a species of men tall, well made, white, and with features exceedingly regular.

Of a different race seem the savages of Hudson's Bay, and northward of the land of Labrador; although small, ugly, and unshapely, their visage is almost covered with hair, like the savages of Jesso, northward of Japan: in summer they dwell in tents made of skins of the rein-deer; in winter they live under ground, like the Laplanders and the Samoiedes, and sleep together promiscuously without the smallest ceremony. They live to a great age, though they feed on nothing but raw meat and fish. The savages of Newfoundland resemble those of Davis's Straits, they are low in stature, have little or no beard, broad and flat faces; large eyes and flat nosed; they are also far from being unlike the savages in the environs of Greenland.

Besides these savages, who are scattered over the most northern parts of America, we find a more numerous and different race in Canada, and who occupy the vast extent of territory as far as the Assiniboils. These are all tall, robust, and well-made; have black hair and eyes, teeth very white, a tawny complexion, little beard, and hardly a vestige of hair on their bodies; they are hardy, indefatigable travellers, and very nimble runners. They are alike unaffected by excesses of hunger, or of eating; they are bold, hardy, grave, and sedate. So strongly, indeed, do they resemble the Oriental Tartars in colour, form, and features, as also in disposition, and manners, that, were they not separated by an immense sea, we should conclude them to have descended from that nation. In point of latitude, their situation is also the same; and this further proves the influence of the climate, not only on the colour, but the figure of men. In a word, in the new continent as in the old, we find, at first, in the northern parts, men similar to the Laplanders, and likewise whites with fair hair, like the inhabitants of the north of Europe; then hairy men like the savages of Jesso; and lastly, the savages of Canada, and of the whole continent to the gulph of Mexico, who resemble the Tartars in so many respects, that we should not entertain a doubt of their being the same people, were we not embarrassed about the possibility of their migration thither. Yet, if we reflect on the small number of men found upon this extent of ground, and on their being entirely uncivilized, we shall be inclined to believe these savage nations were new colonies produced by a few individuals from some other country. It is asserted that North America does not contain the twentieth part of the natives it did when originally discovered; allowing that to be the fact, we still are authorised to consider it then, from the scantiness of its inhabitants, as a land either deserted, or so recently peopled, that its inhabitants had not had time for a considerable multiplication. M. Fabry, who travelled a prodigious way to the north-west of the Mississippi, and visited places where no European had been, and where consequently the savage inhabitants could not have been destroyed by them, says that he often travelled 200 leagues without observing a single human face, or the smallest vestige of a habitation; that whenever he did meet with any habitations, they were always at immense distances from each other, and then never above 20 persons together. Along the lakes, and the rivers, it is true, the savages are more populous, some sufficiently so as to molest occasionally the inhabitants of our colonies. The most considerable of these, nevertheless, do not exceed 3 or 4000 persons, and are dispersed over a space of ground frequently more extensive than the kingdom of France. I am fully persuaded there are more men in the city of Paris, than there are savages in north America, from the gulph of Mexico to the furthest extremity north, an extent of ground larger than all Europe.

The multiplication of the human species depends more on society than nature. Men would not have been comparatively so numerous as wild beasts, had they not associated together, and given aid and succour to each other. In North America, the *Bison*[E] is perhaps more frequently to be seen than a man. But though society may be one great cause of population, yet it is the increased number of men that necessarily produces unity. It is to be presumed therefore that the want of civilization in America was owing to the small number of the inhabitants, for though each nation might have manners and customs peculiar to itself; though some might be more fierce, cruel, courageous, or dastardly than others; they were yet all equally stupid, ignorant, unacquainted with the arts, and destitute of industry.

[E] A kind of wild bull, different from the European bull.

To dwell longer on the customs of savage nations would be unnecessary. Authors have often given for the established manners of a community, what were nothing more than actions peculiar to a few individuals, and often determined by circumstances, or caprice. Some nations tell us, they eat their enemies, others burn, and some mutilate them; one nation is perpetually at war, and another loves to live in peace; in one country, the child kills his parent, when arrived at a certain age, and in another the parents eat their children. All these stories, on which travellers have so much enlarged, mean nothing more than that one individual savage had devoured his enemy, another had burned or mutilated him, and a third had killed and eaten his child. All these things may happen in every savage nation; for a people among whom there is no regular government, no law, no habitual society, ought rather to be termed a tumultous assemblage of barbarous and independent individuals, who obey nothing but their own private passions, and who have no common interest, are incapable of pursuing one object, and submitting to settled usages which supposes general designs, founded on reason, and approved of by the majority.

A nation, it may be replied, is composed of men who are no strangers to each other, who speak the same language, who unite, when necessity calls, under the same chief, who arm themselves in the same fashion, and daub themselves of the same colour. With truth might the remark be made, if these usages were established; if savages did not often assemble they know not how, and disperse they know not why; if their chief did not cease to be so, whenever it suited their caprice, or his own; and if their language was not so simple as to be, with little variation, the language of every tribe.

As they have but few ideas, their expressions turn upon things the most general, and objects the most common; and, though the majority of their expressions were different, yet the smallness of their number renders them easily understood; and more easily, therefore, may a savage learn the languages of all other savages, than the inhabitants of one polished nation acquire a bare comprehension of the language of any other nation equally civilized.

Unnecessary as it may be to enlarge on the customs and manners of these pretended nations, yet it may be important to examine the nature of the individual. Of all animals a savage man is the most singular, the least known, and the most difficult to describe; and so little are we qualified to distinguish the gifts of nature from what is acquired by education, art and imitation, that it would not be surprising to find we had totally mistaken the picture of a savage, although it were presented to us in its real colours, and with its natural features.

An absolute savage, such as a boy reared among bears, as mentioned by Conor, the young man found in the forest of Hanover, or the girl in the woods in France, would be a curious object to a philosopher; in observing which he might be able to ascertain the force of natural appetites; he would see the mind undisguised, and distinguish all its movements; and, possibly, he might discover in it more mildness, serenity, and peace, than in his own; he might also perceive, that virtue belongs more to the savage than to the civilized man, and that vice owes its birth to society.

But let us return to our subject. If in North America there were none but savages, in Mexico and Peru we found a polished people, subjected to laws, governed by kings, industrious, acquainted with the arts, and not destitute of religion. They lived in towns where the civil government was superintended by the sovereign. These people, who were very populous, cannot be considered as new colonies sprung from individuals who had wandered from Europe or Asia, from which they are so remote; besides, though the Savages of North America resemble the Tartars, by their being situated in the same latitude, yet the natives of Mexico and Peru, though they live, like the Negroes, under the torrid zone, have not the smallest resemblance to them. Whence then, shall we trace the origin of these people? and whence proceeds the cause of the difference of colour in the human species, since the influence of climate is, in this case, entirely overthrown?

Previous to answering these questions let us pursue our inquiries respecting the Savages of South America. Those of Florida, of the Mississippi, and of the other southern parts of this continent, are more tawny than those of Canada, though not positively brown, the oil and colours with which they rub their bodies, giving them an olive hue which does not naturally belong to them. Coreal says, that the women of Florida are tall, strong, and of an olive complexion, like the men; that they paint their arms, legs, and bodies, with several colours, which as they are imprinted into the flesh by little incisions, are indelible; and that the olive colour of both sexes proceeds not so much from the heat of the climate as from the oils with which they varnish their skin. He adds, that the women are remarkably active; that they swim over great rivers with a child in their arms, and that they climb up the loftiest trees with equal agility. In all of these particulars they entirely resemble the savage women of Canada, and other countries of America.

Speaking of the Apalachites, a people in the vicinage of Florida, the author of the "Histoire Naturelle et Morale des Antilles," says, that they are of a large stature, of an olive colour, and well proportioned; and that their hair is black and long. He adds, that the Caribbees, who inhabit the Antilles, are sprung from the savages of Florida, and that they even know, by tradition, the period of their migration.

The natives of the Lucai islands are less tawny than those of St. Domingo and Cuba; but there remain so few of either that we can hardly verify what the first travellers mention of the inhabitants. It has been pretended that they were very numerous, and governed by chiefs whom they call *caciques*; that they had priests and physicians; but this is all very problematical, and is of little consequence to our history. The Caribbees, in general, according to Father du Tertre, are tall, and of a good aspect: they are potent, robust, active, and healthy. Numbers of them have flat foreheads and noses, but these features are entirely the work of the parents, soon after their birth. In all savage nations this caprice of altering the natural figure of the head is very frequent. Most of the Caribbees have little black eyes, beautiful white teeth, and long smooth black hair. Their skin is tawny, or olive, and even the whites of their eyes are rather of that hue. This is their natural colour, and not produced by the use of the rocon, as some authors have asserted, for several of the children of these savages, who were educated among the Europeans, and not allowed the use of paint, retained the same complexion as their parents. The whole of this savage tribe, though their thoughts are seldom employed, have a pensive air. They are naturally mild and compassionate, though exceedingly cruel to their enemies. They esteem it indifferent whom they marry, whether relations or strangers. Their first cousins belong to them by right, and many have been known to have at one time two sisters, or a mother and her daughter, and even their own child. Those who have many wives visit them in turn, and stay a month, or a certain numbers of days, which precludes all jealousy among the women. They readily forgive their wives for adultery, but are implacable enemies to the man who debauches them. They feed on lizards, serpents, crabs, turtles and fishes, which they season with pimento, and the flower of manioc. Lazy to an excess, and accustomed to the greatest independence, they detest slavery, and can never be rendered so useful as the Negroes. For the preservation of their liberty they make every exertion; and when they find it impossible, will rather die of hunger or despair than live and be obliged to work. Attempts have been made to employ the Arrouaguas, who are milder than the Caribbees, but who are only fit for hunting and fishing; exercises of which, being accustomed to them in their own country, they are particularly fond. If these savages are not used with at least as much mildness as domestics generally are in the civilized nations of Europe, they either run away or pine themselves to death. Nearly the same is it with the slaves of Brazil; of all Savages these seem to be the least stupid, indolent, or melancholy. Treated with gentleness, however, they will do whatever they are desired, unless it be to cultivate the ground, for tillage they conceive to be the characteristic badge of slavery.

Savage women are all smaller than the men. Those of the Caribbees are fat, and tolerably handsome; their eyes and hair are black, their visage round, their mouth small, their teeth white, and their carriage more gay, cheerful, and open, than that of the men. Yet are they modest and reserved. They daub themselves with rocon, but do not, like the men, make black streaks upon the face and body. Their dress consists of a kind of apron, in breadth about eight or ten inches, and in length about five or six. This apron is generally made of calico, and covered with small glass beads, both which commodities they purchase from the Europeans. They likewise wear necklaces, which descend over the breast, as also bracelets round the wrists and elbows, and pendants in their ears, of blue stone, or of glass beads. Another ornament peculiar to the sex is, a kind of buskin, made of calico, and garnished with glass beads, which extends from the ancle to the calf of the leg. On their attaining the age of puberty the girls receive an apron and a pair of buskins, which are made exactly to their legs and cannot be removed; and as they prevent the increase of the under part of the leg, the upper parts naturally grow larger than they would otherwise have done.

So intermixed are the present inhabitants of Mexico and Peru, that we rarely meet with two faces of the same colour. In the town of Mexico, there are Europeans, Indians from north and south America, negroes from Africa, and mulattoes of every kind, insomuch that the people exhibit every kind of shade between black and white. The natives of the country are brown, or olive, well made and active. Though they have little hair, even on their eye-brows, yet that upon their head is very long, and very black.

According to Wafer, the natives of the Isthmus of America are commonly tall and handsome; their limbs are well shaped, chest large, and at the chace they are active and nimble. The women are short, squat, and less vivacious than the men; though the young ones are tolerably comely, and have lively eyes. Of both the face is round; the nose thick and short; the eyes large, mostly grey, and full of fire; the forehead high; the teeth white and regular; the lips thin; the mouth of a moderate size; and, in general, all their features are tolerably regular. They have black, long, and straight hair; and the men would have beards did they not pluck them out: their colour is tawny and their eye-brows are as black as jet.

These people are not the only natives of this Isthmus, for we find among them men who are white; but their colour is not the white of Europeans, but rather resembles that of milk, or the hairs of a white horse. Their skin is covered with a kind of short and whitish down, which on the cheeks and forehead is not so thick but the skin may be seen. The hair upon their head and eye-brows is perfectly white; the former is rather frizled, and from seven to eight inches long. They are not so tall as the other Indians; and, what is singular, their eye-lids are of an oblong figure, or rather in the form of a cresent, whose points turn downwards. So weak are their eyes, that they cannot support the light of the sun, and they see best by that of the moon. Their complexion is exceedingly delicate. To all laborious exercises they are averse; they sleep through the day, and never stir abroad till night. If the moon shines, they scamper through the forests as nimbly as the others can in the day. These men do not from a particular and distinct race, as it sometimes happens, that from parents who are both of a copper-colour one of these children is produced. Wafer, who relates these facts, says, that he saw a child, not a year old, who had been thus produced.

If this were the case, the strange colour, and temperament of these white

Indians, can only be a kind of malady, which they inherit from their parents. But if, instead of being sprung from the yellow Indians, they formed a separate race, then would they resemble the Chacrelas of Java, and the Bedas of Ceylon, whom we have already mentioned. If, on the other hand, these white people are actually born of copper-coloured parents, we shall have reason to believe, that the Chacrelas and the Bedas originate also from parents of the same colour; and that all the white men, whom we find at such distances from each other, are individuals who have degenerated from their race by some accidental cause.

This last opinion, I own, appears to me the most probable; and had travellers given us as exact descriptions of the Bedas and Chacrelas, as Wafer has done of the Dariens, we should, perhaps, have discovered that they were no more of European origin than the latter. This opinion receives great weight from the fact that negroes sometimes have white children. Of two of those white negroes we have a description in the history of the French Academy; one of the two I saw myself, and am assured there are many to be met with among the other negroes of Africa.

From what I have myself observed, independent of the information of travellers, I have no doubt, but that they are only negroes degenerated from their race, and not a peculiar and established species of men. In a word, they are among the negroes, what Wafer says, the white Indians are among the yellow Indians of Darien, and what the Chacrelas and the Bedas are among the brown Indians of the East. Still more singular is it that this variation never happens but from black to white, and also that all the nations of the East Indies, of Africa, and of America, in which those white men are found, are in the same latitude. The isthmus of Darien, the country of the negroes, and Ceylon, are absolutely under the same line. White then appears to be the primitive colour of Nature, which climate, food, and manners, alter, and even change into yellow, brown, or black; and which, in certain circumstances, reappears, though by no means equal to its original whiteness on account of its corruption from the causes here mentioned.

Nature, in her full perfection, made men white; and, reduced to the last stage of adulteration, she renders them white again. But the natural white is widely different from the individual, or accidental white. In plants, as well as in men and animals, do we find examples of this fact. The white rose, &c. differs greatly in point of whiteness from the red rose, which becomes white by the cold evenings and frosty chills of autumn.

A further proof that these white men are merely degenerated individuals, is their being less strong and vigorous than others, and their eyes being extremely weak. The fact will appear less extraordinary, when we recollect, that, among ourselves, very fair men have very weak eyes, and that such people are often slow of hearing. It is pretended that dogs absolutely white, are deaf. Whether the observation is generally just, I know not, but in a number of instances I have seen it confirmed.

The Indians of Peru, like the natives of the Isthmus, are copper-coloured; those especially who live near the sea, and in the plains. Those who live between the two ridges of the Cordeliers, are almost as white as the Europeans. Some live in Peru more than a league higher than others; and which elevation, with respect to the temperature of the climate, is equal to twenty leagues in latitude. All the native Indians, who dwell along the river of the Amazons, and in Guiana are tawny, and more or less red. The diversity of shades, says M. de la Condamine, is principally occasioned by the different temperature of the air, varied as it is, from the extreme heat of the torrid zone, to the cold occasioned by the vicinage of snow. Some of these Savages, as the Omaguas, flatten the visages of their children, by compressing the head between two planks; others pierce the nostrils, lips, or cheeks, for the reception of the bones of fishes, feathers, and other ornaments; and the greatest part bore their ears, and fill the hole with a large bunch of flowers, or herbs, which serves them for pendants. With respect to the Amazons, about whom so much has been said, I shall be silent. To those who have written on the subject I refer the reader; and when he has perused them he will not find sufficient proof to evince the actual existence of such women.

Some authors mention a nation in Guiana of which the natives are more black than any other Indians. The Arras, says Raleigh, are almost as black as the Negroes, are vigorous, and use poisoned arrows. This author mentions likewise another nation of Indians, who have necks so short, and shoulders so elevated, that their eyes appear to be upon the latter, and their mouths in their breast. This monstrous deformity cannot be natural; and it is probable that savages, who are so pleased in disfiguring nature by flattening, rounding, and lengthening the head, might likewise contrive to sink it into the shoulders. These fantasies might arise from an idea that, by rendering themselves deformed, they became more dreadful to their enemies. The Scythians, formerly, as savage as the American Indians are now, evidently entertained the same ideas, and realized them in the same manner; which no doubt is the foundation of what the ancients have written about such men as they termed accphali, cynocephali, &c.

The Savages of Brazil are nearly of the size of the Europeans, but are more vigorous, robust, and alert: they are also subject to fewer diseases, and live longer. Their hair, which is black, seldom whitens with age. They are of a copper-colour, inclining to red: their heads are large, shoulders broad, and hair long. They pluck out their beard, the hair upon the body, and even the eye-brows, from which they acquire an extraordinary fierce look. They pierce the under lip, to ornament it with a little bone polished like ivory, or with a green stone. The mothers crush the noses of their children, presently after they are born; they all go absolutely naked, and paint their bodies of different colours. Those who inhabit the countries adjacent to the sea are somewhat civilized by the commerce which they carry on with the Portuguese; but those of the inland places are still absolute savages. It is not by force that savages have become civilized, their manners have been much more softened by the arguments of missionaries, than by the arms of the princes by whom they were subdued. In this manner Paraguay was subdued: the mildness, example, and virtuous conduct of the missionaries touched the hearts of its savages, and triumphed over their distrust and ferocity. They often, of themselves, desired to be made acquainted with that law, which rendered men so perfect, submitted to its precepts, and united in society. Nothing can reflect greater honour on religion, than its having civilized these nations, and laid the foundations of an empire, without any arms but those of virtue and humanity.

The inhabitants of Paraguay are commonly tall and handsome; their visage long, and their colour olive. There sometimes rages among them a very uncommon distemper. It is a kind of leprosy, which covers the whole of their body with a crust similar to the scales of fish, and from which they experience no pain, nor even interruption of health.

According to Frezier, the Indians of Chili are of a tawny or coppery complexion, but different from Mulattoes, who being produced by a white man and negro-woman, or a white woman and a negro-man, their colour is brown, or a mixture of white and black. In South America, on the other hand, the Indians are yellow, or rather reddish. The natives of Chili are of a good size; their limbs are brawny, chest large, visages disagreeable, and beardless; eyes small, ears long, and their hair black, straight, and coarse. Their ears they lengthen, and pluck out their beards with pincers made of shells. Though the climate is cold, yet they generally go naked, excepting the skin of some animal over their shoulders.

At the extremity of Chili, and towards the lands of Magellan, it is pretended, there exists a race of men of gigantic size. From the information of several Spaniards, who pretend to have seen them, Frezier says, they are from 9 to 10 feet high; they are called *Patagonians*, and inhabit the easterly side of the coast, as mentioned in the old narratives, which, however, from the size of Indians discovered in the Straits of Magellan, not exceeding that of other men, has since been considered as fabulous. It might be by this, says he, that Froger was deceived in his account of the voyage of M. de Gennes; as several navigators have actually beheld both these classes of Indians at the same time. In 1709, the crew of the James, of St. Malo, saw seven giants as above described, in Gregory Bay, and those of the St. Peter, of Marseilles, saw six, to whom they advanced with offers of bread, wine, and brandy, all of which they rejected; but as M. Frezier does not intimate his having seen any of these giants himself, and as the narratives which mention them are fraught with exaggerations with respect to other matters, it remains still doubtful whether there in reality exists a race of giants, especially of the height of ten feet. The bodily circumference of such a man would be eight times bigger than that of an ordinary one. The natural height of mankind seems to be about five feet, and the deviations from that standard scarcely exceed a foot, so that a man of six feet is considered as very tall, and a man of four as very short. Giants and dwarfs, therefore, are only accidental varieties, and not distinct and permanent races.

Besides, if these Magellanic giants actually exist, their number must be trifling; as the savages of the straits, and neighbouring islands, are of a moderate height, whose colour is olive, have full chests, square bodies, thick limbs, and black straight hair; who, in a word, resemble mankind in general as to size, as the other Americans as to colour and hair.

In the whole of the new continent, then, there is but one race of men, who are all more or less tawny, the northern parts of America excepted, where we find some men similar to the Laplanders, and others with fair hair, like the northern Europeans; through the whole of this immense territory, the diversity among the inhabitants is hardly perceivable. Among those of the old continent, on the other hand, we have found a prodigious variety. This uniformity in the Americans seems to arise from their living all in the same manner. The natives were, and are still savages; nor, so recently have they been civilized, can the Mexicans and the Peruvians be excepted. Whatever, then, may have been their origin, it was common to them all. Sprung from one stock, they have, with little variation, retained the characteristics of their race; and this because they have pursued the same course of life, because their climate, with respect to heat and cold, is not so unequal as that of the old continent, and because, being newly established in the country, the causes by which varieties are produced have not had time to manifest their defects.

Each of these reasons merits a particular consideration. That the Americans are a new people seems indisputable, when we reflect on the smallness of their number, their ignorance, and the little progress the most civilized among them had made in the arts. In the first accounts of the discovery and conquest of America, it is true, Mexico, Peru, St. Domingo, &c. are mentioned as very populous countries; and we are told that the

Spaniards had every where to engage with vast armies; yet it is evident these facts are greatly exaggerated; first, from the paucity of monuments left of the pretended grandeur of these nations: secondly, from the nature of the country itself, which, though peopled with Europeans, more industrious, doubtless, than its natives, is still wild, uncultivated, covered with wood, and little more than a group of inacessible and uninhabitable mountains; thirdly, from their own traditions, with respect to the time they united into society, the Peruvians reckoning no more than 12 kings, from the first of whom, about 300 years before, they had imbibed the first principles of civilization, and ceased to be entirely savage; fourthly, from the small number of men employed to conquer them, which even with the advantage of gunpowder, they could not have done, had the people been numerous. Though the effects of gunpowder were as new and as terrible to the negroes as to the Americans, their country has yet remained unconquered, and themselves unenslaved; and the ease with which America was subdued, appears an irrefragable argument that the country was thinly peopled, and recently inhabited.

In the New Continent, the temperature of the different climates is more uniform than in the Old Continent; for this there are several causes. The Torrid Zone, in America, is by no means so hot as in Africa. The countries comprehended under the former zone, are Mexico, New Spain, and Peru, the land of the Amazons, Brazil, and Guiana. In Mexico, New Spain, and Peru, the heat is never very great; these countries are prodigiously elevated above the ordinary level of the earth; nor in the hottest weather does the thermometer rise so high in Peru as in France. By the snow which covers the tops of the mountains the air is cooled; and as this cause, which is merely an effect of the former, has a strong influence upon the temperature of the climate, so the inhabitants, instead of being black, or dark brown, are only tawny. The land of the Amazons is particularly watery, and full of forests; there the air is exceedingly moist, and consequently more cool than in a country more dry. Besides, it is to be observed, that the east wind, which blows constantly between the tropics, does not reach Brazil, the land of the Amazons, or Guiana, without traversing a vast sea, by which it acquires a degree of coolness. It is from this reason, as well as from their being so full of rivers and forests, and almost continued rains, that these parts of America are so exceedingly temperate. But the east wind, after passing the low countries of America, becomes considerably heated before it arrives at Peru; and therefore, were it not for its elevated situation, and for the snow, by which the air is cooled, the heat would be greater there than either in Brazil or Guiana. There still, however, remains a sufficiency of heat to influence the colour of the natives: for those who are most exposed to it their colour is more yellow than those who live sheltered in the vallies. Besides, this wind blowing against these lofty mountains, must be reflected on the neighbouring plains, and diffuse over them that coolness which it received from the snow that covers their tops; and from this snow itself, when it dissolves, cold winds must necessarily arise. All these causes concurring to render the climate of the Torrid Zone in America far less hot, it is not surprising that its inhabitants are not so black nor brown as those under the Torrid Zone in Africa and Asia, where, as we shall shew, there is a difference of circumstances. Whether we suppose, then, that the Americans have been long or recently established in that country, their Torrid Zone being temperate, they are of course not black.

The uniformity in their mode of living, I also assigned for the little variety to be found in the natives of America. As they were all savage, or recently civilized, they all lived in the same manner. In supposing that they had all one common origin, they were dispersed, without being intermixed; each family formed a nation not only similar to itself, but to all about them, because their climate and food were nearly similar; and as they had no opportunity either to degenerate or improve, so they could not but remain constantly and almost universally the same.

That their origin is the same with our own, I doubt not, independent of theological arguments; and from the resemblance of the savages of North America to the Oriental Tartars, there is reason to suppose they originally sprung from the same source. The new discoveries by the Russians, on the other side of Kamtschatka, of several lands and islands which extend nearly to the Western Continent of America, would leave no doubt as to the possibility of the communication, if these discoveries were properly authenticated, and the lands were in any degree contiguous. But, even in the supposition of considerable intervals of sea, is it not possible that there might have been men who crossed them in search of new regions, or were driven upon them by bad tempests? Between the Mariana islands and Japan there is, perhaps, a greater interval of sea than between any of the territories beyond Kamtschatka and those of America; and yet the Mariana islands were peopled with inhabitants who could have come from no part but from the Eastern Continent. I am inclined to believe, therefore, that the first men who set foot on America landed on some spot north-west of California; that the excessive cold of this climate obliged them to remove to the more southern parts of their new abode; that at first they settled in Mexico and Peru, from whence they afterwards diffused themselves over all the different parts of North and South America. Mexico and Peru must be considered as the most ancient inhabited territories of this continent, being not only the most elevated, but also the only ones in which the inhabitants were found connected together in society.

It may also be presumed that the inhabitants of Davis's Straits, and of the northern parts of Labrador, came from Greenland, being only separated by these small straits, for the savages of Davis's Straits, and those of Greenland, as we have just remarked, are very similar; and Greenland might have been peopled by the Laplanders passing thither from Cape Nord, the intermediate distance being only about 150 leagues. Besides, as the island of Iceland is almost contiguous to Greenland, has long been inhabited and frequented by Europeans; and as the Danes formed colonies in Greenland, it is not wonderful there should be found men who, deriving their origin from those Danes, were white and fair-haired. There is some probability also that the white men along Davis's Straits derive their origin from these Europeans, thus settled in Greenland, from whence they might easily pass to America, by crossing the little interval of sea of which this strait is formed.

In colour and in figure we meet with as great a degree of uniformity in America, as of diversity of men in Africa. From great antiquity has this part of the world been copiously peopled. The climate is scorching, yet in different nations it is of a different temperature; nor, from the descriptions already given, are their manners less different. From these concurrent causes there subsists a greater variety of men in Africa than in any other part. If we examine the difference in the temperature of the African countries, we shall find that in Barbary, and all the territories near the Mediterranean Sea, the men are white, or only somewhat tawny; those territories are refreshed on one hand by the air of the Mediterranean Sea, and on the other by the snows on Mount Atlas, and are, moreover, situated in the Temperate Zone, on this side the Tropic; so also all the tribes between Egypt and the Canary islands have the skin only more or less tawny. Beyond the Tropic, and on the other side of Mount Atlas, the heat becomes more violent, and the colour of the inhabitants is more dark, though still not black. Coming to the 17th or 18th degree of north latitude we find Senegal and Nubia, where the heat is excessive, and the natives absolutely black. In Senegal the thermometer rises to the degree 38, while in France it rarely rises to 30; and in Peru, situated under the Torrid Zone, it is hardly ever known to pass 25. We have no observations made with the thermometer in Nubia, but all travellers agree in representing the heat to be excessive. The sandy deserts between Upper Egypt and Nubia heat the air to such a degree that the north wind actually scorches. The east wind also, which is usually prevalent between the Tropics, does not reach Nubia till it has crossed the territories of Arabia; therefore that the Nubians should be black is little cause for wonder; though indeed they are still less so than those of Senegal, where, as the east wind cannot arrive till it has traversed all the territories of Africa in their utmost extent, the heat is rendered almost insupportable.

If we take all that district of Africa comprised between the Tropics, where the east wind blows most constantly, we shall easily conceive that the western coasts of this part of the world must, and actually do, experience a greater degree of heat than those of the eastern coasts; as the east wind reaches the latter with the freshness which it receives in passing over a vast sea, whereas before it reaches the former, it acquires a burning heat, in traversing the interior parts of Africa. Thus, therefore, the coasts of Senegal, Sierra Leona, Guinea, and all the western regions of Africa, situated under the Torrid Zone, are the hottest climates in the world; nor is it by any means so hot on the eastern coasts, at Mosambique, Mombaza, &c. I have not the smallest doubt, therefore, but this is the reason that we find the real negroes, or the blackest men, in the western territories of Africa, and Caffres, or black men, of a hue more light, in the eastern territories. The evident difference which subsists between these two species of blacks proceeds from the heat of their climate, which is not very great in the eastern, but excessive in the western. Beyond the Tropic, on the south, the heat is considerably diminished, not only from its situation as to climate, but from the point of Africa being contracted; and as that point is surrounded by the sea the air is necessarily more temperate than it could be in the middle of a continent. The colour of the inhabitants of this country begins to assume a fairer hue, and they are naturally more white than black. Nothing affords a more convincing proof that the climate is the principal cause of the variety in the human species than the colour of the Hottentots, who could not possibly be found less black did they not enjoy a more temperate climate.

In this opinion we shall be more confirmed if we examine the other nations under the Torrid Zone, on the east side of Africa. The inhabitants of the Maldivia islands, of Ceylon, of the point of the peninsula of India, of Sumatra, of Malacca, of Borneo, of Celebes, of the Philippines, &c. are very brown, though not absolutely black, from all these countries being either islands or peninsulas. In these climates the heat of the air is temporized by the sea; besides which, neither the east nor west wind, which reign alternately in that part of the globe, can reach the Indian Archipelago without passing over seas of an immense extent. As their heat is not excessive, therefore, all these islands are peopled with brown men; but in New Guinea we again meet with red blacks, and who, from the descriptions of travellers, seem to be absolute negroes, because the country they inhabit forms a continent to the east, and the wind is more hot than that which prevails in the Indian Ocean. In New Holland, where the heat of the climate is not so great, we find people less black, and not unlike the Hottentots. Do not these negroes and Hottentots, whom we meet with in the same latitude, and at so great a distance from the other negroes and Hottentots, evince their colour depends upon the heat of the climate? That there was ever any communication between Africa and this southern continent, it is impossible to suppose; and yet in both we find the same species of men, because the same circumstances occur which occasion the same degrees of heat.

From the animal creation we may obtain a further confirmation of what has been above advanced. In Dauphiny, it has been observed that all the hogs are black; and that on the other side of the Rhone, in Vivarais, where it is more cold than in Dauphiny, all the hogs are white. There is no probability that the inhabitants of one of these two provinces should have agreed to breed none but black hogs, and the other none but white ones. To me it appears, that this difference arises solely from the variation in the temperature of the climate, combined, perhaps, with that of the food of the animals.

The few blacks who have been found in the Philippines, and other islands of the Indian Ocean, seem to originate from the Papous, or Negroes of New Guinea, whom the Europeans have not known much longer than half a century. Dampier discovered the most eastern part in 1700, and gave it the name of *New Britain*; we are still ignorant of its extent, yet we know that, so far as has been discovered, it is not very populous.

In those climates alone, then, where circumstances combine to create a constant and excessive heat, do we meet with negroes. This heat is necessary not only to the production, but even to the preservation of negroes; and where the heat, though violent, is not comparable to that of Senegal, the negro infants are so susceptible of the impressions of the air, that there is a necessity for keeping them during the first nine days in warm apartments; if this precaution is omitted, and they are exposed to the air soon after their birth, a convulsion in the jaw succeeds, which preventing them from receiving any sustenance, they presently die.

In the History of the Academy of Sciences we read, that M. Littre, in dissecting a negro, in 1702, remarked, that the point of the glands which was not covered with the prepuce was black, and the rest perfectly white. From this observation it is evident, that the air is necessary to produce the blackness of negroes. Their children are born white, or rather red, like those of other men, but two or three days after they change to a tawny yellow, which gradually darkens till the seventh or eighth day, when they are completely black. All children two or three days after their birth have a kind of jaundice, which in white children is transitory, and leaves no impression upon the skin; but in negro children it gives a colour to the skin, and continues to grow more and more black. M. Kolbe mentions having observed this fact among the children of Hottentots. This jaundice, however, and the impression of the air, seem to be only occasional, and not the primary cause of this blackness; since it is remarked, that the children of negroes have, the instant of their birth, a blackness in the genitals, and at the root of the nails. The action of the air and the jaundice may serve to extend this blackness, but it is certain that the principle of it is communicated to the children by their parents; that in whatever country a negro may be born, he will be as black as if he had been brought forth in his own; and if there is any difference in the first generation it is imperceptible; from this circumstance, however, we are not to suppose, that after a certain number of generations, the colour would not undergo a very sensible change.

Many have been the researches of anatomists respecting this black colour. Some pretend, that it is neither in the skin, nor in the epidermis, but in the cellular membrane which is between them; that this membrane, though washed, and held ever so long in warm water, does not change colour, while the skin, and the surface of the skin, appear to be nearly as white as those of other men. Dr. Town, in his letter to the Royal Society, and a few others, maintain, that the blood is black in negroes, and from which cause their colour originates; a fact which I am inclined to believe, from having remarked, that among ourselves the blood of those who are tawny, yellow, or brown, is proportionally more black than that of others.

According to M. Barrere, this colour of the negroes is produced by the bile, which in them is not yellow, but always black as ink; of which he affirms he received certain proof from several negroes which he had occasion to dissect at Cayenne. When the bile is diffused, it tinges the skin of white people yellow; and it is probable, that if the former were black, the latter would be black also. But as when the overflow of the bile ceases, the skin recovers its natural whiteness, so on this principle there is a necessity for supposing that in the negroes there is always an overflow of bile, or at least that, as M. Barrere observes, it is so abundant, as naturally to secrete itself in the epidermis, in a quantity sufficient to communicate this black colour. It probable that the bile and blood of negroes are more brown than those of white men, as their skin is more black. But one of these facts can never be admitted as an explanation of the cause of the other; for if it is the blood or bile which, by its blackness, communicates this colour to the skin, then, instead of inquiring why the skin of negroes is black, we must inquire why their bile or blood is so; and thus, by deviating from the question, we find ourselves more than ever remote from the solution of it. For my own part, I own I have always been of opinion, that the cause which renders a Spaniard more brown than a Frenchman, and a Moor than a Spaniard, is also the cause which renders a Negro blacker than a Moor. At present I mean not to enquire how this cause acts, but only to ascertain that it does act, and that its effects are the more considerable, in proportion to the force and continuance of action.

Of the blackness of the skin, the principal cause is the heat of the climate. When this heat is excessive, as at Senegal, and in Guinea, the inhabitants are entirely black; when it is rather less violent, as on the eastern coasts of Africa, they are of a shade more light; when it becomes somewhat temperate, as in Barbary, Mogul, Arabia, &c. they are only brown; and in fine, when it is altogether temperate, as in Europe and in Asia, they are white; and the varieties there remarked proceed solely from the mode of living. All the Tartars, for example, are tawny, while the Europeans, who live in the same latitude, are white. This difference clearly arises from the former being always exposed to the air; having no towns nor fixed habitations; sleeping upon the earth, and living coarsely and savagely. These circumstances are sufficient to render them less white than the Europeans, who want nothing to render life comfortable and agreeable. Why are the Chinese whiter than the Tartars, whom they resemble in all their features? Certainly from the above reasons.

When cold becomes extreme, it produces effects similar to those of excessive heat. The Samoiedes, Laplanders, and Greenlanders, are very tawny; and it is even asserted, that some Greenlanders are as black as those of

Africa. Here the two extremes meet. Violent cold and violent heat produce the same effect upon the skin, because these two causes act by a quality which they possess in common. Dryness of the air is this quality; and which cold is as equally productive as intense heat; by either the skin may be dried, and rendered as tawny as what we find it among the Laplanders. Cold compresses all the productions of nature; and thus it is that the Laplanders, who are perpetually exposed to the rigours of frost, are the smallest of the human species.

The most temperate climate is between the degrees of 40 and 50; where the human form is in its greatest perfection; and where we ought to form our ideas of the real and natural colour of man. Situated under this Zone the civilized countries are, Georgia, Circassia, the Ukraine, Turkey in Europe, Hungary, South Germany, Italy, Switzerland, France, and the North of Spain; of all which the inhabitants are the most beautiful people in the world.

As the principal cause of the colour of mankind, we ought to consider the climate; the effects of nourishment are less upon the colour, yet upon the form they are prodigious. Food which is gross, unwholesome, or badly prepared, produces a degeneracy in the human species; and in all countries where the people are wretchedly fed, they are ugly, and badly shaped. Even in France, the inhabitants of country places are more ugly than those of towns; and I have often remarked, that in villages where poverty and distress were less prevalent, the people were in person more shapely, and in visage less ugly. The air and the soil have also great influence on the form of men, animals, and vegetables. The peasants who live on hilly grounds are more active, nimble, well-shaped, and lively, than those who live in the neighbouring vallies, where the air is thick and unrefined.

Horses from Spain or Barbary cannot be perpetuated in France; in the very first generation they degenerate, and by the third or fourth they become downright French horses. So striking is the influence of climate and food upon animals, that the effects of either are well known, and though they are less sudden and less apparent upon men, yet, from analogy, we must conclude they extend to the human species, and that in the varieties we find therein, they plainly manifest themselves.

From every circumstance may we obtain a proof, that mankind are not composed of species essentially different from each other; that, on the contrary, there was originally but one species, which, after being multiplied and diffused over the whole surface of the earth, underwent divers changes from the influence of the climate, food, mode of living, epidemical distempers, and the intermixture of individuals, more or less resembling each other; that at first these alterations were less conspicuous, and confined to individuals; that afterwards, from continued action, they formed specific varieties; that these varieties have been perpetuated from generation to generation, in the same manner as deformities and diseases pass from parents to their children, and that in fine, as they were first produced by a concurrence of external and accidental causes, and have been confirmed and rendered permanent by time, and by the continual action of these causes, so it is highly probable that in time they would gradually disappear, or become different from what they at present are, if such causes were no longer to subsist, or if they were in any material point to vary.

END OF THE FOURTH VOLUME.

Lightning Source UK Ltd.
Milton Keynes UK
UKHW041044100820
367987UK00004B/1020